DRAGON QUEEN

ELIZABETH KNIGHT

CREATIVE WONDER PUBLISHING

Copyright 2021 © **Elizabeth Knight**

All rights reserved.

This is a work of fiction. Names, characters, places, and incidents are either the product of the author's imagination or are used fictitiously, and any resemblance to actual persons living or dead, business establishments, events, or locales is entirely coincidental. No part of this book may be used to reproduce, scan, or be distributed in any printed or electronic form in any manner whatsoever without written permission of the author, except in the case of brief quotations for articles or reviews. Additionally no part of this book may be used to create, feed, or refine artificial intelligence models, for any purpose, without written permission from the author.

Please do not participate in or encourage piracy of copyrighted materials.

Knight, Elizabeth

Dragon Queen

Editing: Swish Editing & Design

Cover artist: Malice and Mayhem Book Covers

Formatting: Creative Wonder Publishing

ISBN: 979-8-88958-050-8 (Print)

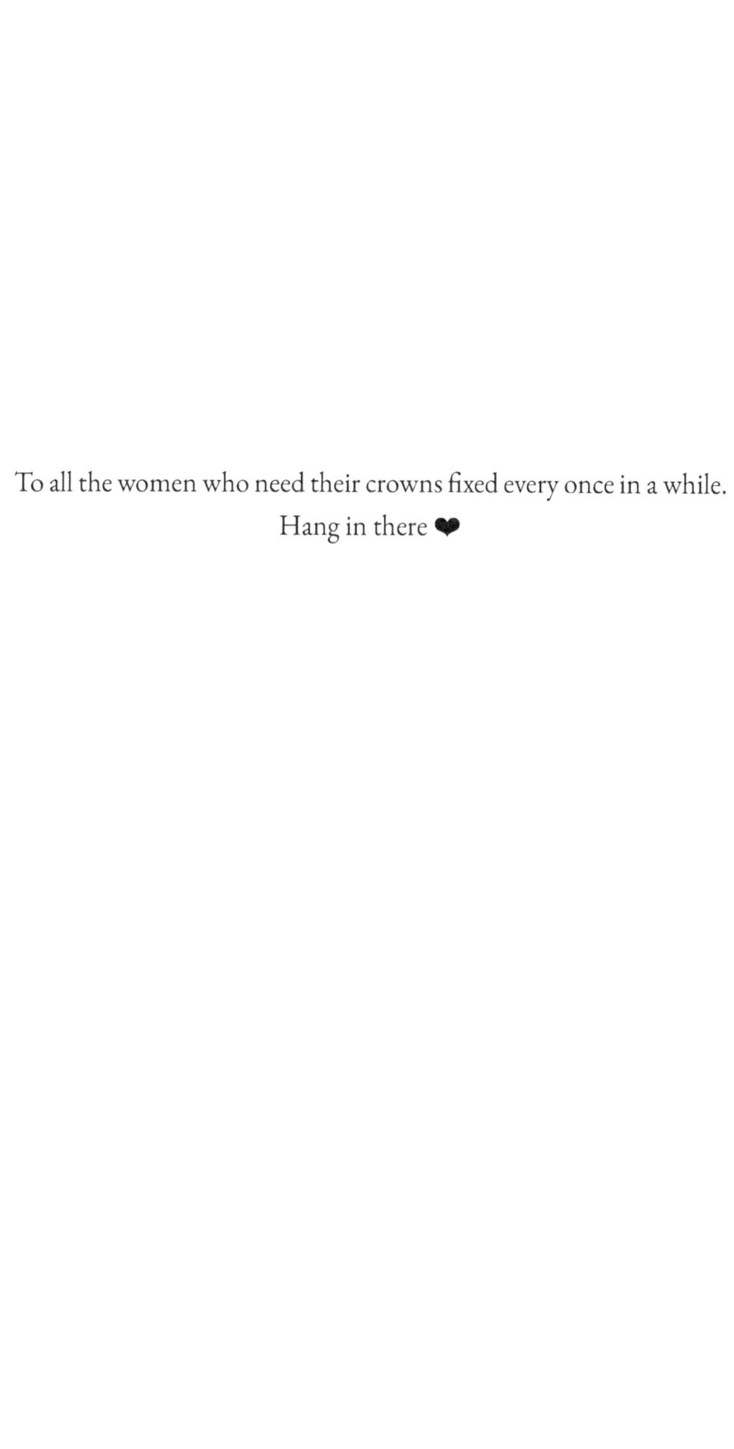

To all the women who need their crowns fixed every once in a while.

Hang in there ❤

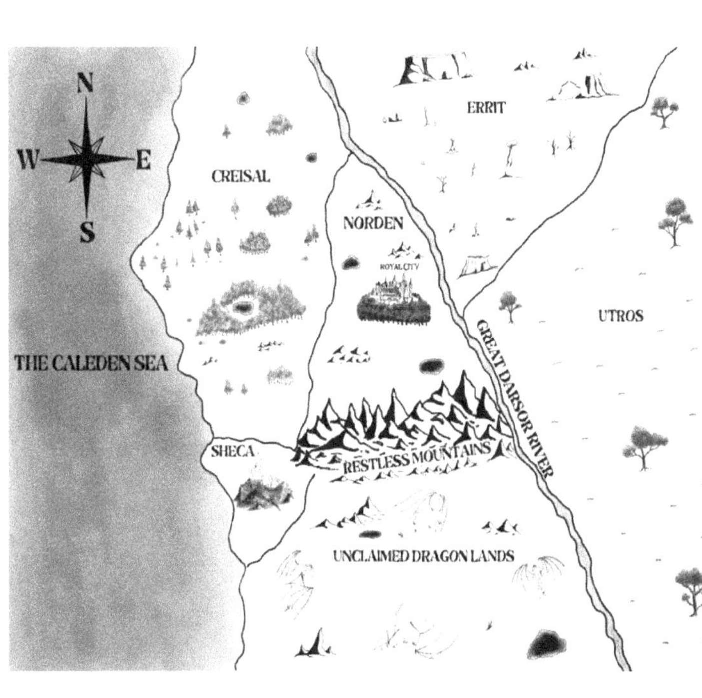

N
W E
S
THE CALEDEN SEA
CREISAL
ERRIT
NORDEN
ROYAL CITY
UTROS
SHECA
RESTLESS MOUNTAINS
GREAT DAESOR RIVER
UNCLAIMED DRAGON LANDS

Contents

ONE

MEETING THE CLANS

The flight leaving the forest and the Lost King behind was long, and the moon's light was the only thing I had to be able to see. I trusted Vasin to keep me safe and know where we were going since the clans went into hiding.

After finding out I'd been taken, all the mercenary clans evacuated to their secret stronghold location known only by a select few leaders. The journey gave me time to think about everything I'd learned and what I would say to the clan when I showed up with the crown prince of the exact people they were hiding from. Jade seemed to think they would listen if I put my foot down, but I wasn't so sure about that. Fear does something to people... like making them irrational and unpredictable.

"WE ARE ALMOST THERE, NOT MUCH LONGER."

"Any words of wisdom on how to handle the first meeting?"

"JADE ALREADY KNOWS TO KEEP GAVIN SAFE UNTIL YOU CAN EXPLAIN, SO I WOULD ADVISE MAKING YOUR POINT AS QUICKLY AS POSSIBLE."

"Really, out of all that dragon wisdom, that is all you have to suggest?"

"SOMETIMES THE BEST APPROACH IS THE SIMPLE ONE. YOU ARE THEIR QUEEN. NONE OF THE OTHER CLANS KNOW ABOUT THE ONE-YEAR TRIAL AGREEMENT YOU MADE WITH YOUR

HOME CLAN. I WILL ALSO BE THERE TO MAKE SURE THEY LISTEN TO WHAT YOU HAVE TO SAY."

I sighed, shaking my head. At least having a black dragon gave you some perks that could be used in numerous ways. I hated when people feared Vasin for being a black dragon out of some misguided superstition of being a bad omen. I knew it was inevitable until they spent time around him and realized he was harmless. Letting the conversation end, I peered down at the mountains below us and tried to figure out where they could be hiding out. This mountain range was steep, with harsh peaks thrusting into the clouds. In the moonlight and shadows, it made them seem ominous and foreboding.

Vasin began to circle a section of the mountain before he swooped down perilously fast to a cliffside that had a wide ledge where both dragons could land with plenty of room. I signaled to Jade so he knew we'd arrived, and Tahir followed after us. The moment Vasin touched down, men came swarming out of the stone like ants. The mountain seemed to glow with an inner light I could only assume came from torches. It appeared they'd carved into the mountain to create a safe haven with lookout points all up the face of the cliff, many of which were filled with shadows of armed men and women.

"Who the hell are you, and how did you find this place?" a man demanded from one of the cliff's vantage points above.

I'm sure he had an arrow trained on me, ready to take us out if we didn't give the correct answer. I took a deep breath and readied to explain, but Jade's raspy voice called out, silencing me.

"Look what she's riding, you dumb shit. Who else would be brave enough to ride on the back of a black dragon other than the queen herself?"

I heard someone swear and others gasp at this information. Many of the men lowered their weapons, but a few were not entirely convinced.

"Someone grab Ballard. He'll be able to tell us if she's the queen," a different voice suggested when no one made a move.

Yes, Ballard would be the voice of reason in this situation. As regent to the clans, he'd been overseeing everything in the absence of a king or queen for many years. Not wanting to push my luck, I sat patiently on Vasin, trying not to shiver. The night had grown cold, and dragons being cold-blooded didn't help matters. I really needed Jade to show me how he made his saddle for Tahir. As my mind wandered, I missed the crowd starting to part and the talking stopping until someone grabbed my leg and yanked me from my dragon. Just as my training was about to kick in, I heard his voice.

"Thank God you're safe," Abbott said into my neck as he crushed me in a hug.

"Can't breathe," I whispered, wiggling, but it seemed he didn't hear me or didn't care.

"Unhand the queen before I make you," Jade growled from somewhere next to me.

The tone of his voice left no room for argument, and if I didn't know he was on my side, I would've been worried Jade might kill him. Abbott relaxed his hold on me but didn't let me go entirely. When I looked up, I found Jade had a dagger resting against Abbott's throat, so close that if he swallowed, he would bleed.

"Jade, what the hell are you doing?" I snapped, turning to face him, my anger flaring. "Put your dagger away. He's my friend, not an enemy."

Jade's pale green eyes flicked to me, bright against his rich skin tone, then back to Abbott before he removed his dagger. "I thought he was hurting you..."

"Seems you picked up a new friend while you were away, mouse," Cole commented, joining us. He raised an eyebrow at me, then looked over at Jade. "Can I hug her, or are you going to pull a dagger on me too?"

Jade looked at me, then back at Cole. "If you pose no threat and the queen allows it, then who am I to stop you?"

"Yes, who are you?" Abbott questioned, rubbing his neck and glaring at Jade. "How did Cassarah end up in your care?"

While the two glared at each other, which was so unlike Abbott, Cole clasped my hand and pulled me over to him. Getting a hug from Abbott was normal, but Cole had never been the type to do so. It told me right away how worried he'd been. He draped one arm over my shoulder and pulled me close to his side and out of the way of the two posturing males.

"Guys, chill. Jade and Tahir, his dragon, are from the Hell Hawk clan, and they saved my life," I answered, trying to break the tension.

"Yeah, and some thanks I'm getting for doing it. It's not even my job to keep her safe. I didn't even know we had a queen," Jade commented with a sneer.

I wasn't sure why his words hurt, but they did, not that I would let him know. I needed to toughen up and not take things so personally if I were to be queen. I mean, I'd only known Jade for a day. He kept me alive and made sure I got back home. What more could I ask of the man? He was doing his duty for his clan and queen, so no reason to look into it more than that.

"The clans are grateful to you, Jade, for returning our queen to us safe and sound." Ballard's voice cut across the silence as he walked up to us, Becka and Helena on either side. "It seems you have brought another with you as well, Cassarah."

I'd all but forgotten about Gavin, who was standing between the two dragons, trying not to draw attention to himself. Ducking out from Cole's side, I walked up to Gavin and grasped his hand in a show of camaraderie.

"This is Crown Prince Gavin."

Everyone gasped, and some lunged toward us, but Vasin and Tahir let out rumbling growls that made them pause. Some started to shout curses at him, then me for bringing him here, while others started to raise their weapons.

"He is under my personal protection!" I stated loudly, doing my best to be heard over the chaos. "I have given my word as Queen of the Mercenaries that we will keep him safe until I can get him back home."

This statement did not help matters, but instead, it made things worse. Ruled by their fear, they disregarded the danger the dragons posed and started to throw rocks, brandished weapons, and even a few of the men above drew their bows. It was just as I feared. Everyone was going to turn on me, and I was going to get us both killed. I should have known it would be too much for them to learn they had a queen and have me bring the enemy into our hidden camp. My heart started to race, and I tried to come up with something to say or do that would make these people see reason.

As if my Birthright felt my danger, my hands began to glow with the faint blue light my bow was made from. The energy in me was building like it never had before. If I didn't do something with it, I would explode. I fought to keep hold of it, not wanting to let it spill out of me and cause some unknown havoc, but my control wasn't strong enough.

Blue light burst forth, blinding me from seeing what was happening around me. I could feel Vasin by my side, our bond singing with the amount of power pouring from me. I tried to rein in the power in vain, but it lashed out at me, unwilling to listen until it accomplished what it set out to do. Once I surrendered to it, I could feel its intent.

It was looking for someone. No, not just one person—it was seeking out multiple people.

It sensed my need for protection, and it called out to those who would keep me safe. The brand on my arm from Vasin started to heat up and pulse, causing me to cry out in pain and clutch my arm to my side. I dropped to my knees, unable to deal with the power and the pain coursing through me. Feeling my pain, Vasin roared so loud the ground under my feet began to shake, causing a new reason for the people around me to start screaming. Finally, my power settled back into my body, having accomplished what it set out to do, leaving me disoriented and drained.

It was so quiet on the cliffside that the hammering of my heart was deafening to my ears. My body ached like it had that first day of training, causing me to groan as I tried to stand. My body decided it had been beaten enough and refused to listen to me. It was also at this moment that my wound from the wagon escape added its voice to my melody of discomfort. I closed my eyes, trying to will my legs to work, refusing to show weakness if they were going to kill me.

I heard someone's footsteps walking over to me, causing me to open my eyes. I found a hand held out in front of me. The hand was covered in black ink that snaked up his arm in swirling patterns so detailed I could look at them for hours. They seemed to enhance the already large muscular arm that was the canvas. Following the design, I looked at a man I had never met. His rich brown eyes watched me with interest, which I could only guess was a reflection of how I was looking at him. He had a long, full beard that was a soft, sandy color but seemed to set off his bronzed skin in the torchlight. His head was shaved but for a section of long, braided hair on top. It was striking on him. A lesser man would have looked ridiculous. I tentatively took his hand and felt a jolt of leftover power spark between us. He sucked in his breath, tightening his grip on me as he pulled me to my feet.

"Thank you..."

"Dayson of the Bronze Reapers, My Queen," he answered, his voice so deep I could feel it in my toes.

"He is one of your chosen guardians." Vasin stepped up beside me, offering his support.

"Is that what my powers just did, picked my guardians? I thought the clans submitted their choices for me to consider," I questioned.

"Many generations ago, when our powers were stronger, it chose for the kings or queens. As the magic has weakened over time, they switched to a new system. Your powers are the strongest seen in centuries. You have called eight to your side. They all bear your mark."

Looking down at my left arm where Vasin and my Birthright had branded me, I saw it was still glowing. Instinctively, I grabbed Dayson's left arm and looked. Sure enough, the same mark was glowing on his tattooed skin. I looked up at him again, and he smiled down at me with pride showing in his eyes.

Dayson dropped to one knee and bowed his head. "I am honored to serve you, to give my life for you. I would happily fulfill the duty bestowed upon me if you will have me, Queen Cassarah."

I looked up past him to the crowd of people who slowly dropped to a bent knee, heads bowed. Some kept sneaking glances at me with shock and awe written on their faces. Others seemed angry and scowled in Dayson's direction as if unhappy with him being picked.

"Call the others to you so they can be accepted," Vasin said, nudging me with his nose.

"I call forward the rest of my guardians to be recognized," I announced, unsure of who would be walking up and scared that the two I hoped would, didn't.

I sighed in relief when Abbott, Cole, and Jade came, kneeled, and extended their left arms so I could see my mark. Two other men joined, and much to my surprise, so did Becka and another woman I'd never met.

"I have never read about female guardians before."

"They are your personal guards for times when having male guardians is a disadvantage. Many queens used them as advisers as well as protection. Every woman needs female support in a world dominated by males," Vasin explained with humor in his words.

Ballard walked up to stand on my left, a soft, encouraging smile on his face. I smiled back at him, comforted to have him supporting me, having been one of the few people who had believed in me from the beginning.

"Do you mind if we officially make you Queen before we swear your guardians to your service?" Ballard asked in a low voice for my ears only.

My smile faltered.

Was I ready to take over leading these people on the brink of war? This was the moment I had been working toward long before knowing who I truly was. It was time to let go of the old Cassarah and embrace my calling. I nodded my agreement and turned to face my people.

Two

It's Good to be Queen

Ballard stepped out before me and raised his hands out to those kneeling before us. "My clansmen, I present to you Cassarah, born of Chadrick, pair-bond to the black dragon, Vasin, the symbol of our people, thus proving her claim to the throne." Ballard's voice echoed off the mountainside, filling the night air.

Turning to face me, he pulled out a necklace from a pouch on his hip and held it aloft. "Kneel, Cassarah, as proof that even though you will rule our people, you are still of the people."

Dropping down to my knees, I bent my head and waited for the words I knew from my training he would speak.

"Do you solemnly swear to govern these people of the five clans? To be their shield and protector in times of war, to uphold our rights and customs, furthering our way of life, to surround yourself with advisers and to listen to their words," Ballard recited the ancient words.

"I so swear it," I answered as loudly and confidently as I could.

"Then may this pendant serve as a reminder of your oath for the rest of your days." Ballard slipped the necklace over my head.

Standing again, Ballard took my hand, pulled me to my feet, and thrust our hands up. "Long live Queen Cassarah!"

The crowd rose to their feet, whooping and hollering their acceptance, where they were ready to kill me moments ago. If I were honest with myself, I didn't blame them. Fear did that to people. Thankfully, the display of my powers and an angry black dragon were all it took to win them over. I wasn't naïve enough to think this was the end of it. I'm sure I will have doubters, but I would enjoy the moment for now. As the crowd settled down, I turned to the men and women still waiting for me on bended knee. Raising my arms out wide, I drew everyone's attention.

"My first act as queen is to establish my guardians by accepting those who have been called to my side." I walked over to Dayson, who was the closest to me. "Do you swear on your honor that you will be faithful to your queen and her people now and in the future, never causing them harm? And you will observe homage to your queen completely against all persons in good faith and without deceit?"

"I so swear," Dayson said, kissing my outstretched hand.

Next, I moved to Abbott and repeated the same oath.

"I so swear," Abbott answered, his face full of sincere determination.

Cole winked as he listened to me recite the oath, making me smile. "I so swear... little mouse." He tacked this on quietly enough for only me to hear.

When I came to Jade, I wasn't sure what he thought of this. His face was blank and gave me nothing to go on, but when his eyes met mine, I saw a look of awe and reverence in them. This surprised me more than any other reaction he could've had. I half expected him to be upset with being called as one of my guardians.

His answer came almost before I had gotten all the words out. "I so swear 'til my last living breath, My Queen."

Then I came to one of the men I hadn't met yet. He had thick, straight, shoulder-length black hair. His skin was fair and made for a striking contrast against his dark hair. When he looked up at me, I noticed his eyes were almond-shaped and the color of coal. Even though his face was finer-boned, it didn't detract from the lethal presence he carried.

"Your name, my guardian?" I asked softly.

"Izel of the Jade Talon clan," he answered.

"Greetings, Izel," I said, smiling at him before I recited the oath.

"I so swear," Izel answered before dropping his gaze back to the ground.

Moving on to the last of the men, I noticed that as dark as Izel is, he was the opposite. He had short, tousled white-blond hair, his eyes a pale icy blue that glittered in the firelight. He grinned at me, his excitement practically vibrating off him.

"Payson at your service. I'm from the Wind Fist clan," Payson announced, his grin growing bigger.

I couldn't help but laugh at his eagerness. "Are all the people from your clan so exuberant?"

"Nah, that's all me."

"Hmm, Payson, do you swear on your honor that you will be faithful to your queen and her people now and in the future, never causing them harm? And you will observe homage to your queen completely against all persons in good faith and without deceit?" I asked.

"Hell yeah!" he yelled, causing people close enough to laugh at his response.

"I'm glad you're excited about this, but I need you to give the correct response for this to be official," I murmured, trying to hold back my laughter.

Payson rolled his eyes before answering, "I so swear."

Nodding, I moved to the two women and knew the oath I would ask of them would be different. I'd never learned about female protectors before, but I could feel the flow of knowledge Vasin was sending my way to guide me.

"Becka, do you swear to renounce all other allegiances, to support and defend our people and your queen against all enemies, whether they are foreign or of our own blood? That you will bear the honor of being my shadow and my adviser? That you will speak wisdom and guidance, carrying out my orders as your sovereign ruler?" I asked, holding Becka's gaze, letting her know how much it meant to me to have her by my side through this.

"I swear, My Queen." Becka smiled.

Coming to the last person, I took in her strong features. Half of her hair was shaved, and the other half was waist-length blonde hair, braided tightly against her head to keep it out of her way. Like Dayson, she was covered in black ink, adding to her fierceness. Her hazel eyes observed me with a cool detachment that made me wonder if she would accept my oath. This was a woman who would not be forced into anything, regardless of what my powers thought.

"I am May of the Bronze Reapers," she introduced herself without me asking, her voice strong, clear, and commanding.

Taking a deep breath, I asked her the same thing I had of Becka and waited to hear her response. May's eyes never left mine. It was as if she was trying to see into my soul. Who knows, if she had a Birthright, she might be able to. As the silence stretched and tension grew from the men to my left, I gulped, hoping no one else could see how nervous this woman made me.

"I do not give my word lightly, and when I choose to stand behind someone, it is a person I believe in and trust to lead with wisdom and strength. Before I answer your call, I request you answer one question," May stated, catching me off guard.

"You dare question your queen? You are no clansmen of mine, May," Dayson growled, storming over, eyes flashing.

I held up a hand, halting him from doing whatever he had planned. When I saw he wouldn't go against my command, I turned back to May. "Ask your question."

"Why you? You are not of the clans. Your family abandoned our ways for the noble life. Yes, the black dragon picked you, but what makes you the person to lead us as we fight to survive? That is my question."

I could feel my stomach dropping at her words. This question had been in the back of my mind since I found out who I really was. I had come to respect these people and their way of life. They fought every day to live free and true to who they were and let their children have the same life.

"I don't deserve to be your queen," I answered, making the crowd gasp as nervous whispers spread around me. "I grew up entirely different from any of you, and I'm still learning every day what it means to be a part of a clan. The loyalty and trust you have for each other is astounding. In the noble world, it's all backstabbing and finding the best way to get ahead while taking someone else down."

I paused, closing my eyes and taking a deep breath, reaching out to Vasin to anchor me as I continued. "I might not be what you were looking for in a queen, but I can promise you this... I will do everything in my power to keep the clans alive. I understand how the nobles think and how they will attack. I have studied all the battles they've fought and found their weaknesses. I will gladly share that knowledge with the clans, and for all that I have to give, I will give. I know I have much to learn, and I'm not above asking for help or letting someone with more knowledge teach or advise me. I might not be the queen you wanted right now, but one day, I hope to become a queen you are proud of."

May's eyes lit up with a fire I hadn't seen when she asked me her question. Standing, she pulled out the sword she had on her hip, causing people to gasp and the men to take a step closer. Once again, I halted them, knowing this was a very important moment and what I did would weigh heavily in the eyes of the clansmen around us.

May grasped her sword, slicing her palm, not even flinching as blood welled and dripped from her fingers. Kneeling once again, she bowed her head and held her hand to me. "I swear my allegiance to you, My Queen, and I give you my life as well. As long as breath is in my body, I will guard you and speak the truth to you, even when you may not want to hear it. I seal my vow with blood and my life be forfeited if I ever betray you."

Taking the knife from my boot, I sliced my hand, grimacing at the pain, and grasped her hand. "I honor your vow with a seal of my blood."

Reaching out, I clasped her hand so our wounds touched, and the oath we had given each other snapped into place. Everyone around us clapped and yelled their support, some hugging each other and others smiling. Now that she was standing at her full height, May grinned down at me before she pulled me into a hug that engulfed me.

"Little queen, I have a feeling you and I will get along just fine," May whispered to me before she stepped back, and Becka swooped in to hug me.

It was moments like this that I realized how truly messed up my life had been before I met them. For twenty-one years, the only people who showed me kindness were my father and Becka. Now, I was surrounded by people who wanted the best for me. I'm sure it wouldn't be long before the doubters raised their heads, but I was going to live in the here and now. Cole walked up, took my hand, and tugged me behind him as he headed into the cave fortress.

Three

Family is Who You Chose

"Where are we going?" I laughed as Jade appeared at my side, glaring at Cole's hand wrapped around mine.

Cole looked over his shoulder at me with a smirk. "What if I said I wanted some time with you to myself? You've been gone for four days. I've missed you, little mouse."

"You shouldn't be dragging her around while she's injured," Jade growled.

This information caused Cole to stop so suddenly that I crashed into his back, letting out a yelp.

"What did you just say?" Cole snapped.

"You're not a very good mercenary if you couldn't spot the injury she has. Aren't we trained to spot weaknesses?" Jade taunted, crossing his arms with a cocked brow.

Cole held me at arm's length and truly looked at me. "Fuck!" Before I knew what was happening, I was scooped up into his arms, and he stormed off deeper into the cave. "Why didn't you say anything?"

"With all the excitement, I didn't have a chance," I reasoned, not liking he was making this my fault. I'd almost been killed by the very people who were celebrating outside, not to mention everything else that happened in the past forty-eight hours. Cole just grunted as he continued on his mission. To what end, I wasn't sure.

The inside of the mountain fortress was unlike anything I could have imagined. Just past the entrance, it opened up to a massive cavern with zigzag walkways up to cutouts in the stone. Soft lights flickered in most of them, leading me to believe they were rooms for those hiding out. Fabric curtains blocked you from being able to see in, but the warm glow still showed, along with the torches placed along the walkway. I peered up to see how far the path went, and I couldn't track it, getting lost in the darkness above. We turned off the main path and took one that branched off to the left, separating this area from those used by the other clansmen. Jade grabbed a torch, and Cole paused to let him go ahead of us, lighting our way as we went until we came to a round opening with thick wooden doors sealing the entrance.

"We need your necklace to open the royal rooms," Cole informed me as he set me down.

I'd all but forgotten the necklace Ballard gave me upon my coronation. Grasping it, I saw it was a sword with a dragon wrapped around it, but the bottom of the sword was the teeth of a key instead of a point. Walking up to the wooden doors, I inserted the key, and after a little wiggling, I managed to get the lock to turn. Jade pushed open the heavy doors and entered first, lighting the lanterns hanging from the ceiling. The room was large but sparse, with only a bed, a simple table and chairs, and a copper tub taking up space. Once all the lanterns were lit, the room had a cozy feel, even though we were trapped inside a mountain.

"Take a seat. I'm going to get some supplies and let the healer know you need to be looked at," Cole instructed before he headed back out of the room.

"You really shouldn't let him talk to you like that," Jade commented from where he leaned against the wall of my room. "You are the queen, and he is your man to command, not the other way around."

I tilted my head slightly as I examined Jade. His rich caramel-colored skin seemed to shine in the lamplight, making his black, dreaded-hair darker with the shadows. The combination caused his bright green eyes to pop as he looked everywhere but at me.

"Why is it that you have such a hard time with him controlling me?" I asked, having this nagging feeling that this was more of an issue for him than me.

Jade flinched at the question, but he finally met my gaze. "Let's just say I know what it's like to have people feel like they can control you, writing off your wishes as unimportant."

Just as I was going to ask him something else, Abbott, Dayson, and Becka burst into the room with the others of my guard joining them in a more controlled manner.

"Cassarah, why didn't you tell us you were hurt?" Becka cried, rushing to my side. "Seriously, this isn't like it was back home. You don't need to suffer in silence."

"What does that mean?" Dayson growled, his large body puffing up with anger. "Who would dare hurt the queen? Tell me, and I will make sure they breathe their last breath!"

Becka got to her feet, blocking the big man from me, hands on her hips. "You better watch yourself there, Reaper. Not every situation is that simple. Right now, we need to deal with the situation at hand. Cassarah is hurt, and she needs to be taken care of. Understood?"

I couldn't help but smile at seeing Becka scolding someone other than me for a change. That was my best friend, fierce as the red hair on her head and loyal to those she chose. Thankfully, I was among those people. I would hate to see what happened when she truly took her temper out on someone now that I knew how she was trained.

"Apologies, Your Majesty. Young Becka speaks reason. I will have to work on my temper so I do not dishonor you again," Dayson acknowledged as he took a deep breath, reining in his anger.

Feeling the need to smooth out the tension in the air, I made to stand, but a heavy hand fell on my shoulder. Looking up, I found Abbott had moved to stand next to me.

"Please, just until it's been looked at. I would hate for it to get worse," Abbott pleaded with a tender look in his gray-blue eyes.

Nodding, I settled on the bed in a more comfortable spot. "Look, everyone, a lot has happened, and there are even more pressing issues we have to deal with. Before I can get into everything, I need something to eat and some sleep. In the morning, we will go over everything."

"I couldn't have said it better myself," a familiar female voice interjected. Everyone parted, so I could see Alto, the palace healer of all people, standing in my room. "It's good to see you again, Your Majesty, although I wish it were under better circumstances."

"How? I don't understand?" I stuttered, feeling completely blindsided.

Alto grinned at me as she set her supplies on the bed next to me. Cole held a bowl of steaming water, and May was beside him with a tray of food. None of them seemed surprised to see her here, telling me I didn't need to worry about her being an enemy.

"You see, I was the insider keeping tabs on everything happening within the castle, but I had to leave as things got worse with Lord Everett. I wasn't as useful in my post either since no one was able to leave the castle grounds without an escort to make sure the mobs of angry villagers didn't attack us," Alto shared as she had me lie back, propped up by some pillows on the bed before she cut away my bandage and the leather of my pants up to my knee.

When Alto saw the state my leg was in, her eyes shot up wide with shock. "How have you been able to even walk on this, let alone act like nothing's wrong? My Queen, this injury is quite severe!"

Nervously, I licked my lips, stalling for the best answer to give here. I knew everyone in this room would eventually find out about my past, but I wasn't sure this was the best way to break the news. "Can we please leave that answer for another time? Let's just say that pain is not unfamiliar to me, and I've learned how to manage it."

All the men behind Alto stiffened at my words, but thankfully, no one pressed the matter further.

"Very well, Your Majesty, I will do as you ask. Let me know if any of this becomes too much to bear, and I can give you something to manage the pain," Alto said, gently squeezing my good leg before she started working on my wound.

Whatever she used to clean the wound burned like fire, causing me to let out a hiss as she worked. I reached out, grabbing the blankets and keeping my eyes shut tight so I could focus on shutting off the pain. I was out of practice, but old habits die hard, and I managed the only way I knew how. Then, someone slowly untangled my death grip and wrapped their fingers through mine as they spoke softly and soothingly.

"You are not in this room but far away in the sky on your dragon's back. Imagine the world below you, unable to touch you as you soar through the sky, leaving all this pain behind. Up there, you are safe and protected. No harm can come to you while your dragon carries you."

The longer he spoke, the more I could picture what he was portraying to me, and the pain faded away with the wind in my face. I felt nimble fingers combing through my hair as I relaxed further, feeling as if I truly was disconnected from my body. Soon, I let myself drift into the feeling and fell into a peaceful sleep.

When I awoke, I stretched out, feeling more rested than I'd ever felt in my life until the stab of pain shot through my leg, reminding me where and who I was. Slowly, I sat up and looked around the room only lit with two lanterns—enough to see by but not too disruptive. On the table in the center of the room was a tray of food they must have left behind when I passed out. Carefully, I shifted my legs off the bed, making sure not to hit the injured one, but instead of my feet hitting the floor, they landed on what felt like a body. Quickly, I snatched my feet back up, causing me to groan at the throbbing that started afterward. *Why did this hurt so much now when it hadn't before?*

Peering over the side of the bed, I found Izel, of all people, blinking up at me with his dark gaze. Neither of us said anything at first. He just sat up and turned to look at me with his legs crossed and body relaxed.

"How are you feeling, Your Majesty?" he asked, his soothing voice calming me from my shock.

"Cassarah, please," I responded automatically. "I understand everyone else has to show respect, but I feel like my personal guard in the privacy of my rooms can talk to me like I'm still a person."

Izel seemed to take a moment to observe me before he spoke. "When we are in private, I will do as you ask, but I will address you as your title deserves in all other situations."

"What did you do to me last night?" I asked, remembering bits and pieces of what he'd been telling me.

"Forgive me if I overstepped my role as your guardian, Cassarah. You see, my Birthright allows me to open people up to suggestions. I have to be touching them for it to work, but I convinced you that you were not in pain but safe and far from the situation. Once you were calm and the pain was gone, I thought it was best to have you rest. There was no need for you to experience that pain when there was another option."

"Thank you. It's the first time anyone has intervened like that. As I said, pain is not new to me, and I can manage it, but it doesn't mean I want to. I've lived life on my own for the most part, given no other option but to endure whatever was decided for me. The kindness you've shown when you don't even know me means more than you know," I explained, unsure if he understood what I was saying.

"It is my honor to serve and protect you however I can, Cassarah. If you allow me, I'll help you to the table so you can eat. I assume that's where you were headed before you discovered my presence," Izel said, rising to his feet.

I smiled, nodding my head. "As grateful as I am for the rest, my stomach is now protesting my neglect with food so close."

He scooped me up and carried me to the table, kicking out the seat before he set me down. "Is this a new thing that everyone will be doing? I promise just because I'm now queen doesn't mean I can't walk."

Izel sat across from me with a smirk pulling at his lips. "Alto made it known that you are not to put any pressure on your leg for at least a week while it heals. If you would like to change that, you'll have to argue with her. I warn you, though, she isn't one to be dissuaded."

"So you're telling me I have to be carried everywhere for the next week? We have a war to get ready for. What kind of message does that send?" I questioned, feeling like all the work I'd done to gain their respect was washing away before my eyes.

"A good leader knows when to lean on others as well as support those around them. It is not a weakness to need help, Cassarah," Izel scolded me.

I sighed, letting my head fall into my hands. "I'll be nothing but a burden to you guys."

"I doubt that. There's not one among us male guardians who isn't at least a little pleased to have you in their arms..."

My head shot up to meet his gaze and saw the interest that shone in them. "All of them?"

"All of them."

Four

Time to Meet the Clan Leaders

"How long have I been asleep?" I asked as I munched, feeling a little awkward with the silence that fell between us.

Izel tilted his head to the side as he thought about my question. "My guess is that it is close to midday. Your body clearly needed the rest, and I wasn't going to wake you when the others could manage things for now."

"What do you mean, manage things? What's going on?" I demanded, worry causing me to drop the bread I was eating. "Has something happened to Vasin or Gavin? Speaking of the crown prince, where did he end up in all this? I can't believe I forgot about him!"

I shot to my feet without thinking, and the shooting pain in my leg took my breath away, making me immediately fall back onto my chair.

"Calm yourself, My Queen," Izel murmured as he rested a hand on my shoulder. "Dayson and May have been looking after him..."

He was going to say more but then seemed to think better of it.

"Where are they looking after him?"

It was written all over his face that he didn't want to tell me, but he sighed and answered, "In a cell. The rest of the people refused to let him wander around and didn't listen to us guardians when we wanted to put him under guard in a dwelling away from the others."

"He's in a cell? Take me to him right now!" I shouted.

"As you wish, Your Majesty," Izel answered as he bent down to pick me up.

Izel moved swiftly and smoothly down the trail, bringing us to the cavern's main area where I saw people gathered around the firepits, working and cooking while children played under the watchful eyes of their mothers. How could they sit here like nothing was wrong when a man who'd done nothing to them was sitting in a cell? Had I been wrong about these people? They spoke of the clans and their love and loyalty to one another, yet when I told them Gavin had my protection, they ignored it. My heart sank when we left the main area and entered another tunnel that led deeper into the mountain. At the end, there were two guards armed and at the ready with grim looks on their faces. When they saw us approaching, they stood at attention, bowing to me as Izel stopped before them, setting me on my feet.

"Is it true that Crown Prince Gavin is locked up here?" I asked, needing to hear it from someone who wasn't one of my guardians.

The two men looked at each other with a worried look. "Yes, Your Majesty, he is in a cell with two of your guardians."

"Did my guardians ask you to remove him from the cell?" I pushed.

"Yes."

"Then could you explain to me why he is still there?"

"The clan leaders disagreed with your guards that he should be free to wander. That it would be better to keep an eye on him here," one answered, not meeting my eyes as he spoke.

I turned to Izel. "Now correct me if I'm wrong, as I'm still learning the finer details of being queen, but aren't you supposed to be able to speak for me in matters I cannot oversee myself?"

"That is correct, Your Majesty," Izel answered with a glint of irritation in his eyes over the matter.

Bringing my focus back to the two guards, I tried to hold back my anger, knowing it wasn't their fault. They were listening to the leaders they had been following their entire lives. I was new, and unlike what Ballard had me believe, not everyone was happy to have royalty back in the clans.

"Would you be so kind as to get my guardians and Prince Gavin?" I asked, falling back on my mother's training to keep my emotions from showing. "It seems there needs to be a meeting with the clan leaders over this matter. Therefore, I will keep him with me until we can find a more fitting resolution to this issue."

Both guards bowed and headed deeper into the tunnel to do as I asked.

"Izel, it seems I have yet another thing to add to my growing list of things to handle. How long would it take to get all the clan leaders together? I feel the matter of who is in control needs to be addressed first and foremost, or nothing will get done." I sighed.

"Once Dayson and May join us, I will personally gather them," Izel answered, resting his hands on my shoulders.

Instinctively, I leaned into him, letting him take some of the weight off my leg. If you'd told me six months ago that I would allow someone I hardly knew to touch me in such a manner, I would have laughed. Initially, Abbott and Cole had been extremely careful with me, keeping their physical interactions minimal. Once I stopped flinching whenever they reached out toward me, casual touches became more common, and I grew more confident.

It didn't take long for the guards to return with Dayson, May, and Gavin following them. Gavin seemed a little frazzled, with his thick, curly blond hair wild and dark shadows around his deep blue eyes from lack of sleep. When he saw me, his relief made me feel even worse about the whole situation. I bet a crown prince didn't have much practice being a prisoner, and in the past few days, he's been held captive by two different groups. If I wanted any chance of building relations with the king and queen, I needed to fix this quickly.

"Are you all right, Your Majesty?" I asked once they reached us.

"I am very thankful to be out of that cell, but your guardians made sure I was looked after and had everything I needed," Gavin answered, giving me a half-hearted smile. "It seems you have come to my rescue once again, Lady Cassarah."

My cheeks heated with his words. "Just doing my part as someone who was once your subject."

"My Queen, if I have your leave, I will leave you with Dayson and gather the clan leaders as you asked," Izel cut in, drawing my attention back to the other people standing here.

I wasn't sure if it was a side effect of the prince's Birthright that I always seemed to lose myself in his presence. "Yes, thank you, Izel. I'll be fine."

Izel waited until Dayson was by my side before he let go of my shoulders, bowed, and headed quickly out of the tunnel.

Tilting my head up to see Dayson's gaze, I resigned myself to what I had to ask next. "It would seem I'm not allowed to walk on my own two feet, so if I might impose on you—"

Before I could finish the sentence, I was swept up into his arms. I wrapped mine around his neck, holding him tightly as he immediately started out of the tunnel. "There is no reason to formally request my help, Your Majesty. I'm your guardian and here to assist and keep you safe. Letting you walk on that leg would mean I am failing at my true purpose."

I let out a bark of laughter at his words. "It is not your job to carry me around like an infant, Dayson."

"On that, we will have to disagree. Now, what is this about Izel gathering the clan leaders?"

Sensing I wouldn't win this argument, I allowed him to change the subject. "Seeing as it was their call to overrule me and my guardians and keep the crown prince locked up, I felt we needed to sort out a few things."

May chuckled from where she was walking next to us. "This is going to be fun. How do you think those old coots will take being scolded by our new queen, Day?"

"Seeing as one of them is my father... not well," Dayson muttered.

"Your father is the leader of the Bronze Reaper clan?" I gasped.

"My Queen, you picked sons from all the leaders of the other clans," May chimed in, far too pleased with being the one to share this information.

"Vasin, in the days when the magic picked out the guardians for the king or queen, were they offspring of the clan leaders?"

"DURING THAT TIME, THERE WERE NO CLAN LEADERS. THIS STARTED ONCE A NEW KING OR QUEEN BECAME MORE INFREQUENT."

"Do you think my magic picked them because they were?"

"I'M NOT SURE THERE IS AN ANSWER I CAN GIVE TO THAT QUESTION, BUT I DO KNOW YOUR MAGIC WILL ALWAYS DO WHAT IS BEST FOR YOU AND THE CLANS. IF IT FELT THAT HAVING THEM AS YOUR GUARDIANS WAS THE BEST OPTION IN BONDING THEM ALL TOGETHER ONCE MORE, THEN YES."

"Do they have a place here for you to be comfortable? With everything that happened last night, I feel like I abandoned you and Gavin."

"Dear Cass, do not worry about me. I am fine now that you are back. I could feel how tired you were on top of being in pain, so I do not mind. Try not to worry about things that do not need your worry. This place was made to house dragons, and I have Tahir to keep me company. He has been sharing his stories of his adventures with Jade."

"Anything I should know about?"

"No, I will let the man tell you himself when he is ready, but I am no longer worried about you being safe with him since he bears your mark."

"Does that do anything special?"

"Yes, but we will deal with that once you're finished with your clan meeting. One step at a time, Cass, and remember, you are not in this alone."

Letting out a huff, I pulled my attention back to my current surroundings, being carried into a good-sized cave with a large table in the middle of the space. This had to be a strategy room because in the middle of the table was a massive map of our country and the lands that bordered it. Dayson set me down at the head of the table and pulled out a chair, but I ignored it to hobble over to the map. I leaned over the table and absorbed everything I saw. This had to be one of the most detailed maps I'd ever seen of the place we called home. It had more to it than most I'd used with my father and showed places I didn't even know existed or we'd mapped out.

"There are Unclaimed Dragon Lands?" I asked no one in particular.

"You have a dragon, and you don't know this? Where do you think all the dragons who don't bond with someone go?" a snide voice asked behind me.

I stiffened at his words which sounded so much like something my mother would say to me. Gripping the back of the chair next to me, I turned, putting all my weight on my good leg to face off with whoever this man was. He was far older than me with a harsh-looking face as if he'd been out in the sun too long for many years. His white hair was pulled away from his face in a low ponytail, giving him an even more severe appearance. His ice-blue eyes gave away which of my guardians he was a father to. I hadn't spent much time with Payson, but he seemed to be the exact opposite of his father, which I was now very grateful for.

Plastering a pleasant smile on my face, I greeted the man. "Who might I have the pleasure of addressing?"

"Porvan, clan leader of the Wind Fist clan and father to your guardian, Payson," he answered without any sign of respect for who I was to his people.

Porvan might not see me as his queen, but I would attend to that issue later. There was no way I could let him show me such disrespect in front of the other clan leaders. If I completely lose the respect of one, then the rest will quickly follow after. That was just a fact. From all my training, I knew this is where battles were won and lost. If the leadership couldn't work together, then everything would fail. Porvan would have to fall in line or be executed—there was no in-between. If I banished him, he had too much knowledge that would cripple us, even if it might give me more favor with the people. I prayed I might win him over, or my first act as queen would be to kill the father of one of my guardians, and that was not the best scenario. I decided to wait on the matter since Ballard, three other men, and the rest of my guardians entered the room.

"Looks like we are all here. Let's take our seats, shall we?" I offered as I took a tentative step forward.

I managed to keep the pain off my face, but I knew I wouldn't make it to my spot on my own. Without asking, Payson walked right up to me and took my arm in his so I could lean against him. Clinging to him, I managed to move without much of a limp, refusing to look weak in front of the wolves in the room watching for any sign I might crumble. This was my audition, and it had to be perfect.

FIVE

I DON'T THINK THEY LIKE ME

As everyone seated themselves, I turned to Dayson once I reached the head chair. "Could you please bring over a chair for Prince Gavin and put it on my left?"

I saw the flash of surprise at my request since that spot was normally reserved for the queen or the king's wife or lover. This was all about strategy, and I needed them to know I was serious in my request to keep Gavin safe, and the fact they had disregarded it would not be overlooked. I might not be able to fight them physically in my condition, but I knew mentally I could back them into a corner, forcing them to see reason.

"Why is *he* here?" one of the other men snarled. "Who let him out of his cell?"

By his size alone, I would guess he was the clan leader of the Bronze Reaper clan and Dayson's father. They looked similar in many ways, along with sharing his quick temper with his son. I could already tell with Dayson, it was out of his desire to protect me, and I was hoping it was the same for his father.

"I let him out. He never should have been placed there at all. Prince Gavin is under my protection. I gave my word as Queen of the Mercenaries. Would you ask me to dishonor that promise?" I asked, raising a brow.

Dayson set the chair on my left side, and this caused the clan leaders to shoot to their feet, shouting.

"You dare to put him in such a position?"

"Once from a traitor's family, always a traitor. You sold yourself out to the kingdom!"

"This will not be tolerated. He must be removed at once, if not killed!"

Ignoring them, I locked eyes with Gavin and nodded for him to take his seat. He looked at them, then back at me before squaring his shoulders, putting on his royal air, and leisurely settling himself beside me.

"Enough!" Ballard roared, slamming his fist on the table. "How dare you address your queen in such a manner! The lot of you should be put to death for such a display of disloyalty and slander!"

I raised a hand, motioning for Ballard to sit back down as I rose. This was a moment I couldn't let anyone else speak for me. I needed to do this on my own. They had to admit I was good enough to be their queen.

"Gentlemen, allow me to introduce myself. I am Queen Cassarah of the Raven Rose clan and leader of *all* the mercenary clans that still exist. I was once of the royal court that this man's parents ruled, but I have shed that loyalty, being I cannot rule if I am ruled. Don't you agree?" I inquired, pausing to give them a moment to let that sink in. "Now, why don't we all take our seats, and if you could be so kind as to share with me who you are. If I am to defend myself and my actions, I would like to know who my accusers are."

It seems Mother's training had more uses to it than I thought. They are like a bunch of unruly children who don't want to share a toy with the new kid.

"Vasin, can you enter the inner cavern at all?"

"Cass, nothing will stop me from getting to you, but yes, I can do that with ease."

"Excellent. Would you be so good as to stand guard outside the doors of the room I am in right now? Anyone who isn't my guardian, Gavin, or Ballard is to be eaten if they step out of this room."

"By the sounds of it, I might eat them anyway if they have offended you this much."

"That won't be necessary. I just need to get them to take me seriously. Once we get over this hurdle, I'm sure they will see reason."

Thankfully, they all took their seats again and seemed to be passing looks at each other as if completely caught off guard by me. Then Porvan stood, body ramrod straight, as he met my gaze, determination clear on his face. It would seem I hadn't been wrong to ask Vasin to join us for this conversation.

"I am here, Cass, and I might add that I haven't had a chance to eat yet."

That caused me to smile, and I had to force myself not to snicker at Vasin's joke.

"Is there something you wish to say, Porvan?" I asked as his face turned into a scowl, thinking I was laughing at him.

"Either the prince is removed, or we will leave this room, and you will not be recognized as our queen," he declared.

Both brows rose at this statement. "My, it sounds like this was an agreed-upon choice, but how could it be? None of you knew I removed Prince Gavin from the cell until you saw him here. This leads me to believe you planned to turn your back on me from the moment you stepped foot in here. Does that sound about right?"

Porvan gaped at me, shock written all over his face that I wasn't the least bit bothered by this news. "Did you really think the black dragon would pick someone so easy to dethrone?"

"Dragons are not people. They don't see things the same way we do. How could he know you were the right person to be our queen? It's been a very long time since the last black dragon, and that man it picked was a fool who died in a skirmish, leaving us stranded to deal with the aftermath of his mother's battle. We shattered after that, and we won't let another poor choice of a ruler kill us off," one of the other clan leaders snapped. I would guess he was Izel's father.

"If you would like to ask Vasin personally on that matter, he's right outside the door, but I should warn you that he hasn't had a chance to eat yet," I informed him, gesturing toward the door.

The man blanched, and he turned his worried gaze to Porvan, their chosen leader, it would seem.

"Is it your plan to keep us locked in here against our will?" Porvan growled.

I gave him a bright smile. "Not at all, but if you choose to leave, then you will not make it far. If, on the off chance, that doesn't sound like something you want to do, then all I ask is you hear me out. After hearing all I have to say, if you still don't wish to have me as your queen, then I will revisit that with you."

Porvan seemed to realize I had him neatly tucked in between a rock and a hard place, but the lesser of two evils was to listen to what I had to say. "Very well. What is so important for us to hear that you would go to these lengths?"

"I'm so very glad you asked, but first, I would love the pleasure of knowing who else sits at the table with me. Or should I ask your sons instead?" I countered, not giving up since it had been my first request.

"You're not one to give up easily, are you?" Porvan muttered.

I decided not to encourage him with an answer and turned my attention to the man I assumed was Dayson's father, hoping he would see reason.

"Garold, Your Majesty, clan leader of the Bronze Reapers," he shared, giving me a nod. "Dayson is my son and May is my niece, but since she's been under my care most of her life, I see her as a daughter. You hold both of my children in your hands."

"They have both already made a fine impression and done what they could to keep me and those under my protection safe," I admitted, giving Garold a soft smile. "I look forward to getting to know them better."

I shifted my gaze to the man next to him who shared his viewpoint on Vasin's ability to pick out a good ruler. "I am Xio, clan leader to the Jade Talon, and you know who my son is. Let it be known that if you get my one and only son killed over protecting that prince, I will not hesitate to kill you."

"Father!" Izel snapped, coming to stand on my right side as the other guardians moved closer to me. "I let what you said before slide because our queen didn't address it, but this is going too far. Don't let it get to the point that I must kill *you* instead."

I didn't know Izel that well, but seeing such an aggressive outburst toward his father surprised me. Reaching out, I wrapped my hand around his wrist and gently squeezed it to remind him where he was.

"Izel, be at peace. I do not fault him for being protective of his child. His words are out of love for you... be grateful for them. I never had a parent come to my defense." When I felt him relax under my touch, I returned my attention to his father. "You get one pass, Xio, and you just used it. Be wise and don't force my hand with another threat on my life. I assume that would leave other children alone and without a father to keep them safe." His expression told me I hit the nail on the head with my deduction.

When I woke up today, I had no idea I would be making sure no one died by my hand or my guardians'. There are some things no training or books could teach you, but I had plenty of life experience with volatile energy. Only this time, I had weight to throw around, and I planned to use it to my advantage.

"That leaves us with the clan leader of the Hell Hawks," I stated, turning to the last man in the room. He also happened to be the one who had said nothing since entering the room.

His dark brown, almost black eyes watched me with careful study. Out of all of them, he was the only one who did not look like his son, and it made me wonder what their true connection was. The clan leader had dark umber skin that his red shirt contrasted with spectacularly. His black hair was shaved off, leaving him with a bald head that the firelight of the lanterns glistened off of. Even though he wore long sleeves, I could tell he was fit with how his muscles moved under his shirt. He was also appeared to be the youngest of the clan leaders.

"My name is Acton, Your Majesty. Jade is tied to me as we share a mother, but he is no family of mine," Acton informed me, his face cold, keeping his emotions locked down tight.

As much as I wanted to ask more about that, I knew it wasn't the time or place but something I should address with Jade. Back in the forest, he told me he might not be welcome here, and now I understood why he might think that.

"While I do hope we can find a way to work together, that is the least of our problems at the moment. What do you know of Errit and the army that has crossed over the Great Darsor River into our country?" I asked, diving right into the meat of things.

All the men scowled or showed confusion at my words, which didn't bode well for us. If the Lost King could slip past us, and the people whose survival was to know these types of things, we were in deep trouble.

"There is no such thing," Porvan announced. "Our clan is right at the border of Errit and Creisal to the west. If there were movement of that kind, we would know."

"What if they crossed into Utros just south of Errit and then crossed over near the far side of the Restless Mountains?" I said gesturing over to the map. "Or if they were smart, they would have crossed in smaller groups over time. We commonly traded with Errit, so caravans always came and went until this past year."

"We are not the gatekeepers of the border, Your Majesty," Porvan spat, then pointed at Gavin. "That is his and the kingdom's duty, not ours."

Now ready to drop the information that would truly tell me if they would see reason or not, I stood, placed my hands on the table, and looked them dead in the eye before I spoke.

"The Lost King, King Edward's first-born bastard son, is back and ready to take his crown from his father, who abandoned him. Care to tell me how we all missed that bit of information?"

SIX

THE UNTOLD HISTORY

"The king has another son?" Acton asked, surprise written all over his face.

I watched the others to see their reaction, and what do you know, Porvan was the only one who showed fear at this news. I sat down, leaned back in my chair, and stared Porvan down until he decided to share what he knew with the rest of us. I was tired of having to ask and drag information out of these men, but something told me the others wouldn't like that he kept this from them.

"He was banished deep in the lands of Utros, carefully guarded and locked in a tower," Porvan blurted. "How could he have gotten out?"

"His Birthright," Gavin spoke up. "Henry can get in people's heads and make them do what he wants them to. I watched him do it countless times to his soldiers and anyone he needed to control."

"How do we know your brother is not controlling you at this very moment?" Xio growled, narrowing his eyes at Gavin. "It would be the perfect strategy."

Gavin just shook his head. "If he took over my brain, then my Birthright would be canceled out, and he needed me to get information out of people without damaging them. His gift destroys weak-minded people, turning them into babbling idiots who should be killed to put them out of their misery."

"This is why you wanted him in here… to get us to spill all our secrets!" Porvan roared, slamming the table, shoving his chair back, and storming toward me.

Dayson and Abbott created a wall of muscle, blocking him from getting close to me as May came to stand right behind me. Cole looked like he wanted to murder the man but hung back with Payson, watching the situation, ready to move at a moment's notice.

"Do you really think that is what's happening, Porvan? Because to me, it seems you have all been keeping your mouths shut tighter than a bear trap. If Gavin were using his powers, you would be singing like a bird. Now, sit down before I make you sit," I ordered from where I remained seated in a show of confidence I definitely didn't feel.

Abbott escorted Porvan back to his seat but stayed behind him to ensure he didn't pull a stunt like that again.

"How did you know about the king's bastard?" Garold asked.

Porvan shifted in his seat, clearly knowing what he was about to say would not go over well. "The king paid us to take him since he couldn't let anyone in the kingdom know. It was before his marriage, and he couldn't have anything stop that from happening."

Garold flinched back like he'd been slapped. "How dare you sit there and tell our queen that she isn't fit to rule us when you've had a hand in something like this! Treachery will always come back to bite you in the ass, Porvan, and now it's your time to bend over and take it. Enough with the pussyfooting around. Tell us everything you know about this bastard who snuck his way onto our lands."

I had to hand it to Garold. He didn't mince words, but I agreed with him on all fronts. It was time we all came clean about things.

"Richard, a member of the Raven Rose clan, was his inside man and is also the one who kidnapped me. They wanted to smuggle me into Errit and lock me up. For what purpose, I don't know, but my guess is that it would be tied to the fact I can speak to Vasin and access his knowledge. Gavin was also abducted to be used by the Lost King as he grows his army of Errits and our own people who have been brainwashed or forced into it. This is no longer just a matter of the mercenaries trying to survive. If the Lost King takes Royal City, then all will be lost, and we will need to flee," I admitted, watching the faces of all the people in the room and the understanding they now have. "I propose that we reach out to Queen Mary and let her know that Gavin is safe and with us. If we can get the king and queen to work with us, then we have a greater number of fighters and dragons."

The room fell quiet at my words, and tension filled the air at my proposal. I knew I was asking a lot of them, but we didn't have the luxury of wasting time fighting about who's right or wrong. Porvan needed to share what he knew, giving us something to work off of, even if it was from so long ago. Knowledge was power, and the Lost King had decades to plot this revenge, and having the Errit kingdom behind him added to his power.

"Are you sure that is wise, Your Majesty?" Acton asked, resting his chin on his hand. "Wouldn't keeping Gavin's presence here a secret be more to our advantage?"

"Not if we are working to combine forces. This is the perfect time to mend the divide between our people, and Gavin is the perfect person to help. If he is willing to play the middleman and convince his mother to talk to us in a neutral location, then we have a chance to share part of what we know and give her son back if he chooses to return," I elaborated.

"You want him to stay with us?" Xio interjected, apprehension written all over his face.

I turned and spoke directly to Gavin. "Prince Gavin is his own person, and I believe everyone should have a say in their future. If we manage to make an agreement with the king and queen and Gavin would like to remain here as their ambassador, I will happily accept. Likewise, if he decides to leave and return to the palace and his role as crown prince, I wish him all the best."

The astounded look on Gavin's face told me what I already knew—never had someone let him choose his own fate. I had first-hand experience with this, and I would never take that option away from someone if I could help it. I couldn't explain it, but I felt a connection to Gavin on a level I don't know if any of the people around me understood. Gavin understood the obligations of the royal court and the lies and viciousness of the people in that world. I would never have to make him understand why my mother did what she did to me, no matter how horrific it was, because that's what you did to get ahead in our world. Now I had the chance to give Gavin what Cole and Ballard gave me—a choice of where your fate took you.

So as not to force his answer, I turned my attention back to the clan leaders. "Tell me all you know about what's currently happening in our kingdom. Then I would like Porvan to share the rest of his story involving the king and his son he smuggled away."

It took far longer than I would have imagined for us to cover everything the clans had been keeping an eye on. Much of the information wasn't useful to our current situation, but it did give me a feel for the rest of our country. Royal City was the epicenter of our kingdom and the largest city we had. There were other small towns and villages, but nothing much of note happened in them since it was mostly farmers and livestock. The closer we got to the border of Errit and Utros, the towns died out, making it far easier to slip in and out of the country. We had guards stationed at the major bridges connecting our lands, but even they had reported that things were quiet. The only thing of note was the lack of vendors and merchants crossing to sell goods, which I'm assuming is where this talk of an arranged marriage came into play. If Henry was using it as a ruse to get his brother into Errit instead of having to kidnap him, that failed when Gavin refused the offer, and his younger brother was promised instead.

"I believe we should take a break. I'm not as young as I once was to work through the night," Ballard suggested, pushing back his chair. "It would be my suggestion to reconvene tomorrow since I believe we still have much to cover on this matter."

Now that he mentioned it, and I gave myself a moment to actually notice what was going on with my body, I was thankful for the adjournment. "Yes, I think that will be best. This is not a matter we will be able to fix overnight. We don't have much time, but we need to be fresh and rested to come up with the best plan of action. You are all dismissed. My dragon would like to greet you on the way out. I promise he will not eat anyone... for now."

"Why would you tell them that? I wanted to see their reaction when they found me waiting for them."

"We made good progress. Do I think they are loyal to me... no, but they are loyal to their people and need my help. So, we will let them live for the time being."

Vasin huffed, and a plume of smoke wafted in from the open door, followed by a very unmanly gasp. I smiled to myself, wondering which clan leader it had come from.

Cole moved in as if he were going to help me out of the chair and carry me out of the room, but I rested a hand on his chest, stopping him. "I think we all need a moment to talk about what just happened in here before we step outside this room. Please sit," I said, motioning for my guardians to join me at the table.

Ballard looked at me with a raised brow, questioning if he should go or stay. "Join us, Ballard. You know these clan leaders in a way the rest of us do not."

"As you wish, Your Majesty."

I gave it a few more moments, knowing that Cole wouldn't be able to keep silent much longer.

"What the fuck, little mouse... why didn't you let us kick their asses? What they did would be considered treason, and you would have been well within your rights to kill the bastards!" Cole spat, his fists clenched.

"You would really have me kill their fathers because they didn't like me? They have been the leaders of their people for a long time, and I'm an outsider who just became their queen. I was expecting pushback, though I didn't know it would be quite so aggressive," I pointed out, rubbing my temple to ease the growing dull ache. "My goal is not to be a tyrannical leader, but I know through all my studies that I can't let them think I'm a pushover... hence, why I brought in Vasin. It was my hope the threat was big enough that they wouldn't force me to act on it."

"It was a smart move, Your Majesty," Abbott assured me.

Groaning, I hid my face behind my hands. "Please don't do that, Abbott. I know you all feel it's the proper way to address me, but I can't handle it from you guys." I lifted my head and looked at all of them. "When we are alone or with Ballard, I need you not to use my title. I refuse to be a queen who will sit at the top and look down on her people... that's not how this is going to work. I intend to make sure everyone knows they matter to me, and I am one of them. No matter what happens throughout this battle, I need you all to keep me grounded in Cassarah, the broken girl who chose her destiny. The more they get to know me, the better I can help them."

May grinned at me while Becka shook her head with a knowing smile. Jade surprised me by scowling as he looked down at the table, unwilling to meet my gaze as Payson looked confused. As for Cole, Abbott, and Izel... well, they just agreed to my request, unsurprisingly, since two of them knew me the best, and Izel and I had already covered this issue.

"Why?" Payson asked. "Don't you want them to respect you as our queen?"

I tilted my head a little as I rolled his question around my brain a moment before answering. "Respect is a funny thing and can be earned in a few different ways. I want to gain their trust and respect through actions... keeping my word and walking alongside them through our hardships. If I do not understand my people's needs, how can I help them? Indirectly, this will help with the clan leaders as well. Once they see I'm no different than they are, I think their minds will open up to working better together for our people."

"Damn, if they could have heard that answer, they would already be tripping over themselves to get your forgiveness." May chuckled. "I certainly chose the right queen to pledge my life to."

Everyone agreed, the atmosphere lightening up as they started to understand what I was trying to do.

"About the carrying thing—"

"Nope, sorry, little phoenix, but you have no say in that matter," Abbott interjected, cutting me off. "Alto told us you shouldn't walk on it for a week to start, and that's what's gonna happen. We could always put you in a cart and pull you around if that makes you feel better, but I don't think it would work very well in the cavern."

I glared at him, irritated he knew just what I was going to ask. "Fine, but I want you all to know it is not something I expect from you, so if you do not wish to be my pack mule, then I will not make you."

"Who says no to holding a pretty woman in their arms?" Dayson asked with a wink.

Cole and Jade scowled at the big man while Abbott watched them both with a contemplative expression.

"Cassarah, I think we can call it a day. Let your guardians take you back to your rooms to read and eat something. It is far later than you realize. We have been in here for hours," Ballard said as he rose. "Tomorrow will be another long day of talks and planning. That is if we can get them to agree on anything."

Sighing, I nodded my agreement, which was all the prompting Jade needed to pick me up and head out the door.

SEVEN

GETTING TO KNOW YOU

"Hey, you okay?" I whispered to Jade as he led our group back to my room.

"Why wouldn't I be?" he answered, brushing off my question.

"Look, it's fine if you don't want to talk about it. I get having things you don't want anyone else to know about. My family life wasn't exactly all that wonderful," I murmured, relaxing into his hold.

Jade grunted, but when he didn't say anything more, I let the matter drop. Just past the door to my room there was another I hadn't noticed in the dark, but now a torch was burning outside it. May gestured for Gavin to follow her, and she swung it open, revealing an open space with other doors branching off it.

"These are the guardians' rooms. I figured with everything going on, it would be best for Prince Gavin to stay here with us. There are ten rooms so each of us gets a room to ourselves. It's nothing fancy, but this cavern wasn't meant to be lived in forever," May explained, then turned to Gavin. "The two with the doors open aren't taken, so feel free to pick between the two. There isn't a bathing chamber in this section, but if you need it, we can show you where it is."

"No, all I want is food and sleep," Gavin said, then turned to look at me. "Do you need me for anything else?"

I gave him a soft smile and shook my head. "Nothing that can't wait until tomorrow. Eat and get some rest. The past few days have been hell on you, and I'm sure you didn't get much sleep last night."

"None. I was too anxious to sleep, even with May and Dayson guarding me," Gavin admitted.

"We will all be right next door if you need anything, and I'll make sure food is brought over," I offered, making sure he knew where people he could trust were.

With a slight bow, Gavin headed into the space to find a room and some sleep.

Cole already had my door open for Jade to enter easily, but he halted when I gasped, finding that it had been completely rearranged with more furniture and other things to make it more comfortable. Instead of the small table for two, there was a larger version for six people to sit at. There was even a comfortable couch and overstuffed chair, giving everyone a seat in my room. The bed was still there but had been shifted to allow for more space, the covers had been changed, and the bed was made.

"What is all this?" I asked as Jade set me down in front of the armchair.

"The room hadn't been prepared for you to have eight guardians and a crown prince who might be spending time in your rooms," Abbott teased as he sat on the couch. "Truthfully, we didn't have much time to think about this room being used. It was such a frenzy getting everyone here and then trying to make a plan to get you back."

My head snapped to face him. "You were looking for me?"

"Don't be an idiot. Of course, we were looking for you, little mouse. You got taken right under our noses by one of our own. Why wouldn't we come after you?" Cole snapped.

Jade whirled, and a dagger was once again at Cole's throat. "How many times do I have to tell you not to speak to her like that, Raven?"

Cole slapped Jade's hand away from him, not in the least bit worried about getting hurt. "I know who you are, *Shadow*. The real question is, does she?"

"You will be dead where you stand if another word comes out of your mouth," Jade snarled, stepping closer to Cole.

Cole moved in a flash, knocking the dagger out of Jade's hand, twisting his arm behind him, and trapping him in an armlock I knew hurt like a bitch. "If you weren't her guardian, there is no way I would let someone like you near her. Filth like you doesn't deserve to be given the honor."

Frozen, I watched in wide-eyed shock at the animosity between them. Once my brain and body caught up, I shot to my feet and took a step to stop them, shouting as I moved. "Stop it right now!" Forgetting about my leg, I slammed it against the low table and dropped to my knees, my hands slapping the stone floor as I caught myself.

"Cass!" Cole cried out, shoving Jade away from him and darting toward me, but Dayson was there first.

"Back off, Raven. You've done enough already," Dayson warned.

Taking my arm, he helped me to my feet, and I limped back to my chair. Dayson dropped to his knee, placing my foot on his thigh and pulling up the leg of my loose pants until the bandage was revealed. You could see specks of blood soaking through the fabric, letting me know I'd agitated it.

"Payson, grab me the supplies Alto left for us over on the shelf by the bed," Dayson directed as he started to unwrap my bandages.

Abbott stood and walked over to Cole, grabbing his arm and dragging him toward the door. "What the hell, man?"

"We're going to get food for her because after they finish cleaning that, we'll be lucky if she's awake long enough to even eat it," Abbott muttered, ignoring all of Cole's protests. "She has all her other guardians. She'll be fine."

Cole turned to look at me, his eyes filled with worry, so I gave him a small smile and nod, sending him off. His shoulders sagged, and he stopped fighting Abbott as he left the room.

"I'm sorry, little bird, you shouldn't have had to see that," Jade apologized, his eyes cast to the floor, braced for me to yell at him.

"Come sit. You've been standing all day," I offered, causing his gaze to snap to mine in confusion. "Please sit. Don't make me order you."

Silently, he drifted over to the couch and perched on the arm, following my request... barely. "This is all new to us. The eight of you come from different places, backgrounds, and clans. It will take a little time for all of you to learn to work together. My plan is to see if I can learn more about guardians of the past to see how things worked between them. I know you are my guardians and protectors, but I really don't know much else about your roles. Queen Emery was the last queen to have guardians, but we are still translating the scrolls from her time. I did get through all of her mother's thoughts. Queen Miranda, the Raven Queen, I believe you know her by, was the last to take all her guardians as lovers. Emery only took two, and her son didn't live long enough for anyone to write down much about him," I shared, trying to distract myself from what Dayson was doing.

He'd gotten my bandage off and was using the bowl of water and a cloth that Payson had given him. The water felt cool against my hot, angry skin, but I knew if I looked at it, it would become far more painful than I wanted to deal with.

"You can read the old tongue?" Izel asked, a sense of awe in his voice.

I grinned, seeing a man who would be like-minded in my love of learning. "Yes, I wasn't as proficient at it as I am now, but my father used to have me learn different languages."

"I don't mean to offend, Cassarah, but isn't that unusual for a noble woman?" Payson asked from his spot on the floor near my chair, holding supplies for Dayson.

"That is true. Most women aren't taught to read or write much more than their name, let alone another language. I might not have come from the best family, but I thankfully had a father who valued knowledge as much as how well a woman can sew or dance," I explained.

Now I had Izel and Payson's full attention while the others also listened in.

"What else did your father teach you?" Izel asked, leaning forward in his seat.

"Actually, this might be good for you and the clan leaders to know—"

"No!" Jade cut in, making me jump at his outburst. "They need to earn that trust. Don't hand over secrets to those you are not sure are loyal to you. I get that you want to impress them and prove you should have the role of queen, but you already have it. They need to accept it."

I paused, watching him before I nodded my head. "Wise advice, Jade. Thank you. I suppose I need to blend my knowledge of the royal court with what I know of the clans. Raven Rose has shown me what a family unit can be like and how they trust and work together to survive, but I'm guessing not all clans are that way."

"The Ravens are the most well-off of the clans, being that they were tied to royalty. Others have struggled far more, forcing us to extend our limitations on what jobs we will take, hardening us. The Wind Fists are on the border of Norden and Errit, pulling jobs from Errit just to keep their people fed. Normally, we do not venture outside our country, but we do what we must," Payson shared, his shoulders hunched, eyes downcast, like I was going to be upset by this information and take it out on him.

The signs of him being abused, most likely by his father, screamed at me. I couldn't believe I'd missed it before now, but he always managed to hide it behind a smile and a laugh, whereas I always hid it in silence and gritted my teeth to bear it. I hissed as Dayson had to redo a few of the stitches, catching me off guard. I closed my eyes for a moment, took a deep breath, and opened them again to continue the conversation.

"As we get to know each other, I would love to learn more about what each clan is really like. I see all the reports, but they don't explain what daily life is like," I said with a tight smile.

Izel frowned as he stood, walked over to me, and squatted beside my chair. "Don't do that. There is no need to hide your pain from us. We are guardians and prepared to keep you safe, but that also means from yourself. It is not good to smother your pain like that because, at some point, it might kill you if we don't know what's going on with you. Jade was right to tell you not to share your secrets with the clan leaders, but we are your sworn and bound allies in every way we can be. Let us be there for you, just like you want to be there for our people. Even queens need someone to lean on."

Without thinking, I reached up and rested my hand on his cheek, seeing the sincerity in his eyes. The small flame that Abbott, Cole, and Ballard had been trying to grow in my heart burned a little brighter, hearing Izel's words. This wouldn't be easy for me to do, having spent so long covering up my needs and emotions. He made it sound so easy to trust in them, let them in, and see the true core of who I was.

"Dearest, Cass, does it finally make sense now that I'm not the only one telling you this? Cass, you are no longer the girl trapped in her room, beaten for her strong mind and will. Let them help heal the damage your past has dealt you and be reborn as the Mercenary Queen," Vasin coaxed, his calming voice drifting through my head.

"I will try, but I'm sure you will need to repeatedly remind me to let them."

"That is something I can do."

Izel startled me as he covered my hand with his, pulling me back to those around me. "I don't know how to do that very well, so I'm going to need your help." Slipping my hand off his face, I looked up at the others. "All your help, since it was literally beaten into me that I wasn't worth being cared about. My value was in what I could gain for my parents in prestige and status within the court. Believe it or not, I've come a long way, but there is still a lot of room to grow."

"We would be honored to help you, Cassarah," May spoke, her eyes filled with compassion and understanding. "This group will be your new family and teach you what that should look like. We all might be a little screwed up in our ways, but we'll have each other's backs."

EIGHT

I KILLED A MAN

Just as Dayson finished redressing my leg and getting it wrapped in a clean bandage, Abbott and Cole entered with three other people behind them, carrying trays of steaming bowls and fresh bread. Soon, all the table space was filled with food and drinks, making the room smell amazing and causing my stomach to grumble, sharing my excitement for the food. Abbott grabbed a tray and set it in my lap, making sure it was stable before he let go.

"Just so you don't fret, I made sure to drop a tray off to Gavin, but he's already passed out. It'll be there for him when he wakes up," Abbott shared as he filled my cup with water.

Reaching up, I grasped his arm and gave it a gentle squeeze. "Thank you."

"Of course, Cassarah. I'm happy to help, and he seems like a decent guy for a prince," Abbott teased, remembering when we met and how formal and stiff he'd been, thinking I was a noble woman. "Now eat so we can get you in bed before you sleep in your soup again."

"That happened one time! It also was at the beginning of my training when you had me do the obstacle course four times, then I had training with Becka," I grumbled.

Becka laughed, hearing me. "Oh, you mean back when it was learning how to fall off a horse since you couldn't keep your seat?"

"Having no stirrups and expecting me to be able to do all those maneuvers is just torture. Inali almost didn't let me ride her again after that week. I had to bribe her with apples and sugar cubes before I could put the saddle on," I shot back before shoving a spoonful of stew into my mouth.

"Everyone goes through hell the first month of training but look at you now. No one would ever know you didn't grow up here," Becka announced proudly. "That is something you should be proud of."

"Trust me, I've seen her fight, and she is no novice. Didn't even hesitate to do the deed," Jade interjected. "She also went head-to-head with Lord Everett and won."

Becka, Abbott, and Cole gaped at him, then looked at me in shock.

"You bested the king's captain of the royal guard?" Abbott asked as if he didn't believe Jade.

"Fuck that... you killed someone?" Cole demanded; his brows creased. "Are you okay?"

I moved to set the tray of food down since I was no longer hungry, but Izel stopped me. "No, they can wait. You need to eat so your leg will heal."

It was becoming clear to me my guardians were all naturally overprotective of the people they were responsible for. I'd never had people hovering over my well-being like this, and it had only been twenty-four hours. The dark side of my brain warned me it wouldn't last because everyone wanted something, and when they got whatever I could give them, they would leave me. Then my heart told me to listen to what May told me—they care and want to be my family. But the only family I'd ever known would sell me out to the best option for them. What would they think when I told them I forgot I'd killed people? I'd never once had a single moment of sadness about what I did to free Gavin. Could it be that there was evil in my blood deep inside me like mother always told me?

A hand caught my chin and forced me to look up to meet light green eyes that seemed to see right into my soul. "Little bird, what you did in that camp saved Prince Gavin, me, yourself, and gave our people time to devise a plan. Don't you dare feel ashamed. We are going to war, and every war has casualties. Those men will not be the last to die by your hand. You are a strong queen, and I am honored to be at your side as we enter this battle."

Jade's words hit me in the heart as if he had stabbed me with his own knife. How could he possibly know what I was feeling so perfectly? I'd seen him fight, and that alone told me many people had died at his hands.

"Know that I will be here when you need me. With so much going on, it might not affect you now, but eventually, it will. It's how you know you still have a soul. Don't force it. Your mind will tell you when you are ready to deal with it and not a moment before," he murmured, keeping his voice soft. "Promise me you will find me when that time comes. This is not something you want to do alone. Promise me."

I could tell from the look in his eyes he wasn't going to let this go without an answer. "I promise."

"Good. Now finish your stew so you can get settled for bed," Jade ordered.

"You are all worse than a hen sitting on her eggs," I groused as I broke off some bread and scooped it into the bowl.

They chuckled at my words, grabbing their meals and settling comfortably around the room. I watched as they all chatted, talking about their training and the horror stories that went along with it. It was comforting to sit back and watch, seeing them trying to find common ground with each other. Dayson was loud and expressive with his body gestures as he got into stories, most of them being about his competitiveness. Cole would try to one-up him with a story of his own, being he was equally competitive. Payson followed the conversation, adding in a joke or two at the right moment to send everyone into fits of laughter, making him smile wide, pleased with himself. Abbott had no trouble flowing in and out of the conversation but didn't share anything too personal and avoided anything to do with before he came to the Raven Rose clan. Thinking about that, I didn't even know what clan he'd been born into. From what little I knew of them, my guess was between the Hell Hawks and Bronze Reapers, yet neither seemed to quite fit.

"Oh yeah, well, I'd like to see you do a job where you had to hide on a horse in a stampede to get away!" Becka challenged Dayson, her green eyes flashing at the assumed slight at her abilities.

"The thing is, Red, I wouldn't have been caught, therefore never needing to pull such a ridiculous stunt." Dayson grinned, crossing his arms.

May burst out laughing. "You big idiot, you never would have been able to do the job. Killing a man in a brothel is women's work, and you know it. Who would want to fuck your hairy ass?"

"Watch it. I haven't had any complaints with the ladies I blessed with my prowess," Dayson growled.

"Hard to have someone tell you how bad it was when they're not there in the morning," Payson chimed in. "My guess is that you pass out like a bear in the winter after the first eruption."

Dayson lunged at Payson, but Izel grabbed the man's arm, stopping him. "We are not in a pub. Do not brawl like animals in the queen's chambers. If you morons are going to be like this, then leave and settle this in your own space."

Dayson and Payson muttered under their breath about being scolded, but they settled back into their spots as if nothing happened. It would seem that Izel was the peacemaker, rules follower, and mother hen who valued order and civility around him. He was extremely levelheaded and seemed to be able to notice when to step in or to leave it to someone else better suited to the issue. Jade was the only one out of the group who kept to himself, simply watching and observing, much like I was. The only difference was that none of the others tried to include him, whereas they would occasionally ask my opinion on a matter they were discussing. Cole's words came back to me as he asked Jade if he told me who he was. Then there was the matter of his half brother, telling me he'd disowned Jade. Vasin knew what his secret was and didn't seem bothered by it in the least, giving me some peace about the matter. I trusted Vasin above all others to keep me safe from harm and to do what was in my best interest.

"It looks like someone is falling asleep in her chair. Might be best for us to let her really go to bed," Abbott announced, cutting off the conversation and jerking me out of my introspection. "Who do you want to stay with you tonight?"

I frowned at him, cocking my head. "Why would I need anyone to stay?"

"Well, after having torn some of your stitches, there is no way in hell we will let you walk on it. Plus, I'm thinking you might need help getting ready for bed. One of the girls can deal with that, and whoever you pick will sleep on the couch," Abbott informed me.

"Wasn't I crowned queen? What you just said sounds a lot like you're ordering around your student. Surely you wouldn't do that to your queen?" I teased, knowing he was falling into his old habits.

It was now Abbott's turn to scowl at me dramatically. "I believe it was you who told us to keep you grounded and remind you you're one of the 'people.' "

Rolling my eyes, I turned to Becka. "Would you mind helping me get ready for bed?"

"Ah, just like old times. I was wondering when you would put on your royal airs and demand your personal maid back," Becka answered with a wink and smile.

"Now, who's going to stay?" Abbott pressed.

"I vote for Cole since he's the one who caused her to damage her leg more. He should be responsible for the consequences," Jade suggested.

"Fuck you, Shadow!" Cole snapped, glaring at Jade. Abbott coughed and gave Cole a pointed look. "Little mouse, if you want me to stay, I would be more than happy to do so."

"Whatever." I sighed, my tiredness rushing over me, making me unwilling to fight the issue any longer. "Abbott won't let this go, so I hope the couch is comfortable. Otherwise, you could bring in an extra mattress or cot, since I'll clearly have people sleeping in here for the next week."

Abbott gave me a bright smile. "That is a wonderful idea, Cassarah."

"All right... out, the lot of you and take those fucking dishes with you. The queen needs to get ready for bed," Becka said, clapping her hands and shooing everyone out the door. "Thank God. I never thought I would get a moment alone with you."

"That was never a problem before. I was always alone," I murmured as she helped to pull me out of the chair and hop over to the bed.

I made sure not to put any pressure on my bad leg since it ached bone-deep after everything. Once I was seated, Becka rummaged through my trunk at the foot of the bed. Someone must have thought to take it from my room back at the clan lodging.

"Cassarah, you know, with me around, there was never a chance you were alone. You're my best friend, practically my little sister. The only change in this is that you finally get the chance to make other friends. If I'm being honest, you're doing better than I thought you would. I was worried you'd be too shy and timid to open up to anyone else," Becka commented as she helped me undress and slip on my nightgown.

"I'll have to take your word for it because I do not feel like that. The only reason they're spending time with me is because they're my guardians, and I'm their queen," I countered.

Becka scowled at me with her hands on her hips. "Right, and Jade wasn't crazy overprotective before you put your mark on him. Hell, Cassarah, he pulled a knife on Cole faster than I've seen anyone do. Whatever you two went through on your little journey totally made you friends."

"In fairness, I wanted to stab Cole many times… I still might on occasion."

Becka tossed her head back and laughed. "Oh, girl, if that isn't the God's honest truth. I'm surprised that man has survived this long with so many trained killers around. My money's on the fact it's out of respect for Ballard."

"What do you make of the others?" I asked, curious, as she handed me a basin of water and a cloth to wash my face.

A silence fell between us as she collected her thoughts. "After meeting their fathers, I have to say I feel better about the men you picked. I totally approve of May. She is amazing once you get past the tough bitch exterior. Whenever we had gatherings of the clans, she and I always liked to see who could do better in the friendly events they would set up to test our skills. From what I know of the others, they are kind of the most desired men of our generation. The only one you missed out on was Payson's twin, Paxton, but he left the clan a few years ago after a huge fight with his father. No one will talk about it. I'm not sure he will even tell you if you ask, but it had to be something major if he up and left without even saying goodbye to Payson."

"So everyone knows each other?"

"Would you say you know people at court if all you could do is pick them out of a crowd? All the boys cared about was whether they could beat each other. Past that, they didn't waste any time on getting to know one another and shit like that. Especially since the Wind Fist clan is very particular about who they let their people around. The fact they gave up Abbott still blows my mind. I don't think for a second it was because they couldn't feed him. No, his mother, a respected clan member, married a Hell Hawk. They are known for being the wild child of the clans. They pick all the jobs we think would be too risky to get involved in. Being on the border of Utros, there isn't much for them to do with that country staying neutral and never picking sides but their own in battles. When Porvan said they took in King Edward's son, I was completely shocked. That is very unlike them."

The amount of information that Becka just unloaded on me made my head spin. "I think we're going to need to pick this up in the morning. I'm not remotely able to process all that right now, and some of it sounded important."

"Well, then, m'lady, I wish you goodnight. I'll let Cole know he can come back over if you really want him to stay tonight?"

"It would be him or Abbott. I'm just not as comfortable with the others yet, and Izel slept on the floor last night. He deserves to sleep in his own bed tonight," I answer, flopping back on the bed and wiggling around until I maneuvered myself under the covers.

"Sleep well, Cassarah. I'm really glad you're back with us and safe."

I didn't even hear the door close. By the time my head hit the pillow, I was out.

NINE

NIGHTMARES AND MONTHLIES

"*D*ragon Queen..."

A voice lilted through my head.

"*You think you're safe, tucked away in the mountains where no one can find you?*"

My eyes popped open, and all I saw was darkness. *Had the lanterns gone out? Who was in my room with me? Why hadn't Cole noticed there was someone here in my chambers?*

"*Once you've let me into your head, I can always find my way back. There is nothing you can keep from me. All I have to do is wait for you to fall asleep, and you're an open book for me to read with ease...*"

No, there was no way the Lost King could get inside my head this far away. It just wasn't possible. I had to be dreaming. This was my mind playing tricks on me. Jade warned me there would be nightmares. Could this be what he was talking about?

"*Poor little queen doesn't even have the support of her leaders. How can you even trust that they won't sell you out just to get rid of you like Richard did?*"

"You're not real!" I screamed into the darkness. "If you are, then it proves how much of a coward you truly are if you keep hiding in the shadows. Face me like a real king, and I'll show you how strong I am!"

"Pretty words from a pretty woman. It's too bad I don't enjoy the fairer sex because I feel you would be a delight to break." As he talked, his words seemed to almost caress my skin as if it were his hand ghosting down my curves.

I shuddered at the sensation, feeling nauseous at the unwanted contact. Every day, I thanked whatever gods would listen that a woman's virtue was paramount. Otherwise, I know my mother would have also stolen that from me. Instead, I feared it, knowing that if I were found deflowered, I would be cast out or even killed, no longer of any value to my mother. So even though I knew he wasn't really here and couldn't hurt me in that way, the panic that coursed through my body making my heart pound like a drum was very real.

"Not so brave now, are we, Dragon Queen? Everyone has a weakness, but are you willing to find out what that weakness is and extort it for your own gain? That is why I'm going to win. I won't let anything or anyone get in my way, even if I have to walk over the entire nation's corpses. I will have my crown and rule over this land just as I have with Errit. Then I'll move on to Utros and Creisal, leaving you nowhere else to hide but the dragon wastelands. No one can survive their harsh climate."

"No! I will not let you do this. Whatever it takes, I will become the queen who can save this world from you."

His laughter filled the darkness, the sound clawing against my skin, causing me to cry out.

"Cassarah, wake up!" Cole bellowed at me, shaking my shoulders.

Slowly, my eyes began to clear, and I could see his terrified face leaning over me in the soft light of the lantern. I gasped, taking in a deep breath as if I'd been holding it during my dream. When I exhaled, it came out more like a sob. I reached up with both hands and curled my finger around Cole's shirt, needing to feel he was real, here with me, and I wasn't trapped in the darkness with the crazed man who thought himself a king. Cole wrapped his arms around me, pulling me tight to his chest, allowing me to hide my face in his neck.

"Shh, little mouse, I've got you. Nothing's going to happen to you with me at your side, I promise," Cole whispered as he stroked my back gently.

This was exactly what I needed, and I broke down, letting out all the fear I'd felt while trapped in that dream. He just continued to hold me and whisper in my ear, but I was so lost in my head, I didn't really hear it. Feeling his constant touch grounded me as I tried to pull myself back together, slowly but surely. When I stopped crying and my breathing calmed, I expected him to let me go, but he didn't. Instead, he lifted the sheet and tucked me into his side as we lay back down. My body sagged with relief that he wouldn't leave me, even after I'd gone all hysterical on him. The need to know someone was truly here with me was strong, and I was grateful he knew what to do without me asking.

"Do you want to tell me about it?" he asked after a moment, stroking my hair as my head lay on his chest.

I nuzzled into his chest, taking a deep breath of the calming, deep pine scent of our mountain home. "The Lost King was taunting me. He got inside my head, Cole. He tried to get me to kill Lord Everett to prove he could control me. If Vasin hadn't arrived in time, I would have done it. I'd have been a slave to that madman."

"What was he saying in your dream?"

"That he knows what's in my head, like our location and the fact the clan leaders don't want me." I moved my head to stare up at Cole's face. "He asked if I would be willing to do whatever it takes to beat him, even if it was to the point of innocents being killed."

"How did you answer him?"

"Whatever it takes is what I said, but I won't cross that line. If I did, I would be no different than him, Cole."

He didn't say anything, just held me tighter and continued to run his fingers through my hair.

Eventually, I fell back asleep. When I woke up, I was alone in bed with Becka bustling around the room, dumping large buckets of steaming water into the bath. Groaning as I rubbed the sleep and grit from my eyes, I sat up, looking around the room to see if he was still here.

"I sent everyone out because you need a bath," Becka shared when she caught me searching. "I know you don't like it when we help you, but we can't let your leg get wet, so this will be easier if you just sit there."

"Good morning to you too," I mumbled, shifting so I sat on the edge of the bed and swung my legs for my feet to rest on the floor.

Becka turned to look at me with a hand on her hip and a scowl on her face. "You're getting soft already. This is way later than you normally get up."

"I didn't sleep well last night, and being in a cave means I have no sense of time in this damn room," I grumbled, feeling testy.

Becka stalked over to me, grabbed both sides of my face, and forced me to look up at her. "Could it be? Is Cassarah having a bad day and showing her emotions for all to see? No, not the perfect Lady Cassarah who suffers in silence like all the great noble women."

My temper flared at her teasing, and I jerked her hands away. "Leave it be, Becka. I'm not in the mood to deal with your badgering about my habits."

"Wait, is it that time of the month for you already?" Becka looked at me surprised and checked the front of my nightgown to see if there was proof. "Oh, man, the boys are going to be in for a treat if it is." She laughed as she pulled me up to stand.

I refused to say anything, but I feared she might be right. Ballard's wife, Helena, had been giving me herbs to drink every day with my evening tea, and I'd already been a week without them. She did warn me that I couldn't be on them forever, but we both agreed it was smart while training not to have to deal with my monthly bleeds. It would now seem I was going to get that part of my life back after I'd all but forgotten about it.

"Couldn't I just start taking the herbs to get it to stop again?" I asked, my eyes begging Becka to tell me I could. "I do not need this to happen right now when I'm dealing with the clan leaders and on the brink of war."

"Sweetie, you're the queen. You'll always be dealing with idiots and on the brink of war. You managed to deal with it before you left home, so I'm positive you can do it now," Becka countered.

I all but growled at her as I sank into the steaming bath with my bad leg draped over the side. It was extremely uncomfortable and awkward to manage, but that didn't slow my best friend down one bit.

"Did you forget how that was *managed*?" I snapped. "I was locked away in my room for the week until I was suitable to be seen back in public. The only person I interacted with was you."

"It will be fine. Every woman in the world has to deal with this, and none of the clan's women get locked away. We'll just warn the rest of the guardians that you might be a little more unpredictable and leave it at that. They will be smart enough to leave it alone, and if not, we have May to slap them upside the head. You will need to let Alto know, though, so she can get you new herbs to make sure you don't get pregnant. I doubt you're ready to be a mother."

I laughed at that. "You need to bed a man to accomplish that, and for that to happen, you have to have someone interested."

Becka paused in her scrubbing of my scalp. "Cassarah, I know you aren't that blind. You have at *least* three men mooning over you like lost puppies. Not to mention that I know Cole was in your bed last night with you." My head snapped to look at her, eyes wide as I gaped at her like a fish. "Yes, I know. You had a nightmare, and he was there because you asked him to be, but that is a slippery slope, my friend. You let them into your bed, and it's much harder to say no when the heat of the moment takes over."

"Are you saying you've been with a man?" I gasped, shocked at the idea.

"Ha, ha, ha. Yes, you little prude, I've been with a man or two, if you must know. Women of the clans are far freer with our bodies than noble women. We don't see ourselves as breeders to gain riches through our offspring. Sleep with them, keep them if you want, or toss them back into the wild. It's our choice. Now, do that far too regularly, and you'd be known as easy, and it might make settling down harder, but no one will stop you. Hell, you're the woman who gets to pick however many her guardians she wants to be with. Although I'm not sure how that will work this time since they are magically bound to you instead of choosing the other way," Becka mused as I sat in stunned silence.

Of course, it was no surprise I was expected to pick a husband or husbands from my guards, but to hear her talk about how free every other woman was shocked me. Being so focused on training, I didn't really have time to study the social norms of all the clan members in Raven Rose. I was too focused on learning the past and how to be the queen. This revelation was so foreign, yet interesting and liberating to know. I wouldn't be locked in a room for my monthly bleed, nor was I considered unclean from it, either. By the sounds of it, everyone treated it as normal and moved on, not needing to draw attention to it.

Finished with the bath and feeling better about things, Becka helped me get dressed and prepared me if I did start bleeding. Once again, everything seemed far more manageable with pants holding everything in place, making me feel more at ease.

"What do you say about going to the main area and eating breakfast with everyone?" Becka asked as she made quick work of braiding my hair.

I smiled up at her through the small round mirror. "I think that sounds like a wonderful idea."

Ten

Don't Poke the Queen

As small-statured as Payson was compared to my other guardians, it did not diminish his strength. He carried me with ease, and his gait was light as we made our way down to the main cavern area. The cooking fires blazed with large black cooking pots hanging over them, filling the air with the nutty aroma of the porridge they were making. When we passed through last time, I was far too distracted by my need to get Gavin out of a cell to notice the long wooden tables with benches lined up in rows. Payson set me down on a bench closest to the entrance so everyone would see me as they headed to find a seat. I licked my lips nervously, worried that after everything settled down, they would feel the same way as the clan leaders did about me.

I didn't have to wait long as a group of young children came racing over to me, all talking at once.

"Queen Cassarah, is it true you didn't grow up in Raven Rose?"

"Where are your mommy and daddy?"

"Could I get a ride on your dragon?"

"When I grow up, I want to be as pretty as you, Queen Cassarah."

Flustered, I didn't know how to answer some of these questions or what I should tell them about myself and my past life. I decided not to be ashamed of my family history like so many generations before me had been.

"Settle down now, or I won't be able to answer the questions you've already asked me." I laughed, giving them my full attention. "No, I didn't grow up in Raven Rose or any of the other clans. I lived in a large house in the countryside outside Royal City. That is where my parents are now. They didn't want to leave our home, so I decided it would be easier to just come here on my own."

"That's so brave!" one little girl gasped, clutching her doll to her chest. "I don't think I could leave Mommy behind."

"It was hard, but I knew it was the right thing to do. Sometimes when we grow older, we have to make a tough choice, but I think it was worth it to be with all of you," I assured the girl. "Now, as for getting to ride Vasin, I think we might need to ask your mother first, then we'll see if Vasin agrees."

"You can talk to your dragon?" the older of the boys asked, eyes wide in amazement.

I nodded my head, biting my lip so I didn't laugh. I hadn't spent much time around kids, but the ones in the Raven Rose clan always made me laugh, and Vasin was such a good sport to let them climb all over him.

"Children, let our queen eat in peace!" a woman chided, herding them away, giving me a small bow and a smile. "It's good to see you out and about, Your Majesty."

"Momma, can I ride the queen's dragon? She said I had to ask you first. Please say yes, please?" the boy begged as she dragged him away, shaking her head.

Still watching the kids, I was surprised when a tray of food was set in front of me. Snapping my head around, I found Payson settling in across from me. "Seems you're already charming your subjects."

"From my limited experience, kids are the easiest of the bunch. It's the parents I'm worried about." I sighed, pulling my tray closer. "Thanks for grabbing my food. Not being able to do much by myself is getting very frustrating."

"I fell off a horse and broke my right arm. Thankfully, I do almost everything with my left, but still, you don't realize how often you need two hands. It was weeks before I got back full use of it, so I understand what you're saying," Payson shared as he dipped into his meal, then paused and looked up to meet my gaze. "Cassarah... I'm sorry about my father. He's a bastard and is worse when he feels threatened. You scare the clan leaders, My Queen. Everything you represent is change, and none of them want to lose power. By you even existing, they've lost the prowess they once had. All that to say, don't think their opinions will be the same as everyone else's in the clans. They are ready for a queen to guide them, and everyone knows we need change to survive."

Smiling at him, I reached out and covered his hand with mine, gently squeezing it. "Thank you, that means a lot to me. I don't want to disappoint them, and it was hard to see how much the clan leaders hated me without even giving me a chance."

"I bet you that today might be a different story after all the information that came out. My father is no longer the perfect man he likes to pretend to be since they caught him in his lie about the king's bastard."

I nodded, mulling that statement over as I started to eat my breakfast. The porridge wasn't anything amazing, but I'd learned since coming here that they were more about keeping everyone fed than having it taste amazing. A healthy body can make more money to provide better food and keep the clan safe, but a starving person can do neither of those things. More and more, I was learning how I'd lived a life of opulence, even with all the hardships I experienced.

Yes, I was starved and beaten, but I always knew there would be food when I was allowed. I never questioned that. As for safety, I didn't learn what it felt like until I came to live with the clan, and I was still working on trusting that I was safe.

As we ate, clan members who wanted to meet me drifted in and out of the conversation. It was almost like being at court, but I didn't get the same feeling that they were trying to find fault in me. They just wanted to *know* me. This fueled my desire to be a queen they would always feel like they could come up to and talk about things. At first, the guys tried to move people along so I could actually eat my meal, but I waved them off that idea.

"Leave them be. I'm happy to meet anyone who takes the time to seek me out," I explained.

"My Queen, you still need to be able to eat," Izel countered, looking pointedly at my barely touched bowl.

"I promise I won't die of starvation. I've gone days without food and managed just fine—" Realizing what I'd just said, I slammed my jaw shut so hard that my teeth clicked.

Cole and Abbott knew more than most about what I'd gone through, having helped me to overcome some of my fears and trauma, but they still didn't know it all. That was the old me, and the clan had given me new life, a way to have power over what happened to me, and strength to stop it if I needed to. I didn't want them all to look at me like I was some wounded animal and forever see pity in their eyes. I'd overcome everything my mother tried to do to me, and I was finally becoming who I was meant to be.

"Your Majesty—" Abbott started to say.

"Leave it!" I snapped at Abbott, whose brows went up in shock. "I will not speak about it here."

"As you wish," he answered with a bow of his head.

Taking a deep breath, I let it out slowly, trying to calm my irritation at him for feeling the need to push for information. He knew I didn't like to talk about my mother. He was the only man who had seen me break down. I needed to be strong—a queen they deserved.

"I think now would be as good a time as any to reconvene our conversation with the clan leaders," I announced, looking at the others with a smile I knew didn't reach my eyes. "We have a country to save and an evil king to stop."

"Yes, My Queen. I'll let them know you wish for them to gather," Izel volunteered, getting up from the table.

"May, could you ask if it's possible to have them bring lunch to us?" I asked. "I have a feeling we will be in there all day before we get anything done."

"Of course, I'll go do that right away," May said with a bow and headed into the crowd.

Cole came to stand behind me, resting a hand on my shoulder. "They do not expect you to be perfect, little mouse," he whispered so only I could hear him.

Looking up at him, I met his gaze which held no judgment or pity in it, just understanding. This was a side I'd never seen on Cole before last night. He was always full of snarky comments and a devil-may-care smile. This deeper version was making my heart beat faster in a way it never had. I didn't have an answer for him, so I just nodded and covered his hand with mine.

"Would you allow me to take you to the meeting hall?" Cole asked, catching me off guard. He was never one to ask such things, always more of a do-what-you-want-and-deal-with-the-fallout-after kind of guy.

My eyes flicked over to Becka trying to smother her laughter behind her hand. Narrowing my eyes at her, she started to shake her head no, indicating she didn't say anything about my current affliction. Not sure I really believed her, I scowled and turned to look at each of the men sitting at the table. They all looked a little on edge as if unsure of what to do with themselves, but none would look me in the eye.

"There wouldn't be any reason you all are acting oddly toward me, would there?" I questioned, resting my chin on my hand, waiting for their answer. They shook their heads, still looking down at the trays before them.

Dayson coughed and shifted in his seat under my watchful gaze. "It was me. I warned them you might be dealing with lady business and not to piss you off. Growing up with May, I know the signs, but I doubt you're as violent as she gets."

Part of me did want to punch him right in the gut, but the other wanted to laugh as I pictured Dayson, of all people, having to tell the others I was going to be overly emotional for the next few days.

"I guess I should just apologize in advance for anything I might say or do in the near future," I admitted, my cheeks blushing with embarrassment.

Payson just snorted and collected my tray, stacking it with his. "This couldn't have come at a better time. Give those clan leaders a piece of your mind. It'll shut them up faster than anything else will."

"You're talking about your own father!" I blurted, eyes wide as I stared at him.

He just gave me a playful grin and a wink. "Then it sounds like you should take my advice, seeing as I've known the man my entire life."

Laughter burst out of me at his comeback, setting me more at ease than I'd been a few moments ago. "All right, Cole, let's see if we can get these men to see reason."

"Little mouse, if anyone can surprise them, it would be you. Of that, I have no doubt." Cole chuckled as he lifted me into his arms.

"You know, you're one of the only ones who call me by a nickname no matter where we are. Why is that, and how can I get the others to do it?" I teased, smiling up at him.

His gaze was filled with a fire I'd never had directed at me. "They don't have the history we do. Give them time. I'm sure you'll get your way with them too, if you truly want it."

Why did I feel like that statement meant more than what he was letting on?

ELEVEN

THE TRUTH BEHIND THE LOST KING

B ack in the strategy room, I had Cole set me down at the middle of the long table so I could study the map more as I waited. I'd always known about Creisal and Utros, but they were rarely discussed since we didn't really interact. Though, seeing them on a map was a whole new experience, taking in just how big our continent was. To the west was Creisal and ended at the waters of the Caleden Sea, which the tales claimed was so wide you couldn't see what lay on the other side. Many had tried to sail across, but none ever returned and were believed to be dead. I always dreamed it was because they found a magical place, not wanting to return.

I returned to the problem at hand—Errit, our easterly neighbor, cut off from us by the Great Darsor River, and Utros, just south of Errit. As far as I knew, Utros didn't have an alliance with any of the countries, but could that have changed without us knowing because of the Lost King? He ruled Errit, now commanding their army. What's to stop him from doing the same thing in Utros?

"Vasin, how long would it take a dragon to fly over all of Utros?"

"My best guess would be roughly a week. Utros is a much larger country than ours or even Creisal, for that matter. What are you looking for?"

"We need to see if the Lost King has pulled them under his rule as well as Errit. If I knew he was trying to get his rightful place back, I wouldn't be concerned, but he wants more, Vasin... he wants to rule it all."

"You are right in assuming that a dragon would swiftly get you the information you need, but I'm not sure they will be able to tell you the full story."

"That's a good point. I'll need to send out a dragon rider. This is why we need the queen on our side. They have already trained spies to do just that. I could even send one into Errit, so we have a true sense of how much of it he's taken over."

"This is why I chose you, dear Cass. You are wise and able to see more than others."

I smiled, sending him all my warm thoughts and emotions. *"We need to go flying soon. I'm suffocating at being stuck on this mountain. Now that I've gotten my taste of freedom, I don't think I'll ever be able to give up living out in nature."*

"I would like that very much. Tahir and I have been scouting the area to make sure we are safe, but it would please me greatly to take you with me next time."

"Deal!"

After discussing things with Vasin, I felt more confident addressing it with everyone else. I'd be lost without my pair-bond, and even though we were in the same place together, being apart from him was hard. I'd been spoiled, taking the time as I studied scrolls for Sal to be with Vasin, pretending it was because I needed his help. My dragon and I knew that, at this point, I was almost fluent in reading, writing, and speaking the old tongue after all the work I'd done. I planned one day when things calmed down to teach others so we didn't lose this part of our culture.

"Queen Cassarah, we have arrived as summoned," Porvan announced, causing me to sigh and resign myself to dealing with him.

I shifted in my chair to see the five of them waiting for my directions. Porvan was the only one who seemed to be bothered by the summons. "Please have a seat. We have much to discuss."

"Will you not be taking the head of the table?" Xio asked, his brows knit together.

"I prefer to be able to see the map for this conversation, and sitting at the head of the table will make that impossible," I stated, not understanding why this was such a big deal. "Yesterday, you shared with me all you knew about what was happening in and around our country, but I don't think it's enough. We need more."

The clan leaders drifted to the same seats they took yesterday, leaving me to sit next to Acton and Porvan at the end of the table. *Did they honestly believe he had more power or say in things because he sat there?*

"How do you suggest we get this information?" Porvan demanded, settling into his seat, looking far too pleased.

Apparently, *he* thought he had more power in the matter being in that chair. It was good for them to know it didn't matter where I sat. I was going to outsmart them time and time again.

"As I said yesterday, we need Queen Mary on our side. King Edward is king in name, but I've seen them both deal with a situation, and the queen is the one who has control over her husband. If I can get her to listen to me, I'm sure we can gain their assistance, but I need to know the whole story behind the Lost King," I said, looking pointedly at Porvan. "If you could start at the very beginning of this tale, it would be greatly appreciated."

Porvan shifted in his chair, no longer the relaxed man who thought he had the power in this situation. "I don't see how the past could be all that important to what's happening now."

Idiot.

"Be that as it may, I would appreciate it if you could still tell us. That is unless you are trying to hide more about the situation than you already have," I pressed, unwilling to let him get out of this.

The other clan leaders looked at him expectantly, which was the final nail in his casket. If he didn't give us the full story, it would prove he truly was hiding something from them, causing them to turn on him.

"Look, this all happened thirty-some years ago. I don't know how King Edward got ahold of one of my men, but he did and sent a message to the person in charge... my father at the time. I was brought in on the meeting to decide whether or not we should bring this up to Ballard and the other clan leaders. They voted against doing that, feeling that something this sensitive should be shared with as few people as possible. I was the one they asked to take the boy into Utros and meet up with the people who would become his new family. The king didn't want to know anything other than if the deed was done, knowing if his son was ever discovered, he had deniability," Porvan stated, arms crossed as he spoke. "When my men and I crossed the border and met the family, I was shocked to find it was King Mahon's cousin, Marquees Efrem, and his wife who were taking the child. I shouldn't have been surprised because the king wouldn't have connections with just anyone in Utros. This also told me that King Mahon was in on the deal."

"What reason would the king of Utros have to help out King Edward?" Xio questioned. "Our countries have never worked that closely together. Utros prides itself on being separate from the others, being fully self-sufficient."

"It wasn't my place to ask. I wasn't in charge at that point," Porvan growled out.

"You didn't have your own thoughts on the matter? I find that hard to believe for a power-driven person such as yourself," Garold challenged, leaning forward toward the man. "Or is it that you did something behind your father's back and screwed everything up?"

Porvan let out a breath, his entire body sagging. "The marquees reached out five years later, telling me they couldn't keep the boy. He was becoming a danger to their other children, and they didn't know what to do, not wanting to go back on their deal with King Edward. I took two men with me, planning to take the kid from them and kill him, making it look like an accident, knowing we couldn't have a war starting between us and Utros. They would slaughter us with how large their army was, even though they never used it for anything but guarding their borders. When I got to the small village where they had dropped him off for me to collect, I found him sitting there on the steps of an inn with all the children bringing him things. He was surrounded by food, toys, and clothing, something they had very little of. Somehow, he'd already managed to access his Birthright and used it to get whatever he wanted. It didn't seem to work on the adults who were all yelling at their children for what they were doing, but they just ignored them like they couldn't hear what was being said to them."

"Obviously, you didn't kill him since he's still alive, unless he has another Birthright that can raise him from the dead." Garold sneered, glaring at Porvan. "What the fuck did you do?"

"We tried to get him away from the kids, but he caused them to mob us. I wasn't going to slaughter twenty innocent kids, so we left and waited until nightfall. In the dead of night, we snuck back into the village and kidnapped him, dragging him out into the forest. When I was about to kill the kid, the marquees and his guards came bursting out of the forest, claiming that the kingdom of Norden was trying to murder their child. The whole thing had been a setup, and we were going to be used as the patsy in a war between our countries. The marquees wanted to be king and decided that blackmailing us into assassinating King Mahon was the best course of action."

The clan leaders started yelling at Porvan for walking into the trap. When they didn't settle down, I turned to look at Dayson and tilted my head to indicate the fighting men.

"Quiet!" Dayson bellowed, causing all the men to stop and look at him in surprise. "Sit back down in your seats and act like men, not boys."

Once they all did as he said, he gave me a smile and a wink, which I returned before turning to deal with the *men* of our clans. "Since we didn't end up having a war with Utros, did you kill the king?"

"Yes."

Now everything was making sense. Not only did the Lost King have the Birthright to gain power, but he also had a tyrannical male role model to feed the problem.

"So it would be safe to say that Utros also has the Lost King's back in a battle. Now we are not just fighting Errit but Utros as well," I summed up, rubbing my forehead. "Do you still believe we stand a chance without the king and queen on our side?"

"Wait. You're just going to brush off the fact he helped assassinate one foreign king to put another on the throne? What about the fact that he single-handedly set up this madman to rein terror over all our kingdoms?" Xio demanded, shooting up from his seat in his anger. "I will not just sit here while this traitor is at this table."

"Please, Xio, calm yourself. We still don't have the whole story. I suggest you reserve your judgment for when you have all the facts," I cautioned him.

Letting out a growl, he slammed his fist against the table and again took his seat. "Could we at least have someone fetch us some ale?"

"No, the last thing I need is for any of you to be impaired as we work through this. Drinking will only cloud your judgment and make your anger worse. None of that will be helpful right now," I stated, holding his gaze to see if he would argue my decision, but he didn't. Returning my attention to Porvan, I settled my hands on the table in a show of complete calm. "Was this the last time you had interaction with the now king of Utros?"

"It was not," Porvan answered. "The marquees had me by the balls. If I didn't do what he asked, then he would find some way to destroy my family, clan, and country, and I couldn't let him do that when I was responsible for all of this."

"Do you think King Edward knows anything about this interaction?"

"Absolutely not. This was between me and the marquees. I was young and stupid, just married, and my wife was pregnant with our daughter. I wanted to go to the king, but then I would have to confess what I'd already done, and I would have gotten killed as a traitor."

"Why not turn to us... your clansmen? If everyone had been in the know from the beginning, none of this would have been an issue," Garold interjected, unable to hold his thoughts any longer.

"Nothing would have changed!" Porvan yelled, standing and tossing his chair across the room. "I fucked up, and every day of my life I've been worried something like this would come back and bite me in the ass. You don't get it. If I didn't do as he said, then Henry would have *made* me. By the time he was ten, that bastard could manipulate anyone into doing whatever he wanted."

Something didn't add up with this whole account. Why did it take this long for the Lost King to make his move when he had everything he needed in Utros alone?

"Porvan, what aren't you telling us?" I commanded, reaching the end of my patience with this drawn-out tale of a man's arrogance.

Porvan turned to us, his hair no longer neatly pulled back, now disheveled from running his hands through it. "Paxton, Payson's twin, went after him to end this, but now that Henry is here, it just means he failed, and I got my son killed for trying to fix my mistake."

Now it was my turn to growl at him. "What. Does. That. Mean?"

"My twins are an anomaly. They shouldn't have Birthrights to begin with, being the second-born children. Yet both have one, and Paxton's is to be a void. He can neutralize another person's Birthright. I thought I was in the clear once King Efrem hadn't reached out, but then I was approached again after many years of complete silence. On that fateful day when the messenger came, the boys were with me, and I was forced to tell them part of the story to keep them from telling anyone else. Paxton took it upon himself to end things once and for all since he couldn't be controlled. I tried to stop him, but we got into a very public argument, and he left... never to come back," Porvan said, his eyes shimmering with unshed tears for his son. "Now, I've not only lost a son, but I might even lose our home to this animal."

The room fell utterly silent as we processed all this information. I wanted to give the man a moment to grieve the loss of his son, but it was even more imperative that we figure out a plan to stop the Lost King.

Twelve

And so the Planning Starts

After all this earth-shattering news, none of us knew what to do with it. Then, for the first time since we sat at the table, Acton slowly stood, drawing us all to him, and spoke.

"I, Clan Leader Acton, hereby request a vote to remove Porvan from his position and allow a new clan leader to take his place that will be more fitting in this time of war." Turning to face me, he bowed deeply and sat back down.

The matter was now in my hands. A clan leader had made a request, and it was up to me to approve or deny that request. Setting my hands firmly on the table, I rose from my seat. "By royal decree, I waive the right to vote and remove Porvan from his role for high treason to the clans and our country. He will stand a trial of his peers at a later date, but it will be delayed until after he has helped us defeat the Lost King. His punishment is to be at the beck and call of all clan leaders, royal guardians, and myself for any matter to right the wrongs he has committed." The other four clan leaders bowed their heads in agreement with my ruling. "Porvan, do you accept this ruling and agree to help us, or do I need to lock you away in a cell until the matter can be settled?"

"No, My Queen, you pass fair judgment, and I deserve far worse for the crimes I have done against our people and kingdom," Porvan said, bowing his head to me.

"So it shall be," I intoned, and everyone in the room echoed it back to me, sealing the matter. "Now pick up your chair, sit your ass down in it, and help us fix this whole mess."

Taking my seat, I closed my eyes, took a deep breath, and calmed the nerves that ran through my veins. I'd just made my first royal decree, and it was to remove a guilty man from his position—not the direction I wanted to go, but it needed to be done. Now, all I needed to do was move forward and deal with the knowledge we currently have.

"Porvan, you never told us what the messenger requested or what happened when you didn't do as it said," I inquired.

"It was an order to start recruiting members of the clans to join Henry in his quest to take over Errit. He wanted strong fighters from our clan and the Hell Hawks because the dragons still bonded with them. Payson killed the messenger when I refused the orders, and we never heard from Henry again, but it was also around the same time that Paxton left. I'd hoped it was that he'd killed Henry and just didn't want to come back home to a traitor of a father."

Shifting, I caught Payson's gaze. "Do you have anything to add?"

"No, Your Majesty. I did kill the messenger, but after that and Paxton leaving, I didn't want anything to do with it," Payson answered, giving me an apologetic look. "My father might be an asshole and a traitor, but he is still my father. I should have told you as soon as you told us about the Lost King, but I was afraid of what would happen to my father and myself for keeping it from you."

"That is a matter best left to be discussed at another time," I ventured, giving him a nod as I turned back to the clan leaders. "It is even more important now to gain alliances where we can. I am sending a message to Queen Mary asking for a meeting. We need those dragon riders. Do we have any other dragons pair-bonded to clansmen, or is Jade the only one besides myself?"

"The Bronze Reapers have four since we are closest to the Un-claimed Dragon Lands," Garold shared. "We didn't have them join us here because that many dragons are noticeable to scouts searching for our location."

"There are two others besides Jade in the Hell Hawks, and they are elsewhere for the same reason. It's our protocol. They check in with us every few days, one at a time, to get news and orders," Acton added.

Nodding, I focused on the map, trying to decide what the best use of them would be.

"Vasin, can you reach out to any dragon, or do you need to meet them first?"

"I CAN SEND OUT A BROAD REQUEST, BUT I CAN'T PINPOINT THE COMMUNICATION WITHOUT MEETING THEM FIRST."

"There needs to be a meeting of the dragon riders. We will need them more than ever to get us the information quickly. I believe it would be wise for us to send them out to scout our own lands. We need to make sure Henry hasn't split his army, making them less noticeable because the number of men I saw wouldn't signal he had Utros behind him. Once Vasin meets the other dragons, they will be able to communicate back and forth, giving us real-time details, and we can give them orders back just as fast."

"Send out the request for all clan dragon riders to meet us at a location of your choosing, Vasin."

"IT IS DONE. I WILL LET YOU KNOW WHEN I GET A RESPONSE BACK. HOW MANY ARE WE EXPECTING?"

"Six, but let me know if anyone else answers. You said all dragons could hear your call."

"Dragons do not owe allegiance to any country or king, only their pair-bond. If they would not benefit from this information, the dragons will not make it happen."

"So what you're telling me is that if a dragon that's not a part of the clans hears this call, they will ignore it?"

"That is exactly what I mean. Other dragons cannot communicate like we do, so it will take a lot of effort to drag their rider with them to the location I picked out."

"This ought to be interesting to explain."

When I returned to the people in the room from my conversation with Vasin, I found everyone staring at me expectantly. "I'm sorry, did you say something to me? Vasin and I were working on a plan to get the dragon riders to our location."

"Trust me, you'll get used to telling when she's talking to him. She gets this unfocused look about her," Cole shared, grinning at me. "They were asking how fast you wanted this to happen, but I think you already answered that, Your Majesty."

"Oh, I apologize. I should have explained what I was doing more clearly. Becka, could you please find Alto and bring her here?" I asked and looked around the room. "Do we have any paper or ink here for me to write with?"

Acton pushed back his chair and walked over to a large wooden chest. The lid groaned as he lifted it and pulled out a stack of papers, an ink dish, and oil to mix the ink powder with. I also noticed there were more maps rolled up inside.

"What maps are those?" I called before Acton closed the lid.

"Many are more detailed maps of each country, but some are outdated," Acton explained. "Would you like for me to bring them over as well?"

"Yes, and anything else in there that you might think to be helpful in planning a war," I answered, my hand itching to write down all the plans I needed to make.

Being able to write things down slowed my thoughts enough that I could make sense of it all more easily. I knew I had ideas forming, but I couldn't quite figure them out, telling me they needed to be put on paper. Acton returned and set everything on the table for me. Swiftly, I started to mix the ink into the perfect consistency. The act alone helped me to narrow my focus on what I needed to figure out. Once I had the ink ready, I dipped the pen and started to write down everything we knew about the situation.

"If any of you need a break for any reason, I would suggest doing it now. Once she gets into this mode, it will take a while before she comes out of it." Ballard chuckled, having experienced this many times as I worked with Sal.

Sal!

My head shot up, and I locked onto Ballard. "Where is Sal? Please tell me he didn't lock himself away in his hut and hope for the best."

"He is fine. Under his home is an underground vault for all the books he has stuffed into that place. We put them in there and then dragged him here with the others. His apprentice isn't ready yet to take over for him, so we need to keep him alive a little longer," Ballard explained with a smile.

"Why isn't he here? It only makes sense to have the man with knowledge on everything to be at these types of meetings," I questioned.

Ballard was careful not to give away anything in his expression, but I knew I wasn't going to like the answer. "Personally, I agree with you, Your Majesty, but others of the clan leaders do not see the value."

I let out a scoff before I could prevent it, clearly displaying my feelings on that statement. "Ballard, would you ask him to join us? I would greatly value his insight on a few matters." Once Ballard left the room, I turned to the remaining three clan leaders. "Now might be the best time to tell you I am a scholar and tactician by nature. All things can be explained or clarified by looking at the past because it seems, as humans, we rarely learn from our mistakes. Did you know that hundreds of years ago, there was another massive war between all the countries? I'm talking before the Raven Queen's time and before the mercenaries were their own people. It is written in the history of our people as a nation in the Royal Library."

"Are you telling us that you read this information yourself? Or is this all gossip from the court dandies?" Xio retorted.

I gave him a sly smile, far too pleased he didn't believe me. "It was quite the riveting tale, to be honest. Our country was the underdog being the smallest, yet there was one thing the other kingdoms didn't have… desperation. They feared being swallowed up by the three other countries, so they changed how they fought. No longer would they take the noble road facing their enemy head-on. Instead, they hid and lay in wait before ambushing them… sounds very much like how we mercenaries fight to this day.

"Interestingly enough, the man who pushed the change was exiled from the kingdom when he gained more respect from the people than the king did. Once cast out, he disappeared into the wilderness, never to be seen until one day, many decades later, he arrived back in Royal City on the back of a black dragon. He was the first King of the Mercenaries, and they begged to know how he'd gotten a dragon to let him ride on its back and listen to his commands. This led to making a treaty with Norden's royalty.

"That lasted until the Raven Queen when it all shattered due to greed on the Norden side of the deal. What I want to know, though, is where they vanished. It was a few years before the mercenaries decided to make their home in Norden once again, so where did they reside until then? It's not even in our own history. Granted, we lost almost all of it during the Great War, so it could have been in our history at one point."

The clan leaders gaped at me as I finished rattling off all this information to them. Apparently, they'd never seen a woman who liked to learn history more than how to fight before. A loud and deep belly laugh sounded in the room, causing us to turn toward the door of the strategy room. There was Sal in his dusty robes, ink-stained, wild white hair, and craggy features, grinning ear to ear.

"Maybe I should make you my apprentice instead of Isabell," Sal gestured to the gangly redhead with freckles splattered all over her face.

I'd seen Isabell around, always working or studying, hunched over various books in Sal's home. She was older than me and was extremely shy, having only uttered five words to me over the past six months of my being around. Granted, she had a hell of a job memorizing every single book and piece of information about our clans, so if we ever lost our books again, it wouldn't be gone forever.

"Should have known you'd see the logic in having me help in these meetings, Cassy girl," Sal stated as he shuffled over to sit next to Ballard.

"He calls her Cassy?" Payson whispered to Cole, shocked.

"Yeah, but he's the only one who can, so don't even try it," Cole warned.

"I wouldn't dream of it."

Just as I was going to add to their not-so-secret conversation, Becka and Alto entered the room. "Please take a seat, all of you. I can't have you hovering around the room all day. You're going to be part of this too."

Thirteen

Messages and Myths

"My Queen, how might I be of service?" Alto asked once we all were seated.

"I need to get a letter to Queen Mary, and I figured you might know the best way to do that," I explained. "You spent the most time inside the castle, so I figured you would know who to get it to."

Alto paused a moment, tapping her finger on the wooden table as she thought. "None of our people are in the castle. I was the last to leave, but I know a few people I would trust enough to get a message to the queen. How fast do we need this to happen?"

"How fast can you get it done? If you need to be in Royal City, we can get you there by dragon at a moment's notice... just say the word," I answered. "Also, do you happen to know if the queen knows any other languages?"

Alto just blinked at me, "I'm sorry, I don't know that information."

"The queen came from Creisal. She knows their traditional dialect, Your Majesty," Gavin interjected. "It's commonly spoken there, but we Nordens don't learn it, so it would be safe to write the letter in that."

I smiled at Gavin, pleased he knew what I was doing. "That can be easily done, thank you."

"Wait, you can write Creisalie?" Xio cut in.

"I can read and write many languages while also continuing to learn more," I answered vaguely, not willing to give up just how many and what kind. "To know the world is your greatest advantage in battle."

This shut up the others rather quickly, allowing me to continue. "How fast can you reach out to your contacts, Alto?"

"If I can be taken back to Royal City, it will go much faster. I'll need money for an incentive. They might be friends, but everyone needs a little encouragement," Alto answered.

"Very well, I will have a letter written for you in the morning, and Jade will take you to Royal City. I trust him to get you in and out safely and undetected. I've seen it done myself."

Alto bowed her head and stood up from the table, leaving the room.

"Queen Cassarah, I caution you on using Jade for such a delicate situation," Acton stated the moment Alto was out of the room.

Meeting Acton's gaze, I tilted my head slightly to the side. "You're going to need to give me more than that if you want me to believe this is truly an issue and not a grudge against your clansman. You already stated you don't claim him as family for some unknown reason, so I find it hard to trust your judgment on this matter. On the other hand, I have experienced how well Jade does in a situation such as this when he rescued me and again when we freed Prince Gavin."

Acton's eyes widened in surprise and a little bit of fear. "I retract my words. If you believe he's fit for the job, I will stand behind your choice. Where my half brother is concerned, I do not see the situation clearly."

"I appreciate your honesty, Acton. It will go a long way with me. Does anyone else have any objections to my plan?" All the other clan leaders shook their heads. I nodded to them and turned to Jade. "How long will it take for you to make it to Royal City from here?"

He started to speak, his face betraying the fact he was going to argue with me, but then took a deep breath. "It will take a few hours to get there and sneak into the city unnoticed. I would expect the mission to take a full day, maybe a day and a half at most."

"That will give us ample time to deal with the clan dragon riders and return to manage the response." I nodded, sitting back in my chair. "I believe that is all I need from the clan leaders. Sal, would you please stay so we can go over a few matters? Oh, and I want a guard with Porvan at all times outside this room. He is still awaiting trial for his actions, and I would like to make sure he doesn't do anything to add to that list."

The clan leaders rose and bowed to me as they left the room, Garold having a secure grip on Porvan's arm. I was relieved he didn't argue with me about the matter and took his punishment quietly. I hoped this wasn't a sign of him plotting something and trying to throw me off his scent, but he had seemed genuinely repentant of his actions. If life had taught me anything, it was that everybody could hide secrets behind a smile or even tears to keep you off their scent.

"How might I be of service to you, Cassy?" Sal inquired.

Shaking my head to clear my thoughts, I picked up my pen and placed a clean sheet of paper in front of me. "What do you know of Utros as a country? There isn't much I've seen noted about them other than they have fertile lands, lots of open plains for livestock, and they generally never like to get involved with other kingdoms after the Battle of the Kingdoms."

"All of that is true, but do you know why they like to keep to themselves and let the others fight amongst themselves?" I shook my head no as he paused for my response. "Not many do. Some say what we know is all hearsay, but I think that it's founded in truth. They are the first kingdom to have lost the dragons' respect, causing them to leave and refuse to breed in their lands," Sal said, waving Isabell over to him. "Give me the scroll I told you to grab, girl." Isabell handed over a very old and fragile-looking scroll that looked like it survived the Battle of the Kingdoms itself. "Do you know what the agreement was with the dragons or when it happened?"

I frowned at him. "No one knows, and the dragons will never say. I've asked Vasin, but he says it's the one thing they have guarded from us."

"Utros had someone who figured it out and tried to use it for their own gain. He was killed by a swarm of dragons who burned down his home, and they even made sure to kill his family to keep the secret quiet. Now, doesn't that seem like something we should pay attention to?" Sal asked as he carefully unrolled the scroll.

A trickle of fear ran down my spine. "Sal, you're not going to tell me you know what that secret is, are you? I don't want to force Vasin to kill me over this."

"No child, that would be downright stupid to do when it's clear they will do anything to keep it from us. This scroll is from the first King of the Mercenaries you talked about before."

"I don't mean to question you, but what does that have to do with Utros?"

"You wanted to know where he went, right? Well, I have the answer to that. Now, you're better at reading the old tongue than I am, so correct me if I'm wrong, but I believe this talks about another country hidden under Creisal and butts up against the Unclaimed Dragon Lands."

I gingerly shifted the scroll so I could read it. The ink they used was faint, and some words were missing altogether from the hide it was written on cracking. It seemed to be a personal journal from Yash, the first King of the Mercenaries, about his journey to find a new land and forge it into his own kingdom that would appreciate his ideals. The lands he stumbled upon after getting lost in the Restless Mountains were thick with foliage, but flat ground was hard to find between all the mountains. Then he found a large open space of lush grass that an entire village could be built upon. A smaller mountain overlooked the flat lands as if guarding it from outsiders. That's where he built his castle with the help of dragons that lived there, preferring the rainier climate to the deserts of the Unclaimed Lands. These dragons helped him and became his family until he grew his kingdom from people who had lost their way in the Restless Mountains as he had. Knowing that if anyone found this lush land, they would try to take it from them, he trained all his people—men, women, and children—to fight and defend their homes.

The dragons added their wisdom as well, helping the new country to prosper. Then one night, the black dragon came to him and explained that their most important secret had been discovered. King Yash and his best men flew with the dragons to Utros and slaughtered the man, removing any chance that the secret could be leaked. Seeing how well the men and dragons worked together this way, King Yash decided to make an elite force of fighters who could best any army. This brought a treaty with Norden, and he helped train their army to fight with dragons as well, making Norden one of the strongest kingdoms outside of King Yash's.

"How can this be?" I gasped, rereading the passage once again to make sure I was right. "He was the one who taught our people to ride and fight with dragons? This doesn't make any sense. Why don't we have more information on this from our past kings and queens? The dragons should have all this information locked away in their memories."

"That I cannot answer, Cassy girl, but I think it might be that they could have been waiting for the right person to learn their secrets," Sal mused out loud.

"You think that's me? Why on earth would you think that?" I scoffed, brushing him off as a crazy old man. "There have been many great kings and queens for the mercenaries. What could possibly make me different?"

"Cassy, you are the first one to have such a connection with dragons. I heard how you were able to contact Jade's dragon. That shouldn't have been possible. You are not Tahir's pair-bond, nor is he a black dragon, one of the only kinds that has been known to share their thoughts with another. What if you are like King Yash, and you can communicate with *all* dragons?"

As Sal spoke the words, a memory of my dream came crashing back into the forefront of my mind. "He called me Dragon Queen… but how could he know?"

"Who? Who called you that?" Sal pressed, his eyes sparkling with excitement.

"The Lost King," I whispered, fear causing a chill to run down my spine. "Could he know this information too, about King Yash? It does involve Utros history. Could this be tied to why I was kidnapped? Oh God! He was in my brain. He had me in his grasp. If Vasin hadn't pulled me out of it, I might have been a weapon used against my own people!"

My breathing was coming quicker and shallower. I could feel my heart pounding as the horror of what might have been flashed through my mind. Suddenly, my chair was pulled back, and Izel was kneeling in front of me, his hands cupping my face, speaking to me. His smooth, silky voice drew me in, and I knew he was using his Birthright on me, but I let him. I needed to calm down, and I wouldn't be able to do it on my own.

"Breathe, My Queen, you are safe. The Lost King cannot harm you here with your guardians at your back. We will not let anything happen to you. Take a deep breath… good… now another," Izel coached, his eyes never leaving mine, keeping me locked in the present with him. "That's a girl. Keep breathing in through your nose and out through your mouth."

Once he saw I was more stable, he dropped his hands from my face, but I snatched up his hand, not wanting him to move from where it was. I wasn't in the throes of panic anymore, but I wasn't ready for his calming effect on me to be removed yet.

"Cassarah, I think it might help if you tell us what happened when you rescued Prince Gavin," Izel suggested, giving my hand a comforting squeeze.

I nodded, licking my lips nervously. "It started when I woke up tied in the back of a wagon, not knowing where I was. My hands were tied to the top of the wagon where my two captors sat driving it. We were close to the Darsor River, and they were talking about how they had to lock me up someplace in Errit and hack off a piece of me to send back to the clans to prove they had me. At that time, I had no idea what was going on or who this mysterious Lost King was. All I knew was I had to get out of that wagon. Only Richard and the two men were there, so I had pretty good odds if I got my hands free. I tried to reach out to Vasin, but he was too far away, and I had to make sure I didn't get caught doing it… bastard told them I could reach out to Vasin with my thoughts. Unbeknownst to me, I ended up reaching Tahir. It was garbled, and I could only read emotions off him. I thought I'd finally gotten to Vasin, and the distance was making it challenging. When a red dragon breathing fire showed up causing chaos, I knew it wasn't Vasin I was talking to."

The memory of the heat from that fire echoed through my brain as I took a moment before I continued. "In the madness, my two captors bailed, the horse broke free, and the wagon was rolling right for the raging river. Up until six months ago, I didn't know how to swim. I'm still not very good at it, and with my hands tied, there was no way I would survive if I didn't get out of the wagon. So I kicked out the damaged sidewall and tossed myself out of the wagon, catching my leg on a shard of wood. Everyone scattered, and Jade came to my rescue, not that I was very thankful or welcoming to him."

"Yeah, she thanked Tahir and ignored me until I started pressing her for information. The sweet queen you have all seen so far wasn't the one I met, that's for sure," Jade grumbled, but he gave me a grin, letting me know there were no hard feelings. "It was only because she tried to lie to me that I figured out the truth."

"Oh, but when he learned who I really was, you should have seen him dropping to his knees, apologizing for being an ass." I laughed. "He filled me in on what happened in the two days I'd been missing and happened to mention the large camp of men in the woods he'd just crossed over to get to me. I figured we better find out what that was about, and sure enough, we found the Lost King's camp where Prince Gavin was being held. The two of us, along with Tahir's help, rescued Gavin, and I might have blown up all of their supplies."

"What little bird isn't telling is that she fought with Lord Everett and won, not to mention that she handled every other person who tried to get in her way," Jade interjected.

"I always knew you could be a badass, mouse!" Cole said, kicking his feet up on the table. "The Lost King won't have a clue what hit him when we get this plan of yours going. I have no doubt it will be brilliant."

Fourteen

Nice Night for a Flight

At some point, lunch was brought in while I worked on writing out my plans and all the moving parts involved in it. My guardians had to pry the pen out of my hand so I could eat, and even then, it was only part of it, my brain too full of whirling ideas to slow down. Time blurred as my hand started to ache. People came in and out of the room when I needed them. We would hash out details and add more things to the list that needed to be done.

"Cass, I'm told you haven't taken a break all day. Come outside and sit with me awhile. The fresh air will do you good. Besides, I feel like there are things we need to talk about," Vasin called out to me, effectively cutting off my train of thought.

"I don't have time, Vasin. We need to get this figured out, or all could be lost."

"Yes, but it doesn't all have to be done by you. There are hundreds of people in that cavern, and it's their home too. Let them help and take some of the pressure off you."

I knew he was right, but my stubborn streak was showing, and I didn't want to let anyone else help me.

"Don't make me come get you."

"You couldn't fit through this door even if you wanted to," I teased.

"ALL I HAVE TO DO IS MAKE IT BIGGER..."

"No, you wouldn't! That could collapse the whole room!"

"THEN IT MIGHT BE WISER TO COME OUT THAN FOR ME TO COME IN, WOULDN'T YOU AGREE?"

I set down my pen and turned to look at the doorway to the room. *"You're sitting outside the door, aren't you?"*

"YOUR GUARDIANS NEEDED TO EAT DINNER, AND YOU WANTED SPACE, SO HERE I SIT, KEEPING YOU FROM HARM."

I took a moment to look around the room and discovered Gavin sleeping in one of the chairs, along with Payson whittling something to pass the time. Other than those two, I was alone in the room. It had become oddly quiet without the others talking or working on tasks I'd given them as I went along. I vaguely remember Abbott asking if I wanted food and telling me they were going to eat. Letting out a heavy sigh, I rubbed my face with my hands as tiredness crept in.

"Ah, did you come up for air?" Payson asked, setting down what he was working on. "Everyone went to get dinner and leave this room for a bit. I would suggest you do the same, but I'm not sure you would listen."

I gave him a tired smile and pushed my chair back from the table. "Vasin is the one who decided that enough was enough, and I needed to be done. It's hard to argue with a person who can literally get inside your head."

At my words, Payson jumped to his feet and walked over to me. "Where might I be able to take you, Cassarah?"

"Seeing as he is right outside the door waiting for me, it won't be too far of a walk if you wouldn't mind helping me?" I asked slowly, getting to my feet and stretching my stiff body.

"I don't know if I should let you walk over there, even with my help, seeing as Dayson had to restitch your leg," Payson cautioned.

"What if I helped?" Gavin asked, scaring a squeak out of me. He chuckled as he walked over to us. "That must be why he calls you little mouse. It's cute."

My cheeks heated at his words, and I couldn't meet his gaze, uncomfortable with the compliment.

"What do you say, Payson? If you steady her on one side and me on the other, we should be able to get her to the door without too much trouble," Gavin encouraged.

"I'm gonna need to keep up the strength in my good leg, right? If I keep getting carried everywhere, it will just get weaker," I reasoned, crossing my fingers, hoping he agrees to at least let us try.

"Fuck it, who am I to tell the queen no? Come on, let's get her out of this room before she changes her mind and has us bring in a bed," Payson said, pulling my right arm over his shoulders.

Gavin did the same on my left side, and we started toward the door. It was an awkward process since I was shorter than them, but we managed, laughing the whole way as we kept stepping on each other. Gavin pulled the door open to reveal Vasin's large head looming behind it in the shadows, making him jump. Only he didn't let out a squeak.

Climb on, Cass. I will make sure you get out safely.

Leaning on Payson, I shuffled over to Vasin's side, and Gavin helped Payson vault me onto Vasin's back like you would a ride on horseback. Settled and confident I wouldn't fall off, I wrapped my arms around his neck, keeping my body flush with his as he started to move.

"Where will you be so I can tell the others," Payson called after me.

"Tell him not to worry, and if they really need to find us, send Tahir. I need some of my own time with you, Cass."

I laughed as I turned to answer. "He says not to worry and just have Jade send Tahir to find us. That tells me no one should be able to get to me unless they come by dragon, and we'll see that easily."

Payson opened his mouth to speak, but Vasin was already on the move. Once we reached an open area, he spread his wings and shot up into the air. I closed my eyes, trusting that Vasin knew where we were going as we left the light below and headed right into the pitch-black darkness. I knew the moment we left the mountain and reached the night air, the wind whipping around me. Opening my eyes, I sat up and looked around, the sun low on the horizon, causing a burst of red and orange like the mountains were on fire. Vasin flew leisurely through the mountain peaks, letting me breathe in the clean, fresh air and soak up the last moments of the sun.

Finally, he landed on a grassy plateau and assisted me off his back, tucking me against his chest where his ember burned, keeping me warm. The night air was getting much colder now that the sun wasn't around to warm the land, warning us that winter was coming. Vasin and I sat in silence, letting me be, and enjoyed watching the stars coming out as the moon took over shedding its cool light over the mountains. It made the world look far more intimidating, casting shadows where there were none before. I might have been frightened if I didn't have a massive dragon with superior night vision watching my back.

"I feel your mind whirling, Cass. What is it that has caused you to worry so intently?"

"Everything we are dealing with now has been looming in the darkness for a long time. In some ways, I feel like it's been building for centuries."

"WHY DO YOU SAY THAT?"

Shifting, I sat more to the side so I could see his head as I asked, *"Why do the dragons need to keep the original agreement so secret? They slaughtered a man and his whole family, burned down his home, and hunted anyone he might have told. For dragons who think so rationally, how could they do something like that unless it was absolutely necessary?"*

"IF THE TERMS OF THE ORIGINAL AGREEMENT ARE KNOWN, IT WILL BE THE END OF DRAGONS AS WE KNOW IT. THEY WERE TRICKED INTO IT, AND NORDEN IS THE ONLY COUNTRY STILL HOLDING ONTO THE PRACTICE, BUT WE ARE FIGHTING TO BE FREE OF THEM. THERE IS A REASON THAT FEWER AND FEWER DRAGONS ARE PAIR-BONDING."

"That is because of the agreement?"

"I CANNOT TELL YOU MUCH, BUT WHAT I AM WILLING TO SAY IS WE HAVE WAITED A LONG TIME FOR SOMEONE LIKE YOU TO BE BORN. WE'VE TRIED OVER THE YEARS TO FREE OURSELVES, BUT WE CAN'T DO IT ALONE." VASIN let out a deep breath, smoke puffing out of his nose in his frustration. *"THE FIRST KING OF THE MERCENARIES WAS ALSO THE FIRST MAN TO PAIR-BOND WITH A BLACK DRAGON. IT WAS BECAUSE OF HIM THAT THEY BECAME THE SYMBOL OF ROYALTY."*

"Vasin, have I trapped you?"

"NO! I CHOSE YOU, CASSARAH. IT IS OUR DEEPEST WISH FOR US DRAGONS TO BE LUCKY ENOUGH TO FIND A PERSON WE TRULY BOND WITH. I KNEW THE MOMENT I FELT YOU ENTER THE CASTLE THAT WE WERE GOING TO DO GREAT THINGS FOR THIS WORLD. NEVER DOUBT THAT I WANT TO BE BY YOUR SIDE." Vasin dropped his head to nuzzle me, reassuring me with actions as well as words.

Out of the corner of my eye, I caught something glinting in the moonlight seconds before an arrow shot over my head and bounced off of Vasin's scales. *"What's happening? Can you see who is shooting at us?"*

As quickly as I could, I pulled myself to my feet and threw myself up on Vasin's back, flopping like a fish on land, trying to get astride him. While I was doing that, Vasin batted another arrow out of the sky with his wing before using his nose to shove me the rest of the way on his back.

"There is a dragon hiding in the peak above us. I can't tell where his rider is, though."

"How did they sneak up on us?"

"I wasn't looking for them. Foolishly, I believed we were safe here. Hold on... I'm taking off. We can't sit here out in the open."

The next thing I knew, we were leaping off the edge of a cliff, hurtling down a few feet before Vasin spread his wings, and we leveled out. Trusting him to keep us safe and not lead this dragon back to our hideout, I shut my eyes. I reached out to Tahir, hoping we weren't too far away. Knowing what I was looking for, it was easier to lock on to him this time. He was napping on the still-warm rocks at the peak of the mountain we resided in. The moment my mind touched him, he was awake. I still couldn't get much from him but emotions and impressions of his thoughts, but no words.

"Tahir, we are being attacked. Get Jade!"

Immediately, I got the impression he understood what I'd told him, and he sent me back a flood of worry and understanding as he went to find his pair-bond.

"I was able to talk to Tahir. He's going to find Jade and come help us."

"I can't tell what allegiance this dragon and his rider hold, but I can tell you he found us because of the call I sent out."

"Dammit, that means somehow it's important to his rider that we're found, but why attack us?"

"I've been trying to talk to him, but he's blocking me out of his mind."

The whoosh of wind sounded above us as the dark brown dragon darted by, wheeling to dive right at us. Clinging to Vasin, he snapped his wings closed, and we plummeted, only to sharply turn right into a narrow space between two rock walls. Vasin latched onto one of the walls and thrust himself up, shooting us skyward, his leathery wings propelling us toward the moon. I shifted until my feet could rest on the place where his wings joined his body, giving me something to help keep myself from sliding off his back. My leg burned at the weight I was putting on it, but that was the lesser of two evils. Falling off and dying as I was smashed against the rocks below was a far worse option.

Now out of the rock and back into the open sky, I swiveled my head around, trying to see where the dragon was. I knew it couldn't be that easy to lose him. Sure enough, the dragon came charging right at us from the left, his rider sitting tall with a bow drawn right for me.

"Cass, hold on with everything you've got. I'm going to have to spin!"

I knew there was no way I could manage to hold on with only my arms around his neck, but we didn't have much of a choice. Clinging to Vasin for dear life, he rolled to the right and banked toward a grove of trees on the mountain side. I managed to hold on for the spin, but when he banked and curved, my injured leg seized up, sending a shockwave of pain through me, and I couldn't keep my grip on his neck. Scrambling, I tried to grab hold of anything as I started to slip. Vasin tried to right himself, but the brown dragon darted in at us, forcing Vasin to jerk to the left.

Once I lost my hold on him, it was impossible to stop at the speed we were flying, and I flew off his back into the night sky.

FIFTEEN

MORE SECRETS REVEALED

The wind rushed past me as I plummeted, drawing closer and closer to the ground below. Oddly, my mind was calm as I kept my eyes on Vasin, watching as he was locked in battle with the brown dragon. He kept trying to break away to get to me, but the other dragon would get in his way, clawing at him, trying to tear into his wings. Then, beyond all reason, the rider leaped off the brown dragon's back and shot toward me like an arrow. Nothing about this made any sense. Why would this person try to come after me when they clearly wanted to kill me?

A roar burst from the darkness as a red dragon shot toward me. Tahir shot flames at the brown dragon as he passed before tucking his large red wings at his side as he dove, chasing after me. There was Jade on his back, strapped into the saddle he'd formed, so situations like mine didn't happen. Tahir shifted so he streaked past me to the right, allowing Jade to reach out and snag my arm, yanking me to him. Jade trapped me against his chest and Tahir's neck as they rolled into the turn, avoiding the ground growing ever nearer. Tahir snapped out his wings and headed back to Vasin, who had the brown dragon's neck in his jaws and the talons of his back legs deep in its belly.

The brown dragon let out a cry of pain as it thrashed, clawing at Vasin, trying to get him to release him. I gasped as the brown dragon's mind slammed into my own, begging me to stop Vasin from killing him. Its panic and fear were overwhelming, but the strange part was the fact that regret was just as intermixed.

"Stop! Don't kill him! He'll speak to you now!"

Hearing my plea, Vasin released the brown dragon and pulled away from him but didn't go far. I watched as the two dragons circled each other like two fighters in the ring, watching and waiting for the other to make a move. Jade kept Tahir farther back, watching the whole thing in case we needed to act. Vasin let out a mighty roar that shook my bones as Tahir joined in flames burst from his mouth, lighting up the night sky for a moment.

"Follow me. His rider has landed below us and has a lot to explain for himself."

"He survived jumping off his dragon?"

"Apparently, but if his answers are not good enough, he won't live too much longer."

I turned my face up so it was more or less nestled in Jade's neck. "Follow Vasin. He is going to lead us to the dragon rider."

Jade didn't answer me. He just caressed my cheek with his own, and Tahir banked to the left, falling in behind Vasin. I breathed in the comforting scent of Jade, reminding me I was still alive. I was probably handling this so well because I was in shock, and my brain refused to let me deal with the fact I almost died. His warmth seeped into my skin, letting me know just how cold I must be right now. How did a simple outing with Vasin turn into a life-or-death altercation with a rogue dragon?

Finally, we landed in a small valley with a river trickling through, shimmering in the full moon's light. There, checking over his drag-on, was the rider, dressed in some strange leather outfit that looked almost like it had bat wings attached to it between the arms and legs. The moment we landed, the rider turned, brandishing a sword, which Vasin promptly ripped out of his hand, tossing it into the woods and roaring at him, once again knocking the man on his ass.

The man refused to back down from Vasin, his handsome face calm with only a slight jut of the chin. His bronze-colored hair was in disarray from his leap off his dragon, but it only gave him an even more roguish look. He might have been trying to kill me, but watching him guard his dragon from mine was impressive.

Tahir hunkered down low, making it easier for Jade to slide me off his back while he unbuckled himself from his saddle. Slowly using Tahir's shoulder, I stood, wobbling as if the ground under my feet was shaking, but it was just my body that was doing the trembling. It seemed the shock was starting to wear off some. Jade vaulted off Tahir and grabbed me around the waist as I almost tripped over a rock.

"Seriously, how many times are you going to play with your life tonight?" Jade growled quietly. "I don't think my heart could take much more after seeing you free-falling, about to splatter on the ground below."

I looked him in the eyes for the first time since he rescued me, and they were ablaze with his fear—fear of almost losing me. I reached out and rested my hand on his chest over his heart, feeling how fast it was beating, even though his body didn't betray his emotions. "Thank you for saving my life once again, Jade. I wasn't sure I was going to survive."

"*Cass! You need to talk to this man right now,*" Vasin snapped at me, causing me to flinch with the anger behind it. "*I'm sorry, I'm not upset with you. It appears I'm having trouble controlling my emotions since this man almost killed you.*"

"Can you help me over to Vasin so I can figure out what the hell is going on?" I asked.

Jade swung me into his arms, carried me over to Vasin, and set me down but didn't budge from his place beside me. He was my guardian and clearly taking that role seriously, knowing I couldn't defend myself very well right now.

"Who are you?" I called out to the man.

He cocked his head and turned to face me in my general direction. "Shouldn't I be asking you that? What business do you have riding on the back of a black dragon?"

"He is my pair-bond. What reason would you have to harm him?" I demanded, utterly confused by the question.

A person didn't ride a dragon unless they were bonded with each other. It simply wasn't done. How else could you communicate with your dragon if you didn't have the bond?

Hearing this, the man stood a little straighter and scowled at me, but there was still something off about how he looked at me. It was almost as if he was looking past me but not truly *seeing* me. "Pair-bond... does this mean you have a mental connection to this dragon? Your souls are one?"

"How do you not know what a pair-bond is? Don't you have one with the brown dragon behind you?" Jade challenged.

"I asked first."

"Yeah, sorry, asshole, but when you almost kill my queen, you lose all chances of getting anything out of us, let alone living for much longer," Jade snarled, wrapping an arm around my waist. "You tell us who you are, or Vasin will slaughter you for hurting his pair-bond."

Vasin backed up Jade's words with a deep, rumbling growl you could feel in your bones. Shocking us all, a small golden creature burst out of the forest around us, flying right into Vasin's face, hissing and letting out a tiny burst of flame. Vasin rose on his haunches and swiped at the tiny dragon, but it darted out of harm's way.

The man let out a sharp whistle, causing the little dragon to let out a screech before settling on his shoulder. I watched as the tiny thing wrapped its tail around his neck while a little clawed hand gripped his ear.

"I humbly apologize for trying to harm your partner, Vasin, the black dragon, as well as the disrespect Ezzu has shown you. She is very protective of me," he said, dropping to his knee. "It has been centuries since we have seen your kind in these parts."

"What is he talking about?" I whispered to Jade.

"I'm not sure if the man's all there. I mean, he jumped off his dragon, for fuck's sake," Jade muttered.

"Tell him that I will consider his apology when he explains who he is and where he comes from, but he is far from forgiven."

I relayed the message to the man. He nodded his head and stood to face me once again. "I am Zan, a soldier of the Sheca Kingdom. This is Ezzu... she is my eyes, and my partner, Ifra. I was on a scouting mission to find the reason why the dragons of our kingdom became agitated earlier today. I saw you and Vasin on the plateau. I assumed the worst, believing you were holding this dragon against his will."

"What? How in the world would *I* be able to hold a dragon captive?" I blurted, shocked at his assumption. "Dragons do not bond with anyone unless they want to. They have the power in the relationship when it comes down to it."

Zan shifted as if unsure of what to think of my answer. "Is this true, Vasin?"

Vasin's answer was to nod and let out a grunt of agreement. *"He needs to tell us more. He isn't giving us the full story.*

TELL HIM IFRA ALREADY TOLD ME EVERYTHING, AND HE NEEDS TO TELL YOU. IT'S YOUR RIGHTFUL INHERITANCE."

"*What are you rambling about? None of this makes sense!*"

"*ASK HIM.*"

I sighed, trying to control my frustration between these men being cryptic as hell with me. "Zan, Ifra has already told everything to Vasin. So if we could cut the crap and just tell me what the hell is going on, I would be forever grateful. It's been a bit of a rough night if you didn't notice."

"Are you truly the Queen of the Mercenaries?" Zan asked bluntly.

I pulled out the necklace Ballard gave me upon my coronation and held it up in the moonlight. "Yes, I am Queen Cassarah of the Raven Rose clan, ruler of all the mercenaries."

Zan gave Vasin another look before he started closing the distance between us, causing Jade to pull out one of his knives, garnishing a hiss from Ezzu at his threat. When Zan got a foot away from me, he once again dropped to a knee, pulling out two daggers and setting them on the grass before him.

Taking his right hand, he placed it over his heart and bent his head. "I, Zandophen, soldier to the Sheca Kingdom, swear fealty to you, Queen Cassarah, ruler of all the mercenaries. Your people have been waiting for your return to the kingdom and the Dragon Castle."

I looked down at the man, up at Jade, then back down at Zan, completely stunned at what was happening. "I-I don't understand."

Reaching out, I put my hand on his shoulder that wasn't occupied to try and get him to stand. Instead, blue light from my Birthright surrounded us. Once again, I felt that same overwhelming pain mixed with power I'd experienced when I'd called my guardians to me.

No, this can't be happening! Why would my powers choose a man who tried to kill me not moments ago? Just how much protection was I going to need to be queen?

Zan hissed as I knew the same mark that graced my forearm was now searing itself onto his, marking him forever as a member of my guardians. Once the power subsided, I stumbled back from him, and Jade caught me before I tipped over, unsteady on my legs. "No! No, this can't be! I don't understand. Why you? Why would my Birthright do that?"

I turned and buried my face in Jade's chest, unwilling to deal with this, reaching the end of what I could emotionally handle. Tears streamed down my face, and I clung to Jade, filled with anger, frustration, and panic at what this all could mean. I knew that Zan represented something important, but so did everything else that had been brought to my attention the last few days.

"My Queen, I apologize for whatever I've done to upset you. I meant no such disrespect in offering up my oath as your subject," Zan pleaded, and I heard him moving closer.

"Take another step, and I'll drop you where you stand, guardian or not," Jade snarled, his voice rumbling under my ear. "You might have been given her mark, but that does not make you one of us. Not until you prove yourself after almost killing her."

"I didn't know!" Zan shot back, his words sharp with his anger. "It's been three hundred and fifty years since the last king left us behind to keep our kingdom safe. My people thought we were long forgotten and never to be found again."

Wiping my eyes with my sleeve, I turned in Jade's arms to face Zan. "Say that again?"

"Four hundred years ago, the last mercenary king we had sitting on the throne in the Dragon Castle took our best men and women to Norden. They were supposed to set up a new place for those going on missions for Norden's king and queen. He left behind a fair amount of us to keep our kingdom running as it always has until he called us to join the others, only that call never came," Zan explained.

"Vasin, is this true?"

"Yes, the third King of the Mercenaries did separate from Sheca and returned to Norden. He never intended to return to the Dragon Castle, though, purposely leaving behind the weaker of his people. Only the strongest of his people were selected to form this new clan... the Raven Rose clan. When it got too large, and we needed to cover more area, he split it into the six clans we now have today."

"How many of you are there still in Sheca, and why has no one ever heard of this country?"

"There are roughly over two thousand of us, and no one leaves the village. We have all the resources we need in our own country, so there's no need to venture outside it. That and making sure the dragons are safe."

Frowning, I glanced at Jade who just shrugged his shoulders. "What do the dragons have to do with anything? They are protected here in Norden, or they leave to live elsewhere."

"I believe that tale will be best left for when you ascend your throne and return to Sheca," Zan countered.

"Zan... I can't leave. We are on the brink of war with Errit and Utros, with a mind-controlling bastard prince of Norden leading the charge. He wants to wipe out everyone and everything so he can rule it all."

"So the time of the Dragon Queen has finally come."

Sixteen

It's All Too Much

"No, I can't take on more. Being queen over the six clans is already more than I can handle. I can't add on another whole kingdom. If your people have survived for over four hundred years, they can wait a little longer," I stated. "Jade, I think it's best if we head back now."

Jade nodded, but his gaze drifted over to Zan. "What do we do about him?"

"I don't care what he does," I answered, knowing that I sounded cruel, but I wanted nothing to do with the dragon throne or whatever he called it. Having Zan with us would just be a reminder of what else was out there waiting for me, and I couldn't handle it.

"Cass, you cannot abandon him. He is one of your guardians, and your Birthright chose him for a reason. You will need him, as much as I hate to admit it."

"There is only so much a person can take, and I'm not strong enough to handle any more right now. I'm afraid that the more I learn from him, the more my responsibilities will grow. They have been left in a time bubble. Those people have no idea what is going on in the world or how things work between us as pair-bonds."

"What if learning from him is exactly what you need? You said it yourself. If we can learn from the past, then we are not doomed to repeat ourselves. After speaking with his dragon, they know the same

THINGS WE DO ABOUT BEING PAIR-BONDED, BUT THAT IS NOT THE WORD THEY USE. WHAT IF I TOLD YOU THAT EVERY PERSON BACK IN THAT VILLAGE HAS A PURE BIRTHRIGHT AND A PAIR-BOND WITH A DRAGON?"

"What? How can that be? Birthrights are fading from existence."

"SEEMS LIKE HE MIGHT BE MORE USEFUL TO US THAN YOU THOUGHT."

"I hate it when you do that, Vasin. You know I can't argue with sound logic."

Vasin just laughed as he wandered over to check on the brown dragon. *"HE SHOULD BE HEALED ENOUGH TO FLY BACK TO THE HIDEOUT. I SUGGEST YOU RIDE WITH JADE, THOUGH, UNTIL WE GET A HARNESS MADE FOR YOU LIKE HE HAS SO THAT I NEVER HAVE TO FEAR LOSING YOU AS I DID TODAY."*

I had to agree with Vasin there. I wasn't sure I was ready to be on my own flying just yet, after everything. Taking a deep breath, I hobbled up to Zan. "Would you like to come back with me? You may have been marked as a guardian to me, but I will not force that on you if it is not something you want."

"Your Majesty, I would be honored to serve as one of your guardians, but I must be honest with you. I'm blind..."

"Blind?" I blurted, stunned by this announcement, even though I'd noticed something odd about him. "How can that be?"

"My blessing is the ability to use the eyes of any dragon I've made a connection with. I've been blind my whole life, so it's not a hindrance to me in being of service to you. Ezzu is always with me, and in battle, I'll have Ifra, so I am able to see far better than any human," Zan informed me as he shifted his vacant gray eyes to meet mine. "If you still want me to come with you, I will, but if you send me back to Sheca, I won't hold it against you."

"I feel that we have a lot to learn from and about each other, Zan, and I can't do that with you being in another kingdom," I answered, choosing to trust in Vasin and my own Birthright for having chosen him for me.

Zan bowed deeply from the waist. "You honor me, Your Majesty."

"The others are going to *love* this," Jade muttered as he wrapped an arm around my shoulder, guiding me back to Tahir. He hoisted me up and strapped us both in snuggly before Tahir launched himself into the air, and we headed back to our temporary home.

Seeing how far Vasin had led Zan away from the hideout, I was impressed with how fast Jade had made it to us. We circled a few times, waiting for Vasin and Ifra to join us before he glided down to the wide ledge we'd landed on only three days ago. The instant Tahir touched down, all my guardians came rushing out of the tunnel and headed right for us.

"What the hell happened, Cassarah?" Cole demanded, reaching us first with Dayson and Izel on his heels.

Jade lowered me into their arms, where Dayson checked me over for any damage done to my body. When he tried to cut up my pant leg to get a better look at my injured leg, I'd reached my limit.

"Put that damn blade away, Dayson, or so help me God, I will stab you with it," I snapped. "Just back off, all of you... please."

The stunned looks on their faces told me I crossed the line, taking my feelings out on them. It wasn't their fault. They didn't know what I'd just been through or that I couldn't handle anything more right now.

"Who the hell are you?" Payson growled, noticing Zan. May joined Payson, hand on her sword, ready to take action if it was called for.

This caused Ezzu to snarl at them, leaping off Zan's shoulder to attack them, but quick as an arrow, Zan gripped the dragon by her tail and coddled her against his chest.

"What the fuck is that?" Payson gasped as he ducked, covering his head with his hands. "Wait, is that a tiny dragon?"

"Leave them be," I sighed and sought out Abbott. He was standing in the middle of both situations, unsure of which to act on, but when he felt my gaze, he turned and walked over to me. "Abbott, I need you to keep an eye on Zan. I'm not getting into the story right now, but Zan is the newest addition to the guardians."

Abbott started to ask me a question but took a moment to search my face before he nodded and walked over to Zan. He held out his hand to the man. Zan hesitated a moment before he took the offered hand and shook it. "I'm Abbott, one of Cassarah's guardians and a member of the Raven Rose clan. Welcome to the team."

"Zandophen, but you can call me Zan. This little hellion is Ezzu, and that's my dragon partner, Ifra," Zan said, introducing himself and the brown dragon behind him.

"Looks like the big guy got into a scuffle. Does Ifra need to be looked at?" Abbott asked.

Trusting Abbott to deal with this, I let myself relax from worrying about what to do with Zan until later. "Jade, would you help me back to my room?"

I knew that if I asked one of the others, they would bombard me with questions, and I just didn't have the strength to deal with it. I would snap at them, and they didn't deserve that from me right now. Jade lifted me into his arms, and we headed into the tunnel without speaking another word. As we passed by everyone gathered in the common area, I couldn't help but feel envious of them living such a simple life, enjoying time with their families and loved ones. None of them had to deal with the fate of thousands of people's lives and try to make the best call to keeping them safe. I knew I could help them, but what would it cost *me* to do so? I'd already had to change so much from the person I was living trapped in my parents' house—not that I wanted to stay that way. Now, I supposedly had another kingdom I was meant to rule over. That would make me a legitimate queen with a castle and everything. Is that what I wanted out of life? Could it be that I was just meant to save everyone and then hand it off to someone better suited for a job of this magnitude?

"Little bird, you need to take a deep breath," Jade whispered as he sat me down at the door to my room, turning me to face him. "Everything you learned tonight can wait. Like you said, they've been able to manage for hundreds of years without you. I'm amazed you haven't had a meltdown before this. You've had more thrown at you in the past few days than anyone could withstand. We can delay Alto and me going to Royal City tomorrow if you need me around."

"No, you have to go tomorrow. That letter getting to Queen Mary is of the utmost importance, and I trust you to see it done. Vasin and I have to meet with the other dragon riders as it is. This will help get me out of this place and away from the clan leaders for a bit." I leaned my head against his chest. "Jade, I don't have the luxury of breaking. I have to be the one to be strong in the face of it all. If I buckle, then everything else will fail. It's been proven time and time again that without a strong leader, everything else crumbles under them."

Jade tentatively wrapped his arms around me, and when I didn't pull away, he pulled me against his chest. "Then let us hold you up when you feel like you're going to shatter. I know we haven't had much time to get to know one another, but I can already see how much each and every one of your guardians wants to be there for you. Your powers chose us all for some reason or another. Some are obvious, and others I'm sure you will discover along the way, but we are picked specifically for you, Cassarah."

"Trust doesn't come easily for me, but I hear what you're saying," I answered, letting myself melt against him, allowing him to hold me up for a moment before I took a deep breath and pulled out of his arms. "Thank you, Jade, for being there when it truly matters. I'll see you in the morning before you and Alto fly out."

"Sleep well, little bird, but if you need me, I'm the second door on the right," Jade said, letting his hand brush against my cheek before he turned and headed to his room.

I pushed my door open and hobbled into my room, glad to be alone with my thoughts for once. It was harder than I thought it would be to adjust to having people around all the time. Changing into my nightgown, I noticed a pile of books and scrolls on the small table next to my bed. It would seem that Sal sent up more things for me to read, and glancing at the subject matter, it was about Errit and Utros. Deciding against reading that before going to bed, I dimmed all the lanterns until the room was dark enough to sleep and fell into bed.

"Cassarah."

My name whispered through my head as if passing by on a breeze.

"Cassarah, wake up. There is much to be done."

This time the voice was more solid and forced me to open my eyes. I bolted up in bed as I discovered I was in the vast white world of Vasin's mind. Somehow, I had managed to harmonize with Vasin in entering this world filled with all the knowledge of the dragons, past and present. Slowly, I turned in a circle, trying to understand what was happening, but none of this made sense.

"I've been waiting a long time to meet you, Cassarah."

Now I could tell that the voice was female and strangely sounded familiar to me. Then shimmering into existence was Miranda, the Raven Queen, whose life I watched in a series of dreams over the past six months.

"Wait... you can't be here... you're dead," I blurted. "Does that mean I'm dead?"

Miranda just cocked an eyebrow at me with her hands on her hips. "Really, that's what you think is going on?"

"How can you be here then?" I demanded, crossing my arms.

"I knew I was going to like you." Miranda chuckled before her face became more serious. "We don't have much time before you wake up, and we won't get to everything right now, but I had to warn you."

"Warn me about what? None of this makes sense!" I shouted, feeling my anger rise.

Miranda reached out and grabbed my arms. "There is so much more I wanted to do as queen, but my time was cut short. I didn't trust myself or the people around me enough when they told me not to go to the castle on that fateful day. Trust your gut. I know you have the right instincts about people, but also know that not everything is as it seems. You will figure out who offers true counsel and who is just trying to use you. The world is far darker than we ever imagined."

"What does any of that mean?"

"We are out of time but know I'm here for you. All you have to do is call out for me here, and I'll come." Miranda faded away once again, leaving me to get yanked out of Vasin's mind and back into my own.

SEVENTEEN

IF THEY LEAVE, WILL THEY COME BACK?

"Hey, Cassarah, it's time to wake up," Becka said, shaking my shoulder. "Alto and Jade are almost ready to leave."

Groaning, I rubbed my face with both hands, trying to rationalize what happened in my dream. Had Miranda really come to talk to me? It must just be all the stress I'm under—there's no way that could've really happened. Dropping my hands, I stared up at the ceiling, letting my body readjust to being back in my own skin. This feeling only happened when I harmonized with Vasin, giving me yet another sign it might not have been a dream.

"Alto wanted to have a look at your leg before she left. Can I let her in?" Becka asked from where she sat on the edge of my bed.

"It would be easier for her to look at it before I get dressed, so please let her in," I answered as I sat up and tossed the blankets back.

I felt like I did on the first day of training—my body ached, my head was foggy, and it felt like I hadn't slept longer than a few minutes. It would seem riding on the back of a dragon during a battle was rough on the body.

"Goodness, Your Majesty, are you well?" Alto inquired as she kneeled before me with a basket of supplies.

"Last night, Vasin and I had a misunderstanding with my newest guardian that led to a scuffle between the dragons. I'm just a little sore and could do with a little more sleep but nothing else to worry about," I answered, waving off her concern.

The last thing I needed was for the guys to go after Zan when they found out what happened last night. I prayed that Jade kept his mouth shut and didn't tell them I almost died. They smothered me enough as it was.

"I think I can help with some of that." Alto rustled around in her basket and handed Becka a few satchels of herbs. "Boil this in hot water until it turns a rich brown color, then add in a pinch or two of this to help with the pain. She can have more for the pain if she needs it later in the afternoon, but no more than three doses in a day."

Becka nodded and headed off to do just as she was instructed. Alto lifted my leg and set it in her lap, removing the bandage. I was pleased it didn't hurt nearly as much as it had before.

"It's healing nicely, rather quickly as well, which is lucky for you. I think giving it a few more days of no walking on it should do the trick. Once I take the stitches out, you should be able to return to life as normal, but I want you to take it easy until then. Dayson told me you popped a few stitches the other day. Things like that will slow everything down," Alto chided as she wrapped it up in a clean bandage.

"Relying on others isn't my strong suit. I've never really had someone other than Becka to look after me. Even then, she was limited to what she could do," I admitted.

Alto's gaze flicked up to meet mine for a moment before she held onto my foot, running her thumbs down my arch. "Can I assume that these scars on the bottom of your feet are from before you left home?"

"There aren't many places on a woman's body where you can whip without fear of the scaring being seen... it would lower my chances of finding an advantageous marriage," I whispered.

Alto cursed under her breath as she released my foot and stood. "Well, good riddance to that part of your life. While Becka is off getting that brewed, would you allow me to assist you in getting ready?"

"I can manage on my own. Becka is the only person I trust to help me," I answered. When I saw the scowl on Alto's face, I hurried to explain, "It's just I hate to feel that vulnerable in front of someone I don't know very well. I was never intimately abused or anything."

"Well, that's a relief, and I can understand not wanting to bare it all in front of people you don't feel safe with."

"Please, I mean no offense," I said, reaching out to touch her arm, needing her to understand.

Alto's face softened as she looked down at me. "Dear child, I'm not upset with you. If you don't want to undress in front of someone or have them touch you, then that is your choice. It should have always been your choice. The fact you question that makes me sad." Taking a deep breath, she sat next to me on the bed. "I know you are not anywhere near this point, but I have to ask... do you understand what happens between a man and a woman when they sleep together?"

My cheeks heated at her question, and I nodded, looking down at my hands. "I've been taught anatomy and been made aware of the purpose of a woman's cycle."

"That's a relief your mother didn't leave you totally ignorant," Alto muttered. "Helena talked to me about what she had you using while you were training and that it's been a few days since you've taken the medicine. I brought up these tinctures for you. Take one a week, and it will keep you from falling pregnant. I know you are not intimate with anyone, but I want to be sure you are prepared for when it does happen. Life never goes according to plan, and this is one thing we can avoid for now until you decide you're ready to be a mother."

"Thank you. I think this might be what my mother had me taking," I shared and smiled at her, amazed by her understanding of everything.

Patting my leg, she stood up and headed for the door. "Don't be too long. Jade and I need to head out so we make good time getting to Royal City."

The moment the door was closed, I stood up and hobbled around, getting ready for the day. As I moved, it helped to ease some of the soreness in my body. Washed and dressed, I waited at the table when Becka returned with a steaming mug and Dayson on her heels.

Before Becka could even hand me the mug, Dayson was on his knees before me, head bowed in subjection. "Forgive me, My Queen. I acted without thought yesterday, and I deserved the scolding you gave me."

"Dayson, what are you talking about?" I asked, utterly confused at what was happening.

Becka just smirked at me, handed over the mug before she gave me a wink, and left the room.

"It was wrong of me to put my hands on you when you hadn't given me permission, let alone draw a weapon to use on your body," Dayson explained.

"Are you talking about when you tried to cut my pants to check my leg?" I questioned. He nodded but still refused to look at me. "That wasn't why I was upset, Dayson. Please look at me. I'm not mad at you."

Dayson lifted his warm brown eyes to me, and I couldn't help but reach out to cup his cheek. "I should be the one to apologize for snapping at you like that. It was wrong of me to take out my frustration on you and the others when all you were trying to do was look after me."

"It still doesn't change the fact I acted without thinking," Dayson countered, pulling away from my touch. "I'm far too quick at making snap judgments. My anger gets the better of me, and I always choose violence and aggression to fix my problems. You deserve more from me than that."

I couldn't help but grin at this beast of a man telling me he needed to improve himself. It was such a contradiction to his outward appearance. "What if you were picked because you are that way? Everything you described is the complete opposite of who I am. Typically, I would rather run from conflict, and you step right into its path. Knowing I have someone like you at my back helps me be more confident, so please don't be so quick to change yourself. Let's give it time in these new roles before we decide we're failing."

Dayson gave me a searching look before a smile broke out on his face. "I've got to stop assuming what you're going to think or say. I get it wrong every time. I never guessed royalty could be so reasonable and logical in their decisions." He stood and reached out a hand to me. "Now that we've gotten that figured out, Jade's waiting to leave until you see him off. Apparently, you promised."

"I doubt that's the reason he's waiting." I laughed as Dayson swung me up on his back like you would a child.

I wrapped my arms and legs around his body, making sure not to choke him.

"Yeah, I wouldn't be too sure about that. It seems you've gotten under that man's skin, and that is not a simple matter."

"It's only been four days that I've known him. He can't be all that enamored with me. Sure, we've gone through some intense experiences, but we hardly know each other," I said, brushing off his comment.

Dayson shook his head as he glanced back at me. "Haven't you ever heard about the bond you make with someone you go into battle with? You and Jade started your friendship by saving the crown prince from the Lost King's army. Now you have him as a guardian, he was the one you called when you needed help last night. I'd say that is the start of a rather deep relationship, whatever it might be."

I thought that over, remembering the journals I've read about generals and other men in the military and the camaraderie they always speak about—the trust they have in their troops and all the talk about how they would die for each other, leaving no man behind.

"But if you follow that logic, it won't be long until I build that kind of bond along with all the guardians."

"Exactly."

"Do you really think it's possible to have that sort of trust last after the battle is over, though? What if it's just heightened emotions when you think you might not survive? Once the battles are over, life goes back to normal, and everyone goes back to their homes, do they still feel the same way about each other?"

I didn't know where I was going with this conversation or what answer I expected. The only thing I could think of that was causing me to question all this was remembering what Miranda had said—not everything is as it seems. Could she have been talking about the people around me currently or when Miranda was alive? Is it possible my powers picked wrong, and one of my guardians isn't looking out for my best interests?

"Then it's a good thing none of us are returning home after this battle is over. You marked us, so you're stuck with us. Although I can't speak for the others, I still think I would choose to stay with you, even if that wasn't the case."

That comment surprised me. "Why?"

"Simple. I believe in you and your vision for our people. Who wouldn't want to stand behind a queen such as yourself?"

"Now you're the one who's going all logical on me." I laughed.

When we exited the tunnel, the morning sun was low, still hidden behind the mountains, casting a bright pink glow about the sky. Tahir was there saddled and ready to go with Jade at his head, scratching behind his jaw. None of the other guardians were out here with us, just Alto who was packing up the last of her things into baskets that Jade would attach to the saddle. Dayson put me down a few steps from Jade and walked over to help Alto secure the basket, giving us a moment.

"How are you feeling?" Jade asked as he walked over to me.

"Tired and sore but in better spirits. Vasin and I are going out to meet with the other dragon riders later today," I shared. I studied him in a slightly different light after talking with Dayson.

Jade reached out and took my hand, drawing my gaze to his. "Please promise me you won't go alone. I know you don't trust him but take Zan. That way, you can bring along two others."

"I'll have to see after I talk to him again. I know he isn't trying to kill me, but I can't promise that," I admitted, dropping my gaze.

Jade let go of my hand to wrap his hand around my face, forcing me to look at him. "Cassarah, I won't be here to help you if you need me. I must know you'll be safe, or I'm not leaving, so it's up to you. Either take the new guy so you can have three men at your back, or I'll be going with you and taking Alto another day."

"You would ignore an order from your queen?" I demanded, irritated he was pressing the issue.

Pressing his forehead to mine, he whispered, "To keep you safe... without question."

The concern I heard in his voice left me with no other choice. "Okay, I'll take him with me, but if I end up in trouble because of it, I'm blaming you."

His answer was to kiss me full on the mouth, causing my body to lock up at the shock of it. Before I could do anything else, he stepped away from me and climbed up on Tahir before he assisted Alto behind him. He didn't look back at me once as he flew out into the sunrise to hopefully bring back the most important answer to our call for help.

EIGHTEEN

SETTING THINGS IN MOTION

Thankfully, Dayson didn't say a word about the fact that Jade had just kissed me as he carried me over to the table where the rest of my guardians were eating breakfast. Zan sat next to Abbott with Ezzu perched on his shoulder while Cole sat across from him, watching his every move with an assessing eye. When Dayson set me down, May came walking up with a tray full of food for us.

"Thanks, May." I smiled, grabbing a bowl and some fresh bread.

"Oh, Becka said you left this in your room, and you have to finish it," May said, setting the mug of brown liquid beside my bowl of porridge.

Taking the mug, I gulped down the brew, expecting it to taste horrid, but once the flavor registered in my brain, I slowed down. It had a nutty taste to it that was actually quite delightful.

"So, what's the plan for today?" Payson asked, leaning his head on his hand and peering at me. "More meetings with the clan leaders trapped in the cave?"

"Nope, Vasin and I are going to meet up with the dragon riders we called for yesterday. I'll need two of you guys to come with me." Resigning myself to the fact that Jade was right, I leaned forward so I could see down the table. "Zan, do you think Ifra would mind if you had another rider?"

Cole exploded from his seat, turning his glare toward me. "You have got to be fucking kidding me! You don't even know him, and you're already going to take him to an extremely important meeting? Have you lost it?"

Izel grabbed Cole's arm and yanked him back down to his seat. "You are the one who has lost your mind. How dare you yell at the queen in such a public place. She ought to slap you for such a display."

"Are you telling me that you're okay with this?" Cole demanded.

"It's not my place to disagree with her, nor is it yours," Izel hissed. "We should talk about this elsewhere without so many eyes watching."

Cole growled and stormed off, leaving me to doubt the choice I'd just made. Gavin, who was to my left, gently placed his hand on my leg and leaned in. "Trust your choice, Cassarah. Not everyone will always agree with you, but you have to know when to stick to your decisions. If you believe this is the best course of action, then follow it through and prove to them that they need to trust in your judgment. I can't tell you how many times I've seen my parents argue with the council they have over matters. You are their queen and you must worry about the big picture. Cole isn't worried about the clans... he's worried about you. I'm not saying it's a bad thing, but taking that into account with a situation like this is important."

Gavin was right. I knew he was. Jade had been worried about me too, but he also wasn't going to stop me from attending this meeting and wanted the best backup I could have without him there. Cole was more concerned about the threat that Zan posed over the fact I needed more people at my back.

"In answer to your question, My Queen, Ifra would be happy to be of help and is more than able to carry an extra person along with me," Zan spoke up. "If you can give me time to fly back home, I would like to gather a few things and let people know I will be gone for a while. It shouldn't take more than a few hours if you give your leave?"

I felt awful it hadn't even crossed my mind he was leaving everything behind back in Sheca. Of course, he would want to let people know he would be gone. Who wouldn't want to pack their belongings when they moved? I had no idea when or if I would ever make it to this mythical land he's from.

"Of course. I know things happened rather suddenly last night. Did you find a room?" I asked, looking at Abbott, who nodded.

"Yes, it would seem I have now completed filling the space meant for the guardians," Zan shared. "Let's hope you don't pick up any more along the way, or we might have a problem on our hands."

Everyone quickly gaped at him before the table fell into laughter at his words.

"That or I get kicked out on account I'm not truly a guardian," Gavin added, a grin on his lips. "I'm still waiting for her to realize that, but so far, so good."

"Didn't you know hiding in plain sight is the best strategy? If you blend in and act like you're supposed to be there, no one questions it," Payson teased, giving me a wink.

We all chuckled as the others got in on the razzing, giving their best stealth strategy. Much to my surprise, Zan blended in with the others fairly seamlessly. He might not have been born into one of the clans, but he knew the mercenary way of life, and it would seem that's all you needed.

"If I can take my leave, Your Majesty," Zan asked as he stood from the table.

I nodded my agreement. "Yes, you are free to do what you need to settle here more comfortably."

"You have to admit it's impressive that he's a soldier and dragon rider all while being blind," May acknowledged, watching Zan navigate the tables with Ezzu's help.

I felt uneasy with myself at how everyone else was being far more welcoming to Zan than I had. Mind you, they didn't know he almost killed me… at least, I don't think he shared that detail.

"Who else are you going to bring along to this meeting?" Payson asked.

"I thought it would be best to bring Dayson since they will mostly be Bronze Reapers, and it will help them believe I am who I say I am. As for the third, well, that would be you, Payson, since you have the best knowledge of Errit and Utros being close to their borders," I shared. "If only we had another dragon, I would have liked to take you as well, Gavin, but that will have to wait for another time."

"I don't see how I would be much help in this situation," Gavin argued. "Truly, I don't see how I'm much help to you at all other than a show of good faith to the kingdom and wanting to help you accomplish the peace between our people."

I snorted. "Yeah, that's nothing at all. The fact you are willing to be here and be involved after how my people treated you means everything."

"Cassarah, you saved my life. This is the least I can do for a life debt," Gavin countered.

"On that topic, we will just have to agree to disagree. It was the right thing to do. I couldn't just leave you there," I said, pushing myself up from the table. "While we are waiting for Zan to return, I'm going to work on a few things I didn't get to finish yesterday."

Izel stood and walked over to me. "I'll join you this time, if I may."

"I welcome it." I smiled, wrapping my arm around his neck as he scooped me up.

"Could I be of any help?" Gavin asked as he followed us. "I feel like there's more I could be doing to help. I'm quite knowledgeable about the kingdom and Royal City."

"Actually, that will be very helpful. I was going to try and work out what strategy the Lost King might use to take the city. Even if we don't have an answer yet, I think having a plan in place would be wise."

Gavin opened the door to the strategy room, giving me an odd look. "What?"

"For someone who never knew they were supposed to be a queen, you're rather brilliant at it." Gavin smirked as I rolled my eyes at him. "I should know. I was trained since birth to rule, and I suck at it."

"I doubt that!"

"You should see my little brother... he's the brain of the family. The two of you would get along amazingly well."

Izel set me down near the middle of the table, where everything I'd left last night was still sitting. "Since I don't have your brother here, I guess I'll just have to make do with you."

Gavin and I worked together, going over the ins and outs of the castle—where it was weak and what might give us an edge to know. A whole hidden pathway was dug under the castle that no one knew about. It was a guarded royal family secret, but in times of war like this, it was invaluable.

"Are you sure you won't get killed for sharing this with us?" I questioned as he drew the entrances and exits on a spare map of the castle.

"If Mother joins forces with us, then it won't matter. If they don't, I guess you're just stuck with me. Can't get killed if I don't ever return to the castle," Gavin stated, looking up from his work. "You did say I could stay as long as I wanted, right? That I'm under your protection?"

I blinked at him a few times, surprised he would even consider never going back. "Why would you want to stay here? What about your family?"

"Trust me, I wasn't much use to them other than who I would marry. I told you my little brother is the one who should be ruling the kingdom, not me." Gavin shrugged. "I feel more useful here, not to mention the fact I get to be around real people who don't see me as anything other than Gavin."

That was something I could relate to on so many levels. It was the first thing I noticed as I lived with the mercenaries—everyone was equal. Each person had a job and provided for the clan in one way or another. Sure, the clan leader had more say in matters, but they still worked side by side with the other people around them.

"Gavin, if you wish to stay here, I will make sure we find something meaningful for you to do." I smiled.

The door to the strategy room opened, and I peered over my shoulder to see Cole walking in with a tray of mugs. From his body language, I could tell he'd calmed down from his outburst earlier that morning.

"Zan is back and putting his things away," Cole shared as he set a mug in front of me and handed the other to Gavin. "Since you'll be heading out soon, Becka thought you should have another dose of the pain medicine before flying out."

"That much time has passed already?" I asked, sipping my drink.

This time, it was as bitter and earthy as I thought it would have been the first time. Whatever the nutty-tasting stuff was clearly made all the difference in the taste. Stealing myself, I gulped down the rest of the liquid. Thankfully, it was cool enough for me to do.

"It's amazing to me how lost you can get when you start to study stuff," Cole teases, ruffling my hair.

Batting his hand away, I glared at him. "I could say the same about you when you start learning how to crack into a new type of lock. We all have our passions."

"Yeah, I guess that's true." Cole sighed and sat next to me. "About earlier, I'm sorry I lost my temper and started causing a scene in front of everyone. Izel was right to chew me out about it. I didn't handle it well."

"I understand why you're concerned, and in some ways, I agree with you, but I also know that I'm going to have to give him a shot," I explained. "We didn't meet on the best of terms, and I wasn't expecting the whole guardian thing to happen, either. All I did was touch his shoulder, my powers freaked out, and he ended up with a mark."

Cole huffed and leaned back in his chair. "That man is the toughest thing I've ever tried to crack. He didn't say one word about what went down last night. All we got was his name, found out he was blind, and his Birthright allows him to see through Ezzu's eyes, which I have to admit is kind of cool."

"Give me a little more time with him, and I promise I'll tell you guys the whole story," I requested.

"Little mouse, you don't owe any of us an explanation if you don't want to give one. That's the privilege of being queen... no one can demand stuff like that from you. Tell us or don't. I trust you will if it's important for us to know," Cole announced, giving me a half-smile. "Now, are you ready to head off, or do you need to return to your room for anything?"

"Nope, I'm ready to go. I can't wait to get back out into the world for a bit. This underground living messes with your brain. I never know what time it is." I laughed, letting Cole pull me to my feet and lift me into his arms.

"Good thing you have all of us looking out for you, right, Prince?"

Gavin, clearly not expecting to be included in the conversation, took a moment to answer. "Ah... yeah, nothing to worry about with us around."

"Right, we're gonna need to work on that, make it more believable." Cole laughed as we headed outside.

NINETEEN

OFF TO MEET THE DRAGON RIDERS

E xiting the mountain, Vasin and Ifra were both there wait-ing, wings out, sunning themselves.

"Vasin, are you ready to head out?"

"YES, I NEED TO REDEEM MYSELF FOR WHAT HAPPENED YESTERDAY. I WAS A FAILURE AS YOUR PAIR-BOND AND NOT KEEPING YOU SAFE. IF JADE HADN'T MADE IT IN TIME..."

"No, none of that. There was no way we could have been pre-pared for something we didn't know was out there."

"THAT IS EXACTLY WHAT I SHOULD HAVE BEEN PREPARED FOR. IF I LOSE YOU, CASS, THEN THERE IS NO POINT IN LIV-ING. YOU ARE THE OTHER HALF OF MY SOUL. IT'S WHY WE BONDED."

"Someday, you will need to explain all this to me. I don't care if it's on my deathbed, I want to know it all."

"TRUST ME... YOU WILL LEARN IT ALL. YOU'LL HAVE TO KNOW IT IF YOU PLAN ON HELPING US DRAGONS AND YOUR PEOPLE. NOT YET, BUT SOON."

"That works fine. We have a lot to do today."

"Queen Cassarah, I brought something back for you," Zan called out from where he stood beside Ifra. "I hope I didn't overstep in assuming you would want or need this."

Stepping back, he held out a large sheet of leather with all kinds of buckles and straps, giving me no clue as to what it could be.

"Um, thank you," I ventured.

Zan flashed me a grin, the first one I'd seen on his face since meeting him, and it changed everything about him. Zan came across as stern and older than I think he actually is, but with that grin, he turned almost boyish.

"You don't even know what it is, so how can you thank me?" he teased. "It's a dragon harness to keep you and any supplies from falling off your dragon. I noticed that Jade has one for Tahir, but you didn't for Vasin. While I was back home, I grabbed one since we're both going to have inexperienced riders with us."

"That's amazing!" I gasped, wiggling my way out of Cole's arms to hobble over to Zan. "Will you show me how to put it on?"

"Most certainly. It looks more complicated than it is. This will also help getting too cold on long flights from their icy skin," Zan shared as he took my arm and helped me move over to Vasin.

Vasin shifted and lifted his wings so we could get the harness on him easier. I was surprised to see how simple it was to secure it and how much you could load on it.

"Dragons are a part of our society, much like horses are to the average village. They do not mind helping us, and this helps to make it as simple on them as possible," Zan explained as he worked, deftly buckling the straps. "In the event you get into another dragon fight, this will keep you from falling off. But if the need arises that you have to free yourself, the leather is thin enough that a knife can cut through it."

"You've thought of everything," I mused out loud, looking over the contraption. "This does help make me feel better about flying today. As I stand here on the ground, I'm fine. I was leery if I might have trouble once in the air with a rider who isn't as comfortable with flying."

"If I might suggest that you take the smaller of the two. Dayson might be more confident, but he is harder to manage if anything were to happen to him while we are flying," Zan offered.

It struck me then that Zan was a soldier through and through. He looked at everything from all angles and sought out any weakness, ensuring it didn't hinder the mission.

"That is a wise suggestion," I said, shaking my head. "I never would have even thought of something like that. I would have taken Dayson with me since he would be better protected, but if he got hit with an arrow or otherwise hurt, then he'd squash me."

Zan dipped his head, trying to keep me from seeing his cheeks tinged with embarrassment. "I'm only fulfilling my duty as your guardian, Your Majesty."

"Don't be afraid to share your thoughts, Zan. I'm always willing to listen to sound logic. It's the emotional part that I sometimes struggle to see the value in," I shared, keeping my voice low so the others couldn't hear me, reaching out to pet Ezzu's head. "My other guardians can be a bit smothering at times, forgetting I was also trained to defend myself."

Zan nodded his head and looked me in the eye. "It's a balance, Cassarah. You need those who will ignore your orders when they think they will put you in harm's way, but you also need others who will push you to do something that makes you uncomfortable. The give-and-take is what's going to keep you alive longer. If we all wanted to keep you locked in the mountain safe and sound, then that would be a disservice to you. Cole was right to question you bringing me along. He doesn't know the whole story about what happened last night, but he knows you and could tell it wasn't good."

I raised a brow at Zan. "Are you saying I shouldn't bring you?"

"No, I need to go with you, and I would ignore your orders if you told me to stay or leave, being your guardian. The magic you hold is old and powerful. It doesn't make mistakes when picking something as important as a guardian. I was pointing that out so you don't stay mad at him for doing what he thought was best for you," Zan stated.

"Don't worry. We already worked things out." I smiled, pleased that Zan would stick up for Cole even when they didn't know each other. "Cole and I have a little more history than the other guardians. He actually hated me at one point, treating me like a bug under his shoe. Somewhere along the way, I impressed him enough to get him to really train me, and now we're good friends."

"Friends?" Zan asked, surprise written on his face. "You think the way he treats you is typical for friends?"

"Honestly, besides Becka, who was once my handmaid, I've never had friends. So I'm not sure if it's normal." I shrugged, not understanding what he was getting at.

"Hmm," Zan hummed, tilting his head and looking at me like he could see into my soul. "I think being around you will be far more exciting than I originally thought... and that's on top of knowing we're going to war."

"You're an odd one, aren't you?" I laughed, and he helped me climb on Vasin's back.

"Where I come from, you all are the odd ones," Zan teased as he helped me buckle myself onto Vasin's back before he called over his shoulder, "Payson, you're riding with the queen. Time to strap in!"

Payson jogged over, and I noticed he was dressed in dark blue leather with his weapons of choice strapped to his body. His bow peeked out over one shoulder, along with his quiver of arrows with bright blue feathers for the fletching. A short sword and dagger were also on his hips, preparing him for close combat.

"You're armed?" I blurted.

Payson looked up at me with his light blue eyes, grinning like a fool. "I wouldn't be a very good guardian if I couldn't protect my queen, now would I? I know we are meeting with clan members, but who knows what else might be lurking out there, ready to hunt us down and kill us."

"Do I need my weapons?" I asked since he made a valid point.

"Rumor has it that you have one with you all the time," Payson pointed out as he hopped up behind me, but Vasin shifted at the last second, making Payson stumble and fall to a heap on the ground.

"DOES HE THINK I'M A HORSE THAT HE DOESN'T EVEN BOTHER TO GREET ME OR ASK MY PERMISSION TO CARRY HIM?"

"I asked him to fly with us."

"THAT IS ALL WELL AND GOOD, BUT I AM A SENTIENT BEING WHO WOULD LIKE TO BE ACKNOWLEDGED FOR MY GENEROSITY."

I couldn't help but laugh out loud at the irritation in Vasin's voice. "Payson, you might want to remember that dragons are intelligent beings, and even if they cannot speak back to you, they appreciate being greeted."

"My apologies, Vasin. I have disrespected you when you have so kindly offered to let me ride along with your pair-bond," Payson said, bowing.

"THAT WILL DO FOR NOW, SO LONG AS IT DOESN'T HAPPEN AGAIN." Vasin huffed, sending a puff of smoke at Payson.

"Dragons are proud creatures. Keep that in mind, and you shouldn't have any trouble," I assured, reaching down to help Payson up.

"Pissing off a dragon is the last thing I want to do," Payson muttered as he fastened his straps.

Seeing that Zan and Dayson were ready and waiting for us, I signaled them to take off, and away we went.

"*Where exactly are we going?*"

"*To the edge of the Unclaimed Dragon Lands. No one would dare to follow us there.*"

"*But is it safe for us?*"

"*Because you will have me there, it will be fine. Black dragons are rare but respected among our kind, unlike with humans.*"

"*There is a hierarchy with dragons?*"

"*Of course, it is the nature of all things to have a pecking order. I just happen to be at the top. Then there are the golden females, followed by the rest.*"

"*Wait, are you telling me you are King of the Dragons?*"

"*I suppose in your logic that would be the simplest explanation. I do not rule our kind, but if they were to come after me, I would be the strongest... once I am fully grown.*"

"*So, you're still vulnerable because your scales aren't tough enough, and you don't have your fire yet, right?*"

"*Yes, among a few other things, but those are my best offense and defense against other dragons.*"

"*I've noticed you can now make smoke, though, so that must mean you're getting closer to breathing fire.*"

"*When a dragon's pair-bond is in danger as much as you are, our bodies tend to speed up the process of being able to protect them.*"

"*You're welcome,*" I teased, smiling to myself as I heard him grunt.

"Cassarah, you know we are heading into the Unclaimed Dragon Lands, right?" Payson yelled in my ear.

Twisting slightly, I looked at him over my shoulder. "Yes, there's less chance of anyone messing with us out here."

"What about the wild dragons? They live out here because they don't like people."

"Vasin said not to worry about it. He'll deal with the other dragons."

"He isn't still mad at me, is he?"

"Why, are you worried he'd let a dragon eat you or something?"

"Would he do that?" Payson asked, sounding panicked.

I laughed at the stricken face he had at my sarcasm. "No... well, not over something that trivial. If you did something to hurt me, then all bets are off, whether you're a guardian or not."

"Good thing I don't plan on doing that any time soon," Payson said, giving a nervous laugh.

"*That better be a joke, or I'll dump him right now.*"

"*Why are you being so crabby toward him? Payson has done nothing to warrant it other than the small oversight before we left.*"

"*I can't place it, but I don't trust him.*"

"*Are you sure it's not just his dad you don't like? Judging the son based on what the father has done is unfair. If we did that, I would still be locked away in my parents' home or married to some grizzled old man.*"

"*What you said is true. I will think on that further, but for now, he has a long way to go to prove himself to me.*"

Twenty

Unclaimed Dragon Lands

As we got nearer to the Unclaimed Dragon Lands, all forms of plant and animal life fell away until all that was left was sand and rock. It was no wonder no one wanted to venture into these lands—you'd have to be a dragon to survive. I'm sure there was life somewhere out there, but without the ability to fly, there's no way anyone could survive it. The temperature also warmed the farther south we went, making me wish I hadn't worn the long-sleeved leather jacket but unwilling to take it off with Payson so close. The sun was high in the sky and blinding as it reflected off the sand and Vasin's scales.

Slowly, we started to circle and drift lower into the foothills of the Restless Mountains. I wondered if the dragons had a name for them since they'd lived here longer than us, something to ask Vasin later. I spotted two other red dragons waiting for us with their riders sitting under a tent for shade.

"Can you tell who they are?"

"Both are from the Hell Hawk clan. They were on their way to report back to Acton when their dragons brought them here."

"That will be fun to explain."

"You are the queen... you don't need to explain."

"Right, we'll see how well that goes over."

Zan landed first, while Vasin waited until they had dismounted Ifra before he found a place to settle that wasn't too close to everyone else. Payson quickly undid his harness and slid off Vasin before reaching up to help me down.

"Thank you for the ride, Vasin. It is an honor to be given the privilege," Payson said, bowing slightly to him.

I bit my lip to keep from laughing, but I could tell from our bond that Vasin was pleased with the effort. Payson moved to pick me up, but I stopped him with a hand on his chest.

"Just lend me your arm. I'm going to walk. I can't have these men's first impression of me being weak," I explained.

Almost instantly, I regretted my choice with the ground so unsteady with all the rocks and shifting sand. I kept my back straight and shoulders back, clenching my jaw against the dull throb of my leg. The two men stood once they saw Vasin but waited for us to approach, curiosity in their eyes. Dayson and Zan both fell in behind us as I got closer, showing they were with me.

I pulled Payson to a stop just a few steps away from the men and smiled. "Thank you for coming to meet me. I'm Cassarah, Queen of the Mercenaries."

"So, you're the one who messed with our dragons and had them drag us out here to the wastelands," one of the men snapped. "Do you know how long we've been waiting here while those two refused to do anything but just sit there?"

Vasin let out a roar and started to advance on us, his teeth bared and smoke billowing out of his mouth, making him look terrifying. Both men stared wide-eyed at Vasin before they dropped to a knee and bowed their heads.

"Your Majesty, forgive us for not greeting you with respect. We heard rumors that a black dragon had hatched, but we didn't know if it found its pair-bond. It is an honor to meet you," one of the men greeted, lifting his head to meet my gaze. "I am Tinus, and this is Bast. Those are our dragons, Adils and Groa. We are of the Hell Hawk clan."

Deciding the men would no longer give me trouble, Vasin sat on his haunches, watching the meeting with a keen eye.

"I could have handled it myself, you know."

"We do not have time to play power games with everyone we meet. Seeing me should have been enough."

Letting out a sigh, I stepped away from Payson to stand on my own. "It is good to meet you. I'm sorry you had to wait on us, but this was the only way we could get all of you in the same place. Vasin, my dragon, shared that you are already on your way to the hideout to speak with Acton. Is there news to share?"

Bast looked at Tinus before he turned back to me. "Our clan is close to the southern part of the Restless Mountains and Utros. We discovered an army working its way through the pass."

"We're too late. Utros is already on the move."

"Cass, we already knew they would be involved. This is no surprise. Do not get discouraged."

"If the king and queen don't help us, there's no hope."

"There is nothing more we can do until we have an answer. Use your skills and gather all the information you can to set forth the best course of action. This is what you were born to do. Trust yourself."

"How large of an army are we talking about?"

Bast cocked his head to the side and narrowed his eyes at me. "You're not surprised by this information, are you?"

"Sadly, no. We are on the brink of war with Errit and Utros," I announced.

Bast and Tinus fell silent at my words, but when dragon-shaped shadows passed over us, we all turned our gaze skyward. Four dragons flying in formation circled us before landing a few feet away, kicking up sand and dirt into our faces. Payson pulled me to him so that his shirt protected my face until the air settled back down. Now, without the glare of the sunlight, I saw four brown dragons along with their riders. Dayson headed over, shouting a greeting, resulting in hugs and backslaps.

"Allow me to introduce my clan members to you," Dayson said formally, getting a raised brow from me. "Kormark is the pair-bond to Grim, Helgi pair-bond to Asa, Svan pair-bonded to Ottar, and Jorund pair-bond to Nasi. Guys, this is Cassarah, Queen of the Mercenaries, and her black dragon, Vasin, who is very protective of his pair-bond."

"What's the meaning of all this?" Svan demanded, brushing me off.

Vasin let out a low warning growl, causing the earth to rumble under our feet. The other dragons hissed and backed away from their pair-bonds, lowering their heads as if bowing to us.

"I wasn't kidding when I said he was protective of her," Dayson pointed out, squaring up with the man who was just as big as he was. "She is our queen, no matter how you feel about it, and as one of her guardians, I demand that respect is given to her."

The other three didn't need any more convincing as they dropped to a knee and bowed. Svan took a moment longer, but he too followed suit.

"Thank you for being here. There is much we need to cover and not a lot of time," I stated, waving them to their feet, now fully in agreement with Vasin that we didn't have time for this bullshit. "We are headed for war, and it's closing in fast. I need good, reliable information about what is happening in our country right now, along with Errit and Utros." Looking around, I found that I had everyone's attention. "A man calling himself the Lost King is coming to take over our kingdom, but he doesn't plan to stop there. He wants it *all.* This has been years in the making, and thankfully, I stumbled upon one of his army encampments by sheer chance, but we are still behind on this."

"What can we do?" Kormark asked.

"The best advantage we have right now is they don't know we're coming for them, so we need to keep that edge while gathering all the information and allies we can. I need you to fly out and search the entire kingdom for signs of more hidden soldiers lying in wait. Tinus and Bast spotted another wave of men coming out of Utros through the mountains. If we are going to survive this, then we have to know what we are dealing with," I declared, my hands balled up into fists, willing them to believe the urgency of this matter.

"How should we divide it up?" Tinus inquired as he walked over to his dragon, grabbing something from his pack. "Norden is the smallest kingdom, and it's still hard to fly across in one day."

"Is it just the six of us? What about Jade? Where is he?" Bast asked Tinus.

"I sent Jade with Alto on another mission. He is one of my guardians," I informed them.

Tinus' jaw dropped at that information. "Jade is a guardian? How the fuck did something like that happen? Who invites the Grim Reaper to keep them alive?"

Zan stepped forward into Tinus' space and thrust his left arm under his nose. "The magic picked him like it did all of us. Are you telling us her Birthright picked wrong?"

Tinus shoved Zan away, causing Ezzu to leap off Zan's shoulder as he flipped Tinus over his back to land in the dirt. Ezzu landed on his chest and hissed in his face, baring her teeth in warning. Zan whistled for her, and she returned to her spot, crooning and rubbing her face on his cheek.

"Back the fuck off," Bast growled, storming over to back up his partner.

Payson stepped in his way with a dagger pointed right at his groin. "I wouldn't bother them if you plan on ever having children. He attacked a guardian. Zan had every right to defend himself."

"Enough!" I yelled, causing everyone to snap to attention. "Don't you get it? This is so much bigger than us. We could lose *everything* in this war! If you want to fight over petty things like who is or isn't my guardian, then just kiss the life you know goodbye. Let's go... we're leaving. Clearly, none of these *men* will be of any use to us."

Grabbing Dayson's arm, I turned us toward Vasin. As we walked, I reached out to each of the dragons, learning the feel of their minds as they opened up to me.

"Leave them, fly into the mountains, and let them sit here overnight. If they will help, call out to me, and I will hear you."

"Cass, are you sure that is wise? If I'm not here to keep other dragons away, then they might be killed."

"They should have been smarter. If I can't trust them to do as I ask, then this is pointless. You'll be able to hear them if they call me, right? Just in case I miss it."

"Yes, I will know if they reach out to you. I'm proud of you, my dear Cass. The hardest thing in leadership is making the tough call, but you are proving that you are willing to do this."

"Let's hope it's the right tough call, or I've just killed six men and dragons for nothing."

"You will be seeing them again with a much different attitude, I'm sure of it."

"Cassarah, are you sure we should leave? What if the queen says no?" Dayson whispered as he helped me up on to Vasin.

I squeezed his shoulder, looking into his eyes. "Trust me, I have a plan."

"Okay, do you want me to ride with you this time?"

Glancing over at Zan climbing on Ifra, I nodded. "Make sure you thank Vasin, though. He's a little touchy about people just hopping on."

"It would be rude to assume you're welcome on a dragon's back without asking," Dayson agreed as he walked up to speak with Vasin.

Once he got approval, Dayson swung up, strapped himself in behind me, then wrapped an arm around my waist, pulling me against his chest. "What are you doing?"

"I'm a little larger than Payson, so either my hands touch your ass, or I do this..."

Taking a moment to clear my throat, I agreed. "This is fine."

"I like him. He's blunt and doesn't try to hide things from you."

Snorting as I tried to cover my laughter, we leaped into the air, and all the other dragons followed us, along with the shouting of some very angry mercenaries.

"Think this will travel through the clans when they get back?"

"You know it will. That was the other part of your plan, wasn't it?"

"As you said, we can't play power games whenever we meet someone new. Hopefully, this will speed things along in the future."

TWENTY-ONE

DON'T PISS OFF THE DRAGONS

Dayson and I didn't speak on our way back, but the feel of his muscular chest warming my back made it hard to ignore his presence. I was raised to believe that no woman should let a man touch her unless they were engaged or married. Having them carry me around while injured made sense in my brain since it served a purpose. This was testing my ability even to think straight. Dayson was a handsome man in looks and personality, making me even more aware that many queens in the past have taken lovers from their guardians.

With everything that had been going on since I'd marked these men, it hadn't crossed my mind they might be vying for my hand. It would explain the kiss from Jade earlier that morning and why they all wanted to spend alone time with me. None of them seemed bothered when I spent time with them alone—well, Cole had issues with Jade, but I didn't think that was related to this. Even Tinus and Bast seemed to take issue with Jade being my guardian. Vasin dipped suddenly, causing Dayson to tighten his hold on my waist as his other hand landed on my thigh.

"You did that on purpose."

"CASS, I CAN HELP YOU WITH SOME THINGS, BUT ROMANCE IS NOT ONE OF THEM."

"Oh, but let me guess. You'll just provide moments for the men around me to create them on their own?"

"I told you I liked Dayson. I think he would be a very wise choice as a life partner. Cole and Abbott have also shown interest, as have you in small ways."

"No, I have not! It would be wrong to lead a man on if you have no intention of it going anywhere."

"So you don't like either of them as more than just a friend?"

"Vasin, I don't even know how to be a good friend, so how could I be a lover?"

"Does that mean you like them?"

"How do you expect me to answer that when I don't know? There are far too many things to worry about. Trying to involve lovers into the equation is just silly."

"Ah, you said lovers as in more than one. This is good. What about the crown prince?"

"What about him? There is no way he is truly going to be okay giving up the crown. Well, I should say his parents wouldn't be okay with that. Any woman who has Gavin for a husband will be lucky. He is sweet and sensitive. I'm amazed at how well he is adjusting to living with us. If I'm being honest, I thought he would be begging me to send him back."

"Prince Gavin might not want to rule a kingdom, but he has been trained to see the world through a ruler's eyes. He knows what you are trying to do is the best course of action and is supporting you. If Queen Mary says no, I think he will be the first person to say he will change her mind."

"Why so interested in my love life all of a sudden?"

"YOU ARE READY. BEFORE, YOU DIDN'T EVEN KNOW YOUR-SELF BUT LOOK AT YOU NOW... A TRUE QUEEN IS SITTING UPON MY BACK. IT IS TIME FOR YOU TO FIND THOSE PEOPLE TO HOLD CLOSE AND SUPPORT YOU IN YOUR QUEST TO SAVE THE KING-DOM."

"Aren't I already doing that?"

"No."

"You're going to have to give me more than that, Vasin. I don't get what you're trying to tell me."

"ONCE THIS BATTLE IS OVER AND YOU LEARN WHAT A NOR-MAL LIFE WILL BE LIKE, THINGS WILL CHANGE. WHO DO YOU WANT TO MAKE SURE STAYS AT YOUR SIDE? I KNOW YOU, CASS, AND YOU WON'T DARE TO LET YOURSELF DREAM THAT FAR INTO THE FUTURE, BUT THAT IS EXACTLY WHAT YOU SHOULD DO. WHAT IF YOU DIED OR ONE OF THESE MEN YOU CARE ABOUT DOES? DO YOU WANT THEM NEVER TO KNOW HOW YOU FEEL?"

"I don't have an answer for you..."

"THAT IS FINE, BUT AT LEAST NOW YOU ARE THINKING ABOUT IT."

"It's very hard not to when I have a man plastered against my back, holding me."

"YES, WE WILL NEED TO WORK ON YOUR SHYNESS REGARDING PHYSICAL TOUCH. NOT ALL TOUCH IS SEXUAL. OFTEN, IT CAN SIMPLY BE TO GIVE AFFECTION OR COMFORT, MUCH LIKE COLE AND ABBOTT HAVE BEEN SHOWING YOU. DON'T FEAR WHAT YOUR BODY NEEDS. A HUMAN WITHOUT ANY PHYSICAL CON-TACT IS STARVED. YOU, CASS, HAVE BEEN WANDERING IN THE DESERT LOST AND ALONE WITHOUT THAT. IT WILL TAKE TIME TO REBUILD WHAT YOU'VE MISSED OUT ON. PROMISE ME YOU WON'T RUN FROM IT JUST BECAUSE YOU HEAR YOUR MOTHER IN YOUR HEAD TELLING YOU IT'S WRONG."

"I will do my best and try to be more open, but I can't promise I'll be able to do it."

"I can accept that."

Vasin and I fell into a comfortable silence as we leisurely continued back, enjoying the fresh air and the sights of the mountains below. None of us were in a hurry to return to the hideout and the responsibility waiting for us. Out of nowhere, a blast of panicked emotion slammed into me from one of the dragons I'd met earlier. Thankfully, I was strapped in, and Dayson was holding me because I froze. If Vasin had made any sudden movement, I wouldn't have managed to stay on.

"Cassarah! What's wrong?" Dayson shouted as he shook me gently.

"We have to go back!" I yelled, waving my arms and calling out to Ifra.

"Vasin, what's wrong? Can you tell what's going on?"

"They are under attack from rouge dragons. They have not spotted the riders as of yet. Right now, they are just going after the bonded dragons for being in their lands."

"We weren't in the Unclaimed Lands, right?"

"These dragons do not care about borders, only about keeping humans and enslaved dragons from taking more from them."

"Can we make it in time to help them?"

"I told them to head in our direction, leading them farther away from the riders. Once we are close enough, I can handle them, but if things get too bad, I might need to leave you behind. I won't risk you again."

"Hold on tight," I warned Dayson as Vasin sharply turned us around. "The rogue dragons are attacking ours and hunting for their riders."

"What can two dragons with double riders do against them that six other dragons can't?" Dayson asked, both arms now wrapped around me.

Shooting off like an arrow with a powerful heave of his wings, Vasin called out to the other dragons, letting them know we were coming.

"Vasin is more dominant than all other dragons. If he tells them to back off, they will. It just means we need to go back and get the riders I left behind to safety. I thought they would be okay, but it seems I misjudged the possessive nature of rogue dragons and their land."

"You still made the right call. They needed to learn to take you seriously."

"Let's hope I can keep them alive to act on their newfound knowledge," I grumbled and leaned closer to Vasin's neck as the wind buffeted against my face.

At the speed we were flying, it didn't take long for us to spot the ten rouge dragons pursuing the six of ours, and if we didn't see them, we could easily hear the roaring and hissing as they battled. Fire burst from their mouths, and talons flashed in the sunlight as they battled and kept trying to move in our direction. Vasin darted upward so we flew over the mess of fighting teeth and claws, only for him to plunge into the middle of it, letting out his battle cry. Vasin's thunderous roar reverberated off the mountains around us, making it even louder, to the point I almost wanted to cover my ears. The rogue dragons scattered to avoid Vasin's attack as he slapped his wings into their faces and swiped a taloned claw, forcing them to release their victims. They snarled, backing off enough to regroup and charge right for us.

"Vasin!" I screamed in his head, trying not to show Dayson how terrified I was.

Ignoring me completely, he aimed right for them in a game of chicken, but then, at the last second, he thrust his wings out front, bringing himself to a sudden stop. He snapped them open wide, creating a wall of flesh and wing as he once again let out a mighty roar. Only this time, I could feel something different, an energy backing up his actions that felt similar to when I used my Birthright.

Holy shit, my Birthright!

Instantly, I materialized my weapon and sent off a warning shot to the leading purple dragon, nicking its muzzle and causing it to jerk back at the contact. Aiming again, I sent off arrow after arrow, causing them all to dart out of the way to keep from getting hit. This caused so much chaos they stopped attacking and hovered in the air, growling at us.

"Leave them be, and we will leave your lands. Continue to attack, and I will be forced into action," I called out as loudly as I could.

My voice rang out loud and clear with the same power behind it that Vasin had used. The rogue dragons snorted and let out small puffs of fire in their irritation, but after a moment, they turned and left with a swish of their tails, reminding me of a pissed-off cat. We didn't move from that spot as we watched the rogue dragons leave, not feeling confident they wouldn't change their minds and turn on us again.

"Can we get back to the riders safely?"

"WE HAVE NO CHOICE. WE NEED TO REMOVE THEM, OR YOU WILL HAVE BROKEN YOUR WORD TO A DRAGON."

"Let me guess... that's not a good thing to do."

"It is something that not even I can protect you from, Cass."

"Don't you think that's something I should have known about?"

"I didn't know you could command all dragons. That power you put behind your words made it a binding agreement as much as it was a dominant move."

"Why didn't it work when you did it?"

"You gave them an ultimatum to leave or die after proving you could kill them from a safe distance. I was no longer the bigger threat."

"Does that help or hinder us?"

"Seeing as they left, and we can get to the men, I don't see this as a negative."

The six dragons fell in line after us as we headed to pick up the dragon riders I'd left behind not more than a few hours ago. Still flying at top speeds, we got there quickly, and all the riders came running out from under the tent Tinus and Bast had made. Vasin touched down, but I didn't bother getting off.

"We need to go now. I bought us some time, but there is a horde of angry rouge dragons that will kill you if they find you here," I ordered, cutting them off from whatever curses they were going to yell at me.

Thankfully, they didn't hesitate, and all mounted up as we launched back into the air. I decided it was best for everyone to return to the hideout. According to the information I got from Gavin, coming in from this direction, we wouldn't be spotted by any Norden scouts. Our flight back was mercifully uneventful as we arrived at the hideout and took turns landing and settling our dragons for the night. The sun was setting, but we had enough light to see by before it drifted behind the mountains.

Once I was back on the ground and Dayson helped me remove the harness from Vasin, I noticed Cole and Abbott waiting near the tunnel's entrance. Before I could protest, Dayson swung me up on his back, and I either needed to hold on or fall to the ground in a heap.

"What was that?" I groused as I clung to his back like a monkey.

"You were going to try and walk again if I didn't stop you. That leg won't heal any faster if you keep abusing it," Dayson explained as he marched past the two waiting.

As we entered the cavern, everyone was sitting down for dinner, and my stomach complained at the delicious-smelling meal. Peeking over my shoulder, I checked to see if Abbott and Cole were following since they hadn't barraged me with hundreds of questions. They were there, but instead of talking to me, they were quizzing Payson and Zan, which I could live with. Dayson headed straight to the table that seemed to have become our table since it was the only one without people sitting at it.

"Don't you think we should deal with the dragon riders first?" I asked as I was set down. "I'm sure they have questions about what just happened."

Dayson scowled at me as he pointed to a chair beside the table. "Sit."

I gaped at him like a fish, but he only crossed his arms, making his muscles bulge.

"How do you think it will look after playing a savage power game with them just to turn around and go all soft? They can wait until you are ready to talk to them, not the other way around," Dayson pointed out, making it very hard to disagree with him.

"Fine, but can you tell them I want to talk to them *after* I have dinner?"

Dayson grinned and winked at me. "Now that's more like it, Queen Cassarah. You let those assholes cool their heels until you are good and ready to deal with them."

I couldn't help but blush under his praise as he left to do as I asked.

Twenty-Two
Game Night

I t didn't take long for the rest of my guardians and Gavin to join us at the table, all waiting to hear what happened on our journey. Food and a mug of the pain meds were set in front of me as Becka slid in across from me.

"I'm beginning to think we can't let you ever leave this place," she teased. "Every time you leave, something crazy happens. Who gets into a fight with *ten* rogue dragons?"

"First of all, we didn't really get into a fight—"

Payson let out a bark of laughter. "What do you call Vasin playing chicken after he dive-bombed the fight? Oh, or the fact you used your Birthright to hold the line before you threatened them?"

"Yeah, that totally sounds like it was no big deal," Becka scolded, giving me a disapproving look. "Cassarah, what are we going to do with you?"

"I had people with me this time. It just so happened the only way to end things was to meet it head-on," I countered.

"Literally," Zan added. "Let's also not forget about leaving the dragon riders on the edge of the Unclaimed Lands as punishment for their disrespect. I believed they deserved it and hopefully will learn not to underestimate our queen."

At this news, all of them turned to look at me with shocked expressions until May burst out laughing. "You left them there? Oh God, what I wouldn't give to have seen their reactions as you flew away. Those assholes have always been too self-entitled just because they have their own dragon. Let me guess, Svan was the biggest dick of them all."

"Bast wasn't much better," Dayson added.

"Can we all join you when you talk to them later?" May asked with excitement shining in her eyes.

"Um... sure," I answered with a shrug. "I don't think it will be all that interesting for all of you, but I won't stop you from sitting in on any of my meetings."

The rest of the meal was full of talk about the dragons, and Zan added in what he knew about the Dragon Lands, amazing them all. It was nice to see everyone was truly starting to become a team after such a short time. It put me more at ease, hoping that as things became more strenuous with the impending war, we could all handle the pressure that came with it.

"Has anyone heard from Jade at all?" I asked as the conversation came to a lull.

Everyone shook their heads.

"My queen, you will be the first to know when he returns," Izel assured me. "If he comes in late, do you want him to wake you up?"

"Yes, I need to know the answer as fast as possible. My whole plan hinges on them agreeing," I answered as a bubble of panic started to take hold at the thought of them saying no.

"*Cass, calm your mind. There are many other things we can do. Remember, you now have another kingdom to call on if you need to.*"

"*But that means accepting becoming their queen and changing everything for that kingdom and my clans. Don't you think fighting to survive is enough right now?*"

"A queen must do what is best for all people in-volved. If you believe the Lost King knows about Sheca and its people, they will not be safe for long, either."

"I accept that, but I will deal with that once we know Queen Mary's answer."

Dayson returned to the table with three large glass bottles in his hands. "I say we take the night off. You wanted to leave the riders out in the desert for the night, so why not make them wait until morning."

"That means you got distracted finding this mead and forgot to hunt down the dragon riders," May accused as she stole one of the bottles and pulled the cork out to take a swig. "Damn, you got these from Tati, didn't you? That woman is the best mead brewer in the clans."

"I did, but they were a gift to Queen Cassarah, welcoming her to the clans," Dayson pointed out, snagging back the bottle. "You should ask before you steal from the queen."

Looking at the others and the excitement shining on their faces, I couldn't say no. Besides, as Vasin keeps telling me, I need to learn to have fun and build stronger bonds with my guardians.

"Sounds like a great idea, Dayson. Where do you suggest we hold this night of fun?" I inquired.

"Our rooms might be the best," Payson suggested. "We have an open middle room with more space to sit."

Becka jumped to her feet, clapping her hands. "I'll get everything we need to play a few different games. No, Cassarah, I'm not talking about chess. No one would be able to beat you."

I laughed, remembering all the times I conned her into playing with me when my father wasn't around. Becka wasn't bad at the game, but she wasn't willing to plan out as far as I was, nor as patient. Izel brought me to their rooms as the others ran off to get what they thought we would need for this evening of drinking. I hadn't really spent time in their space other than seeing it the first day from the entryway, so I was pleased to see how cozy they'd all made it. Thick furs covered the floor and chairs, making them look comfortable to relax in. Izel sat me on a long wooden bench with furs padding the seat and backed up against the wall for me to lean against. Instead of sitting next to me, Izel sat at my feet, leaning his back against the bench and his shoulder against my knee.

"How is your leg feeling? The others mentioned you've been walking on it more than you should," Izel pressed as he ran a hand down my leg.

Shifting to the side, he put my foot in his lap and carefully pushed my pants leg up until he could see the injury. Gently, he ran his fingers over my skin, feeling for any heat to show it was irritated. The tea that Alto had been having me drink was helping greatly to quiet the dull ache that's been bothering me most of the afternoon.

"I'm ready to have my leg back. All it's doing now is slowing me down." I sighed, trying to hide the shiver his touch was causing. "After this, I will never again take the ability to walk for granted."

Izel gripped my ankle in a firm hand as he pulled my pants leg back down. "Why is it so hard for you to show even the slightest amount of weakness? No one is that strong. Each and every living thing has something that makes them weak. It's a fact of life."

"Before coming to live with the clans, I was never strong," I whispered, causing him to lift his gaze to meet mine. "All my life, I've been weak, never able to stand up for myself or others until Vasin, Becka, Abbott, Cole, Ballard, and even Helena taught me how to fight for myself. Now, my biggest fear is becoming that weak version of myself all over again, having been told I would fail day in and day out. My mother never thought I would amount to anything. I was too smart, too impertinent, and not ladylike at all. Even my father, who showed me the most kindness, turned his back on me when it mattered so that he wouldn't be ridiculed further for having tainted blood. Having had a taste of this freedom, I can't ever go back to being that."

"You, My Queen, are a warrior through and through. Sure, you might have lost sight of it, but I doubt that will happen again," Izel said, reaching up to take my hands in his and pressing them to his lips. "Never have I met a woman as strong in spirit and mind as you are. There are many physically strong women in our clans, but they have sacrificed the part of them that feels as deeply as you do. Your strength is not in just what you can do with this body but with the mind that controls it. Once they see a glimpse of what is going on in that beautiful brain of yours, they will never assume you are weak, and if they do, that is to their detriment, not yours."

"How is it that you can know that? We've only just met."

Mischief glinted in his eyes as he gave me a half-smile. "I'm a trained mercenary, meaning I can spot a person's weakness and strength a mile away. That and you, my warrior, are an open book when you are with me. You let me see you, the real you, when we talk, holding nothing back. It's these moments I'm coming to treasure more than anything else."

My cheeks heated as I flushed under his attention and honest words. His voice was so smooth and sultry it was like I was being hypnotized by the sound of it, almost to the point I might have missed the others entering the room if Izel hadn't looked away.

"All right! We've got the games, the mugs, the mead, and food to eat as we play to keep us from getting blackout drunk." Dayson's voice boomed with excitement as he set the bottles on the table.

Izel shifted to sit next to me, again seated on the floor, watching everything going on like we didn't just have this moment together. On the other hand, I needed to figure out how to get my heart to stop pounding in my chest and my cheeks to cool before some-one else noticed. Just when I thought I'd managed, I caught Cole's gaze watching me with a critical eye, shifting between Izel and me.

"What are we playing first?" Payson asked as he filled a mug with the amber liquid and walked it over to me. "Do you have a favorite game, Cassarah?"

Accepting the mug, I shrugged. "Other than chess and check-ers, I wasn't really taught many games, and I didn't have any siblings to play with, either."

"That makes this even more fun!" May declared, slapping down a deck of cards. "I say we teach her Smugglers Lies."

"What about starting with something simpler?" Abbott in-terjected. "What about knuckles or dice?"

"Oh, we have pick-up sticks too," Becka announced, holding up a tube of brightly painted sticks.

Gavin scoffed. "Don't you know anything? That game needs to be saved until everyone is well on their way to being drunk. It's too easy if you're sober."

Dayson slapped Gavin on the back, making him flinch a little. "I like this prince. He knows how to have a good time."

"Perfect. Zan, do you know what bones are, what points?" Izel asked, rising to his feet and walking over to the table.

Zan gave a wide grin, rubbing Ezzu's head as he took a seat. "You could say I'm confident in my skills at this game."

"Come on over, little phoenix. Let's teach you how this game works," Abbott said, waving me over. Once I was seated at the table, he rested his hands on my shoulder and stood over me. "It's all about getting the highest numbers you can from what you're given. See how each bone has a different shape on each side, they are worth different points."

Caging me in with his body, he tossed out the bones and showed me every possibility that could be done numbers-wise. It was much like paying dice… just without the dice. Even though I was far more comfortable and used to Abbott touching me, there seemed to be something different in his motives for this lesson. He was using any excuse to make sure he was touching me in some way. It brought back memories of having my first kiss after riding the high of winning the fight with him at the capture the flag game before I was taken. Abbott never acted any differently toward me, so I didn't bother to bring it up, especially when I knew that most women in the clans didn't see it as a big deal. Something was telling me it might just be a big deal to Abbott.

"I think she's got it. No need to keep hanging all over her," Cole snapped, shocking us all.

Cole and Abbott might not have been best friends, but I knew they were good friends. This was how Cole typically treated everyone else around him but not Becka or Abbott.

"Something wrong?" I asked before I realized now might not be the best setting to ask such a personal question.

"It's fine. I just know you're smart enough to have learned this simple game the first time he explained it," Cole grumbled.

Payson nudged Cole with his elbow. "Looks like someone needs to drink more and chill the fuck out. Leave them alone. We aren't in any rush to pressure anyone into anything they aren't comfortable with or ready for."

I tilted my head to the side as Payson spoke, knowing what he said didn't make any sense to the game at hand.

Dayson cleared his throat and nudged over my mug. "Have you ever had mead before, Cassarah?"

"No, I've had wine on special occasions, but it wasn't something I was allowed to indulge in," I answered, taking a sip from the mug.

The mead was sweet and crisp, full of spices that gave it a deep flavor. Quickly, I took a bigger gulp, enjoying the taste of it immensely.

"Whoa now," Dayson laughed, grabbing the mug. "Don't drink too fast, or you'll be passed out in the corner before long and miss all the fun."

"Oh, tonight is going to be great!" Payson chirped, grinning from ear to ear. "All right, let's play a round, and then we wager."

TWENTY-THREE

TRY MEAD THEY SAID...

The night was full of laughter. It echoed around the room, filling it with a warmth I had never experienced. It filled some need I didn't even know I had somewhere deep in my soul.

"Cassy-bear, it's your turn," Dayson called, knocking my chair to get my attention along with using the horrible, yet slightly adorable, nickname he decided on. "Beat their asses so I don't have to do their washing for a week."

In this round of pick-up sticks, we decided to team up, and whoever lost had to do whatever the winner told them to. Dayson and I were paired off against Cole and Gavin in the game's final round, and I'd had more than enough to drink so it was hard to tell what sticks were where. Biting my bottom lip, I reached out. I couldn't tell if the table or my hand was swaying out of control, but I was bound and determined to beat them. I settled on a stick that was slightly raised over a group of three others. If I could pick it up without disturbing the ones under it, I was safe to play another round. Grasping the stick between my fingers, I gingerly pulled it up until I felt my feet slipping out from under me. Losing my balance, I tumbled to the floor, but thankfully, I landed on something soft and squishy. I started laughing, imagining how funny it must have looked for me to have been half up on the table to get a better angle on my stick and then to come crashing down.

"Well, at least she's not hurt," Zan said from somewhere above me. "Come on, Cass. Let's get you off poor Payson."

"Oh, is he why the floor feels so soft?" I asked as I nuzzled into the warmth that oddly started to get firm under my attention.

"Cassy-bear, you really don't want to be rubbing your face right there. I don't think you're quite ready to take responsibility for what you're starting." Dayson chuckled, grabbing me around the waist and pulling me onto his lap.

Looking down, I found Payson sprawled out on the floor with his face bright red and unable to look at me. "Did I do something to hurt him? Payson, are you okay?"

"Yeah, blue-balls never killed anyone," Payson muttered as he picked himself off the floor. "I think our queen needs to be cut off. She's swaying more than a sailor."

"Wait, did I get the stick?" I cried, looking back at the table.

"Look down at your hand, love," Gavin murmured in my ear as he passed.

Sure enough, the stick I'd been going after was in my hand. "But did I win?" I asked, frowning at the others.

Cole and Gavin looked at each for a moment then back at me. "Yeah, mouse, you won. We lost."

"Yes! Day, we won!" I yelled, wrapped my arms around his neck, and kissed him soundly on the mouth.

The room went silent as Dayson turned to stone under me. Sitting back, I blinked then let out a gasp of horror. "I'm so sorry, Day. I didn't mean to kiss you if you didn't want me to. Do you have someone else that you like? I can totally apologize to them if you need me—"

I didn't get to finish my panicked rambling as Dayson's lips descended upon mine, stealing my words. His hand curled around the back of my neck, holding me right where he wanted me as he devoured my lips. Nipping at my bottom lip, I gasped, and he took that chance to deepen the kiss, letting his tongue explore further. I had no idea what he was doing, but I didn't dislike it, so I tried to reciprocate what he was doing, and he groaned at the movement. His other large hand on my hip pulled my lower body closer to his so nothing separated us from pelvis to chest. Dayson's head jerked back from me as another pair of hands removed me from his lap. Quickly, I was curled up in Izel's arms while Cole was hollering at Dayson for some reason I couldn't understand.

"Come on, little warrior, let's get you to bed. I think you've had enough fun for one night," Izel said, his soothing voice making it easier to relax into his hold.

"Okay," I sighed, nuzzling against his neck.

I could hear and feel his chuckle as he walked. "My, you get very affectionate when you're drunk. We'll have to keep that in mind for the future. Can't have you making out in the middle of a feast or other important events, now can we?"

Izel set me down and pulled the blankets back before he turned to help me slide under them. "Was Cole mad because I won?"

"No, he was upset with Dayson, not you."

"That doesn't make any sense."

Izel smoothed back my hair from my face and set a cool cloth on my forehead. "It's because he was taking things too far. You are not in a sound frame of mind right now. What if you are mad you kissed Dayson at all when you wake up?"

"No, I won't be mad about that. I'll be worried he won't stay with me after all this is over." I shifted to look up at Izel's face. "You won't leave me, will you? I can't explain it, but I feel safe with you. I trust you."

"I'm not going anywhere, Cassarah. No matter how things go, I'll always stay by your side. Now get some sleep. You'll have one hell of a headache tomorrow, that's for sure," Izel soothed, shifting to get up from the bed.

My hand snapped out, grabbing his wrist. "Stay, please? I don't really like being alone now that I know there's something better."

Izel shifted me over, settled next to me on top of the covers, and stroked my hair. As he lulled me to sleep, I heard him whisper something that sounded like, "All I ask is that you keep me forever, my little warrior, because there is nowhere else I want to be but by your side."

The sound of a door slamming open and then being body-rolled off the bed onto the floor with someone on top of me was not the best way to wake up.

"Don't move," Izel hissed as he shifted off me and army crawled to the foot of the bed.

"It's me, where's Cassarah?" Jade demanded.

When his voice registered in my brain, I popped up from the floor and instantly regretted that choice. Groaning, I grabbed my head and face-planted on the mattress. "Oh God, what is wrong with me?"

"That, little warrior, is what we call a hangover," Izel informed me as he scooped me up and set me down at the table. "I'll be right back. I'm going to grab what's needed to make a remedy for it."

I nodded, letting my head fall into my hands. Then another pair of hands started to massage my head. I flinched then turned boneless as the touch felt heavenly.

"What did they do to you while I was gone?" Jade asked with a smirk in his voice.

"Apparently, they were teaching me to have fun. We had a night off with drinking and games. It really was a good time, and I was happy to see everyone enjoying themselves and letting loose." Turning my head slightly, I glanced up at him, his bright green eyes watching me. "The way you entered, it seemed like you had something important to say."

"Queen Mary wants to meet with you... now. She is open to the idea but wants to talk with you and see that Gavin is truly alive and well."

"This is good. What time is it?" I prayed I had gotten some sleep so I wasn't still drunk.

"It's almost dawn. Alto stayed behind so I could fly faster to get back to you. Little bird, you're in no condition to meet with the queen." Jade sighed, squatting down next to me. "Can I take a wild guess and assume the others will also be suffering from the same affliction?"

"Honestly, I have no idea. I can't remember many details from last night. Is that normal?" I questioned, turning my face fully to the side to see him better.

Jade grinned with humor, making his eyes dance. "Yes, little bird, the whole point of getting drunk is to let your mind forget all it has to worry about and live in the moment. The price you pay for it is not remembering everything, sometimes nothing, along with headaches, puking, and dizziness."

"Why do they do it if the repercussions are so bad? I don't like this at all," I whined.

Jade's face fell for a moment before he brushed off whatever memory he'd been thinking about. "Sometimes people prefer the physical pain over the emotional, but as you gain a tolerance to drinking, the aftereffects lessen. Though, I wouldn't recommend you follow that logic. For you, less is more. Enjoy a drink or two but don't get carried away, and you should have nothing to worry about."

I grunted my response, letting my eyes trace his face as we sat together. "I kissed Dayson… and he kissed me back… like a lot."

Oh God, why am I telling him that?

Jade blinked at me, surprised by my statement. "Did you want to kiss him or for him to kiss you back?"

"Why did you kiss me?"

"I'm not very good at telling people how I feel about them, so I figured actions would be a better option. Every time we go on a mission, there is a chance we won't make it back home, and I didn't want there to be a chance I couldn't tell you that I like you."

"You like me?"

"After a kiss and the confession I just made, you can't tell? I thought you were the smart one," Jade teased, tapping my nose. "Yes, Cassarah, I like you. I like you very much. I know a few others do as well, and I wanted to make sure I got my foot in the door."

I frowned at that. "Foot in the door for what?"

"Being one of your consorts. I'm under no illusion I'll be the only one, but I would like the chance to be considered."

"Jade, we hardly know each other. How could you know that you want to be my lover?"

"Think of all that we've been through. How many people can say they met the woman they are falling in love with by saving her life and moments later attacking an army to free the crown prince of our country? Then there is the second time I saved your life and found out you're the queen of a second kingdom." Jade sighed and brushed a thumb over my cheek. "I've seen you scared, hurt, angry, demanding respect from others, and protecting those around you however you can. If that doesn't tell me who you are at the core, then I don't know what else to look for."

The surge of emotions that flooded through me was so foreign and scary but at the same time exhilarating. I didn't know what to do other than raise my head and lean in to accept Jade's kiss on my lips ever so gently.

"All I ask is that you consider it. Know that I'm interested and willing whenever you are ready to do anything about it. I know we have a war to deal with, and so many things are hitting you left and right. I'm not in a hurry. I just needed you to know how I felt in case anything should happen," Jade murmured, his lips brushing mine as he spoke.

A person clearing their throat broke us apart, and Izel was standing just past the door with a steaming mug. "I have that tonic for you. I'll just leave it and go wake the others. I'm guessing there is news."

"Wait," I called, stopping him in his tracks. "The queen wants to meet with me and Gavin. I don't remember a whole lot about last night, but how drunk did everyone get? Do you think they'll be ready to head out?"

"They will be fine, I assure you," Izel said with a soft smile. "How many of them do you want to take with you?"

I looked back to Jade with a questioning brow.

"We settled on meeting at Hillney Lake near the Creisal border. There have been no reports of any unknown troops or movement in that area. Queen Mary said she would only bring her personal guard of seven people on dragon back," Jade reported. "The agreed-upon time is the middle of the afternoon, ensuring that neither party could move a large number of men to the designated meeting area in time."

As Jade talked, I gulped down the foul-tasting drink, knowing it would help. I just hoped it would help fast enough, seeing as my brain wasn't working as clearly as it should.

"The dragon riders are still here, correct?" I asked Izel.

"Yes, none of them would dare leave without speaking to you," Izel assured.

"Wake them up and get them in the strategy room along with the clan leaders, Sal, and my other guardians," I ordered, waving them off. "Please send Becka in. I'm going to need her help getting ready."

Jade rose, letting his fingers trail through my hair as he walked to the door and left with Izel behind him. As my head started to clear and the pain subsided, I hobbled over to my trunk and tossed back the lid.

What the hell does a mercenary queen wear to a meeting like this?

TWENTY-FOUR
THE CROWN I WEAR

Stripping out of my clothes, I took a cloth and soap, quickly washed my body, and rinsed off in the tub with a pitcher of ice-cold water. Dry and still shivering, I dug through my chest, pulling out all my clothes and laying them out on the bed. I pulled on simple black leather pants, seeing no other alternative that would work while riding on a dragon. Then I noticed something else in the trunk, wrapped in cloth and twine, under the stack of research papers. Pulling it out, I undid the twine, and there lay the most stunning leather top with an accompanying corset. The top was long-sleeved, but what made it eye-catching was the leather dragon scales that rose up in the back, shoulder to shoulder to make a cowl. It was elegant and fierce, just what I was looking for. The corset was made from thick leather that looked like dragon wings wrapping around me in a hug with lacing up the back.

I managed to get the top on fine, but I would have to wait for Becka to help with the corset. Looking down at it, I didn't harbor the same hatred I'd once held toward the torture device. When I put it on, it wasn't a way to show off that I was good breeding stock. Instead, it displayed the power I held. I was Queen of the Mercenaries, demanding the same amount of respect from others that Queen Mary did. I was no longer going to meet her as her subject. I was an equal, and this outfit reminded me of that.

"I see you found Helena's coronation gift," Becka said as she entered the room. "She had it commissioned right after she met you."

"She never doubted I would be queen, and she was right." I smiled, brushing a hand over the leather. "Remind me before anything else happens that we need to spend more time with her. I really miss her cooking too."

"Don't worry about her. She is the wife of a clan leader and regent. She knows how busy you are and would never want to get in the way," Becka shared, putting me at ease. "Want to wait to put that on until I've gotten your hair sorted? I'm not like your mother. I don't need to make you suffer longer than necessary in one of those things."

"Great idea!"

It didn't take long for Becka to braid my hair into rows, making sure it would stay out of my face and adding to the feel of the outfit. The finishing touch was a bronze circlet resembling braided leather with a black gemstone glistening in the lamplight.

"I think you're ready, Queen Cassarah. Shall we shock the men into seeing you as the real deal now?" Becka asked as she looked me over one final time.

"We don't have time for games, Becka. We need to get things organized and settled as quickly as possible," I chided as I hobbled to the door.

"Just because you look like a badass in that outfit doesn't mean that your leg is magically fixed," Becka snapped, grabbing my arm. "What happens if you fall off the edge and die before you even get to this meeting? Let me grab one of the guys. You stay right there. Don't even think about moving."

Rolling my eyes, I stood where she left me, knowing she was right. I did notice it was feeling much better, and the pain was hardly more than an inconvenience.

"Becka said you need..." Abbott started to say but drifted off when he saw me. "Wow, little phoenix, you've truly been reborn and risen from the ashes as a queen. You look beautiful."

Blushing, I dropped my gaze. "Thank you, but I feel like it loses its effect when I still have to be carried."

"I doubt anyone is going to notice when you're dressed like this," Abbott assured me as he wrapped an arm around my waist and scooped up my legs.

"Will you at least let me walk from the entrance to my chair?" I pleaded once we reached the strategy room.

Abbott looked down at me and seemed like he was going to argue but sighed and nodded as he set me on my feet. "I still want you to hold on to me, though. We can't risk you reinjuring yourself."

"I can work with that."

Abbott pushed open the door, and I tucked my arm through his as we slowly entered the room. Everyone was standing by their seat, leaving the middle one open for me instead of at the head of the table. I couldn't help but wonder which of my guardians made it known that this was where I liked to sit. The six dragon riders looked at me with wide eyes tinged with respect and a little fear while the clan leaders stood proudly as I took my seat.

"Thank you all for getting here so fast. I know it's early, but we don't have much time," I explained once everyone was seated. "Jade has returned from Royal City with an answer from Queen Mary. She wishes to meet with me and Prince Gavin this afternoon to prove her son is safe and unharmed before we talk about becoming allies. She will be coming with her personal guard of seven on dragon back to Hillney Lake near the Creisal border. What I want to know is if there is any way that the queen could set up an ambush or if she still has enough pull in Creisal to get them to attack us?"

The men murmured amongst themselves as they digested this news and compared information.

"Your Majesty," Sal spoke up first. "Queen Mary is the second daughter to the king and queen of Creisal, and though she still keeps close ties to her family, her elder sister, Princess Leanna, who is to rule when her parents pass, hates Queen Mary. I doubt Princess Leanna would allow her sister to use their military forces when they are currently dealing with an influx of sea pirates."

"I agree with this. My clan is closest to the Creisal border, and I know that lake well. It is fairly neutral territory with no villages or other dwellings nearby," Xio added. "I think that Queen Mary is being fair in her choice of location. It's also too far from Royal City that troops on foot or horseback would have trouble getting there by noon. Dragons are much faster but more noticeable, especially the queen's golden dragon."

"All right, so the location is fair and yields no advantage to either party. What about the number of her guards?" When no one offered a response right away, I turned to Gavin. "In the mind of Norden royalty, what would you expect if you were in your mother's shoes?"

Gavin looked around the table then back at me. "Since she made it clear the number of people she would bring with her, it was a sign of good faith. If you wish to prove your intention, I would match her count, or slightly less, to show you do not want to be a threat."

"Who in their right mind would show up with less protection?" Garold snapped, shoving to his feet. "How do we know this wasn't the plan all along? If he talks you into having fewer guards, it's easier to pick you off in the end!"

Raising a hand, I halted him from speaking further. "Sit down. If you have something to say, you can do so easily from a seated position. I do not have time for this discussion to turn into an argument among children."

Garold looked at me with a shocked expression as he sank back into his seat, crossing his arms like a child pouting.

"What Gavin said makes sense, but we are mercenaries, are we not? Skilled in the art of stealth and deception to get the job done?" I asked, looking around the table. "Just because I present the queen with less than seven guards doesn't mean that's how many will be there." It took a moment for everyone to understand what I was saying, but eventually, they all caught on. "I will bring Jade and Zan with me, doubling up, so that I will have four guards present while the six of you will lie in wait."

"There is a dense forest not too far from the lake where they can hide out and won't be seen as you approach. It would work even better if you were slightly late," Xio suggested.

I grinned at him. "Now you're finally thinking like a mercenary. Izel, I want you to pair up with Tinus so that you can make sure they get to the right area since I'll have you fly in slightly behind us. Gavin will ride with me. Dayson and Cole, you will also be with me. My other guardians double up with one of the other six riders." I paused a moment, running over this once more in my brain to make sure I didn't miss anything before I dismissed them. "I don't need to tell you this is a vital moment in our existence. If we can't get their help, it could mean the chance of not surviving this war."

The room fell into a heavy silence, telling me they understood the stakes.

"Does anyone have anything further to say?" I asked.

Bast rose to his feet and bowed deeply. "I would like to apologize for the disrespect I've shown you and pledge my honor and allegiance to your service."

Swiftly, all the other dragon riders rose and gave the same pledge to me, heads bowed, waiting for my response.

"I accept your apology and am humbled at your allegiance," I offered as I also rose. "As your queen, I give you my solemn word I will do all I can to protect those under my care, and I ask your help to do so. I know we got off on the wrong foot, but those who give me their trust will have mine in return. Now go, prepare what you must. We leave when the sun hits the mountain peaks."

Swiftly, the dragon riders left, along with Jade and Zan, while I reviewed the last details. "Clan leaders, in your mind, what as a people are we not willing to give up to make this work?"

"We will never become their subjects. Our entire existence, we have fought for our freedom and right to be our own people," Ballard stated, meeting my gaze head-on. The others grunted and nodded their agreement.

"I vow never to let that happen under my rule," I guaranteed.

Acton rose and bowed. "I trust you will make the right judgment for our people, Queen Cassarah."

The other clan leaders also stood and bowed, showing me I'd finally earned their loyalty and respect.

TWENTY-FIVE

A CHAT BETWEEN QUEENS

The flight to Hillney Lake was as uneventful as the landscape we flew over, with the mountains far behind us. Not having had the chance to see my home country of Norden, it was interesting to see it firsthand instead of on a map. The towns and villages we navigated around were not as large as I thought they were, showing me how small our kingdom truly was. Vasin took point on our flight with Ifra and Tahir on either side, keeping a watchful eye out for anything that might want to attack us. After the last few times I'd gone out, it seemed to be something I would have to worry about.

"I don't think I'll ever get over how amazing it is to fly on the back of a dragon," Gavin commented, his mouth so close his lips brushed my ear.

Surprised by his words, I jerked, turning my head and causing him to kiss me on the cheek. Gavin leaned back from me instantly, giving me space as I froze, forgetting everything I was going to say.

"Cassarah, I'm so sorry. I didn't mean to do that," Gavin babbled as his hands fluttered, unsure if he was welcome to keep them around my waist.

Grabbing a hand, I pulled him back against me. "Don't flail around like that. You'll make the others think something's wrong.

They're already irritated they couldn't talk me out of only having the four of them with me."

"Right, sorry... again," Gavin mumbled, taking hold of my hips. "Do you know how much farther it is?"

"We are nearly there, and it seems that Queen Mary and her men have beaten us there. I count seven dragons like she said there would be."

"Anything out in the distance like what we are doing?"

"No, our six dragons are the only ones for miles besides the seven we are meeting up with."

"Good to know that she wasn't lying to Jade."

"From what I gathered from her dragon while I was in the roost, she is an honorable woman. I know you respect her, and I think she's earned that from us after what she did when we first bonded."

"It's crazy to think I haven't seen her since that day. When we came to rescue you, it was Gavin who greeted me, pretending to be just another palace steward."

"Many things have changed, but some have stayed the same. Trust your instincts, Cass."

"Vasin said we aren't far," I called back. "Seems your mother is already there as well."

"That's my mother, overly punctual."

"I'm going to circle once before we land near them. We can't take any chances that foot soldiers might be hidden about."

I waved over at Jade, giving him the signal that we were going to circle, then did the same to Zan. Making a wide berth around the rather huge lake, we didn't spot anything to be concerned about. We spotted where the queen and her men were settled on the wide-open beach with a canopy for us to sit under. Vasin touched down a few feet away so as not to knock the structure over with the wind from his wings. I took a few deep breaths as I undid the straps and waited for Gavin to slide off first. Once on the ground, he held out a hand to me, assisting as I slid down, landing on my good leg as much as possible.

"Are you all right with me walking you over, or would you prefer one of the guardians?" Gavin asked, his hands settling on my hips, keeping me steady on the shifting sand.

I gave him a soft smile. "Don't you think it would make a nice scene to see us walking arm in arm like the friends we are? Your mother would have difficulty finding a way to say we held you against your will."

"What if you are some witch who's tricked me into compliance with your magic?" Gavin teased, tucking my arm around his. "Or I could be hypnotized and not even know what's going on."

"Lucky for us, your mother knows what my Birthright is, but I would love to see you pretend to be under my control. How good is your impersonation of a chicken?" I asked and burst out laughing when he decided to show me.

"Finally, I got you to laugh. Now, don't worry about this so much. My mother isn't all that scary. She's irritatingly rational, like you in some ways," Gavin shared, nudging my shoulder.

I gave him a look of mock horror. "Are you saying that I'm irritating?"

"No, hell no, far from it, actually. The quality is far more endearing from you than my mother." Gavin winked.

Jade, Zan, Dayson, and Cole fell in behind us, decked out in their best uniforms and strapped with weapons. It was comforting to know they were there for me, and I had no doubt they would be able to handle a fight of seven on four, not to mention that I was also armed this time around. My leg might not be fully healed, but it was strong enough to do what I had to if the need arose. As we got closer, Queen Mary rose and headed toward us, her face betraying just how much she'd missed her son.

"Go, greet your mother," I insisted, shoving him forward as Cole came up to take his spot.

Gavin glanced back before he jogged the last few steps to his mother and swept her up into a tight hug. It was a sight I'd never seen before from a mother, and I steeled myself from thinking about my mother. She no longer had any place in my life, and I wouldn't let her cloud this moment with her inability to show affection. Cole squeezed my hand, pulling my attention away from the tender moment to look into his sapphire gaze.

"You okay?" he murmured.

"The tonic Izel made did wonders to clear up the hangover," I answered, purposely ignoring what he really wanted to know. "What about you?"

"Little mouse, the only one who was drunk was you."

My jaw fell as I thought about what happened last night, and I couldn't help but glance over at Dayson. "You mean…"

Cole slowly nodded his head, grinning at me like a cat who got the cream.

"Lady Cassarah, it's good to see you again," Queen Mary called, bringing me back to reality. "I can't thank you enough for bringing my son back to me alive. I thought we lost him once we got the ransom notice from Errit."

"Mother, it's Queen Cassarah now. She rules over all the clans," Gavin corrected.

Queen Mary's eyes widened slightly as she covered her mouth with a leather-gloved hand in surprise. "My apologies. I didn't realize they still acknowledged the old ways of the black dragon. It's been so many years since the last one was seen."

"It's quite all right. I'm still getting used to the title myself," I said, brushing off the unintentional slight.

"Come sit. Your letter made it clear that this was urgent, and I still don't know the whole story about what happened to Gavin," the queen stated, waving us to follow her, keeping Gavin close to her side.

I took one last shaky breath while the queen's back was to us before heading off after her.

"You're gonna do just fine, little mouse. If you can stop a mob of angry dragons, then this is nothing to worry about," Cole whispered as we ducked into the canopy.

Inside the light gauzy material was a table full of refreshments and three chairs ready and waiting for us. Queen Mary settled into one and pulled Gavin down beside her, refusing to let go of her son's hand. Taking the last chair, Cole stood right behind me as Zan joined us, leaving Jade and Dayson outside watching the queen's other five guards.

"Would you care for a drink or something to eat? I don't know how far of a journey it is from where you're staying," Queen Mary offered.

"No, thank you, Your Majesty. I don't mean this to sound rude, but we don't have time for the social niceties of the court on this matter. King Edward's bastard son is on his way to Royal City with an army comprised of Errit and Utros soldiers under his command. Henry has taken to calling himself the Lost King and wants the throne he believes he is entitled to, no matter who or what is in his way."

Queen Mary sat stunned, blinking at me as if trying to process everything I'd just told her. "Edward has another child?"

"I know this isn't what you expected to hear," I admitted, seeing how tightly she clutched Gavin's hand. "From what I know, this happened before you were married. The boy was born, but King Edward didn't want to kill the baby, so he gave up the child to a family who couldn't have any. Henry ended up in Utros and is the adopted son of King Marquees Efrem. The problem is Henry has a Birthright that allows him to control people's minds."

"What?" Reaching out with her other hand, she grabbed Gavin's shoulder. "Did he do something to you? Are you sure that you're all right?"

"Yes, Mother, I'm fine. Henry didn't want to make me his puppet since he needed me for my Birthright. He would bring people into the tent he had me tied up in and forced me to get them to talk. Once they confessed whatever they were keeping hidden, he would have them killed. If Cassarah hadn't come to rescue me, I don't know what would have happened because this attack would have blindsided our country. We owe Cassarah more than just our thanks, Mother."

Queen Mary turned back to me. "Tell me what you know. How much time do we have?"

"That is the information I need your help to gain," I stated. "I need all of your dragon riders to scour our kingdom and into Errit and Utros. I even suggest we keep an eye out in Creisal as well. Henry is smart, conniving, and manipulative... an extremely dangerous combination for a man with his powers. I will be sending out my own riders as well, but I only have a handful, and they won't be able to get all the information we need."

"Where was the group you discovered?" she pressed, waving to one of her guards. "Bring me a map of the kingdom and clear the table."

Swiftly, the guards did as she ordered, and soon, we stood shoulder to shoulder over the map. It wasn't as detailed as ours, but I had studied it enough to easily point out the location.

"They were here along the Darsor River near the border of Utros. I did get confirmation from a scouting party that there was another mass movement of men coming from the south portion of the Restless Mountains," I informed her, pointing out the spot Tinus and Bast had spoken of. "I fear there are others in the north coming from Errit as well, and since we don't have any large towns or villages up that way, it would be easy for them to wipe them out to keep their existence a secret."

Queen Mary looked up at me, studying my face. "I can see why he likes you. A mind as brilliant as yours is hard not to notice."

I blushed under her praise, dropping my gaze back down to the map.

"How long ago did you discover this original encampment?" she asked, returning to the matter at hand.

"Today makes it five days ago," I answered. "But I blew up all their supplies, so I'm hoping that has bought us some time to make sure they haven't traveled far from that spot. My hope is that the second party is coming to join them and restock supplies since it's coming from his father."

"My, you certainly did try to think of everything, didn't you?" The queen chuckled. "So, we need to make sure we send the dragon riders more southeast to start with and another group to the northeast. If I know my sister, even with a Birthright to back Henry up, he couldn't convince her to do anything. She is as hardheaded as they come, but I will send a message to her, making her aware of the impending battle."

"Would she lend you help?" I hedged.

Queen Mary sighed and grabbed paper along with ink and a pen. "I honestly don't know. If I were to ask her about something she would view as trivial, then absolutely not. Seeing as Norden could get wiped out, leaving them as the only kingdom left to conquer, it might get her attention. Curtis!"

Moments later, a burly man entered the tent. "Yes, Your Majesty?"

"I need you to take this letter to my sister. She likes you, so I'm hoping she will actually read it before deciding to ignore what I have to say," she explained as she sealed the letter and handed it to him. "There can be no delay, and I need you to wait until you get an answer before you leave. Is that understood?"

"It will be done as you say, My Queen," Curtis answered, taking the letter and bowing before he left.

"Curtis is one of my most trusted men. He will make sure it gets to my sister no matter what," Queen Mary explained. "Now, we must return to Royal City so we can send out the dragon riders and stage the next part of the plan we come up with."

I froze, unsure of what to say to that. "Um... I can't return to the city. I must tell my people that we have your support and prepare for our part of the battle."

"Cassarah, you might be their leader, but they are still subjects of my kingdom, as are you."

"No, Mary, I am not your subject. When I took the role of queen, I renounced myself as your subject to rule over my people. The mercenaries have never been Norden's subjects. We are people who hail from the land of Sheca where you have no ties to."

"You dare to use my given name so commonly?" she snapped.

I turned, locking my gaze with her own. "I allowed one slight to my title, but I will not allow another. Either I am your equal in this, or I am your enemy. There is no other option."

TWENTY-SIX
ALLIES

The queen's emerald eyes bore into mine, but I would not back down on this. We had spilled so much blood over this issue, I was not going to fail those who had given their lives to keep us free. Now I understood why Miranda did what she did. There was no way rolling over and letting another take control of my people was ever going to happen.

"Then you leave me no choice..." Queen Mary stated, her voice somber. "Queen Cassarah, I would be honored to have you as an ally in this battle. I would also like to request your presence in Royal City for one day so that we might come up with a plan you can take back to your people. We are the main target. It would reassure me greatly if I had a solid strategy moving forward."

My whole body relaxed at her words, and my gaze flickered over to Gavin who also looked relieved at this turn of events. "I believe that is a fair request. I will return with you."

"Vasin, can you send Tinus here with Izel?"

"They are on their way, but it doesn't seem like they are coming alone."

"Very well... they might as well know what's going on."

As my leg started to ache, I returned to my seat to wait for my backup to arrive. "Your Majesty, I have six other dragon riders coming to join us. They were waiting off in the forest, but I will need to send one of them back to my people so they know why I haven't returned."

"Can't say I'm surprised you had people lurking in the shadows, but I appreciate you alerting me to their arrival." Queen Mary smirked as she sat. "How did you know they were coming? Did you have a set time they were supposed to wait before they assumed the worst?"

Now it was my turn to give her a knowing smile. "We might be allies, Your Majesty, but there are some things that I will be keeping to myself. You would never expect another kingdom to give up all its secrets, would you?"

"For only being queen for five days, you've learned to play the role very well. I suppose you can thank your mother for all that education you got."

At the mention of my mother and her *education,* I froze, hearing her words echoing in my head, causing me to lose focus on what was reality or past events. Then a hand descended on the back of my neck, and thick fingers gripped the base of my skull, pulling on my hair and forcing me to look up into Cole's gaze.

"Your mother is not here. She cannot hurt you anymore," Cole assured.

Licking my lips, I gave him a small nod to let him know I was back and the panic attack had subsided. Cole let go of my hair but kept his hand on my shoulder, letting the weight remind me I wasn't alone like I'd once been.

"It was actually my father who gave me the skills I need to perform this role well. The hours we spent pouring over maps and battle strategies were invaluable," I replied, facing the queen once again.

Her beautiful face was stricken as she realized her words triggered my response. Thankfully, the roar of a dragon outside let me know my backup had arrived and gave me an excuse to leave the tent. When

I stepped outside, Jade and Zan were holding guards at knifepoint with Ezzu hovering in the air.

"What's going on?" I demanded.

Jade looked over the shoulder of the man he had in his grasp. "They weren't saying very nice things about you, Your Majesty."

"Bad enough that it warranted threatening our alliance that was just forged?" I snapped. "Let them go this instant and put your weapons away. I don't want them drawn on another Norden soldier unless one of our lives is in danger. Am I clear?"

Zan released his man, shoving him away as Ezzu gave a hiss and sent a small tongue of flame after him before settling on Zan's shoulder. Jade, on the other hand, held my gaze, his eyes full of the argument he wanted to have with me over my order.

"Did you not hear our queen?" Cole bit out from behind me.

Jade's lip curled in a snarl as he kicked out the guard's legs and sent the man tumbling to the ground. "I don't care what my orders are. If I ever hear you talk like that about *my queen*, I will gut you like the worm you are." Finishing off his threat, he spit on the ground near the guard's face and stormed off toward the newly arrived dragon riders.

"Seems that someone is finally showing his true colors," Cole muttered.

I glared at him over my shoulder. "Look, I know you two don't like each other, but I'm gonna need you to save it for when we aren't trying to make new friends. Whatever you feel about Jade, keep it to yourself, or I'm going to send you back home."

Cole narrowed his eyes at me, but whatever my expression showed him made him back down from the fight he was itching for. "Yes, Your Majesty."

I knew he was pissed at me, but I didn't have the luxury of showing any preferential treatment at the moment. I was their queen, and this was far too important to let it get fucked up by testosterone-filled males. The dragon riders and the rest of my guardians approached and dropped to a knee, heads bowed before me.

"How may we serve you, Your Majesty?" Izel asked.

"I will be going back to Royal City tonight, and I will return home the following day. I need to send one of you back to inform the clan leaders of this update," I informed them. "Svan, you rode here alone, so I'll send you back with a letter for the clan leaders."

Was I getting back at a man who was a bit of an ass when we first met... maybe?

"Yes, My Queen, am I to depart right away?" he asked, showing no hesitation at my orders.

"In a moment. I will need to write the letter," I answered. "As for the rest of you dragon riders, you will accompany me back to the city along with my guardians."

"Yes, Your Majesty," they all answered, giving me a salute.

Turning on my heel, I reentered the tent, wrote my letter, and sent Svan on his way while Queen Mary's men took down the canopy and stored everything away.

"Gavin, Lezat is more than able to take an additional person," Queen Mary said as she ran a hand along her golden dragon's neck. "There is no need to ride with Queen Cassarah back home."

From where Gavin stood by my side next to Vasin, he shifted his gaze between his mother and me. He looked as if he was going to say something to me but instead, his shoulders slumped, and he headed off to his mother's side. I tried not to let on how much the fact that he walked away from me stung. From everything he'd been telling me, he wanted to stay with me, or had I been wrong? Did he say all that about staying until I kicked him out to placate me?

"Cass, I'm sure there is an explanation. He's been gone from home for over a week. It could simply be that he

KNOWS HIS MOTHER WANTS HIM TO RIDE WITH HER. GIVE HIM A CHANCE TO TELL HIS PARENTS HE DOESN'T WANT TO BE KING. THAT IS NOT A TOPIC YOU SPRING ON SOMEONE. IT WILL TAKE TIME FOR THEM TO SEE WHAT HIS HEART TRULY DESIRES."

"*You're absolutely right. There is no reason I need to concern myself with this matter. It helps us if he becomes king. At least I know I can work well with him if we are to be allies.*"

"*DON'T BE LIKE THAT, CASS.*"

"*Says the dragon who keeps telling me to get closer to people and get attached.*"

Vasin just sighed and dropped the matter.

"Who would you have ride with you, Queen Cassarah?" Abbott asked, stepping up beside me.

I glanced over my shoulder at him then back over at Gavin. "I'll be riding alone. With eight of you around me, I think it will be safe enough."

"Little phoenix—"

"Abbott, please don't try to fix this. Just leave it alone. He will tell them if he wants to leave or he won't."

Settling his hands on my hips, he hoisted me onto Vasin's back and made sure I was well strapped in. "Don't do anything foolish, please."

"Do you really think Vasin would let that happen? He is far too overprotective to allow me to get into trouble," I answered with a halfhearted smile I knew didn't fool him.

Patting my leg, Abbott headed off to join Bast, and we took off toward Royal City.

"I believe this is the fullest I've seen the roost in my lifetime. Seventeen dragons, including King Edward's, is a sight to see." Queen Mary smiled as all the dragons were being settled in for the night. "Come, I will show you to your room and make sure your riders and guardians have rooms as well."

"With all due respect, Your Majesty, I will be keeping my personal guards with me," I stated, knowing that if they weren't, they would throw a fit, decorum be damned.

Queen Mary glanced over my shoulder then back at me. "Let me guess... if I don't allow this, they will find a way to make it happen, regardless."

"They are overprotective in nature," I answered. "Two of them are my female guards who will be the only ones attending me, so there is no need to inconvenience your staff in such a way."

"You play the game very well, Queen Cassarah, very well indeed." Queen Mary smirked as she led the way into the castle. "Would you agree to a meal before we start planning? I don't know about you, but a long flight always makes me peckish, and it gives us a chance to share the news with my husband and see if he has any light to shed on matters."

"A meal would be lovely, although I do not have any other attire, seeing as I wasn't prepared to stay away from home," I pointed out.

Queen Mary waved off my concerns. "No matter... I will send something up for you."

As we entered the castle, we were met by her steward. He took the others and me to where we would be staying for the night. The room was actually three different ones that interconnected—a sitting room that flowed into the bedroom with a dressing room. Everything was large and ostentatious and reminded me how I'd come to find comfort in the simple way the mercenaries lived.

"Holy shit." May whistled as she took in the space.

"Just wait until you see the small room attached for us to sleep in," Becka shared, opening a hidden door panel for May to peek in. "Can't have the staff too far but also don't want people to know we exist."

"Well, there won't be a problem with all of us finding space to sleep in here," Payson added from where he was sprawled out on one of the many lush couches.

The others continued to poke around the room, looking behind the thick drapes of the windows and peeking into the bathroom.

"Is this what Gavin is used to?" Dayson asked, staring up at the ceiling with intricate murals painted on them. "There's no way he'll give up all this to live in the forest with us."

I poured myself a glass of chilled juice that had been sent up, along with a dress from the queen. I clutched the metal goblet, trying to shake off the fact that Dayson was voicing my fears.

"Do we get to go to dinner?" Payson interjected as he rolled on to his stomach, peering up at me.

Taking a large gulp of my drink, I sat in one of the stiff armchairs. "You will be present at the dinner, but you will not be eating with us. In the eyes of the court, you are my guard dogs, and dogs do not eat at the table. If you were my consort or husband, then yes, you would be awarded that honor."

"Ugh, I can see why you wanted to get out of this place... so many rules," Payson grumbled, punching at one of the decorative pillows.

"Everything has its good and bad traits. Nowhere is perfect," Izel interjected as he joined us in the sitting room. "Tell us, little warrior, what happened at the meeting? Obviously, things went well, but why are we here?"

At his question, the others came and found a place in the sitting room to hear my answer. "Queen Mary felt it was best if we came up with a plan of action before I went back home. Since they are the main focus of the attack, I can understand her reasoning. My hope is that we can make a game plan, and then I can take that information back with me so we can move forward with what we need to do."

"Is she going to give us the dragon riders we need?" Zan asked.

"The queen hasn't said no, but that is also what dinner is about. King Edward doesn't know anything the queen and I have discussed. She is going to tell him about the Lost King and see what his reaction will be to the news," I responded.

"I don't like it. She challenged you, then moments later demanded that you come back here. Who knows what she's trying to pull," Cole growled.

Looking over at him, I held his gaze. "In order for trust to be earned between us, I have to give her the chance to prove herself. Going into this assuming she will sell me out does no one any good."

Cole didn't have a response to that other than to turn his back on me and stare out the window at the fading light.

"Come on, m'lady, it's time we got you dressed and ready for the court dinner you never got to attend," Becka said, waving to me to follow her and defusing the tension in the room.

TWENTY-SEVEN
A ROYAL DINNER

"I had hoped never to have to wear a gown like this again," I muttered as Becka tightened the corset.

"Do you remember when you first came and dressed in pants? Helena told me she thought you weren't ever going to come out of your room," Becka teased. "Now here you are in the Norden castle, having dinner with the king and queen as an equal. How the winds have changed."

Slipping on the dark emerald-colored underdress, I turned to face Becka. "I know I said we have to trust her, but what if she tries to get me to stay, turn my back on my people, and become their mercenary pet or something as they did to Miranda?"

"Then you tell her the same thing you did back at the lake," Becka stated, scowling at me. "The Cassarah I know isn't a pushover. You might have submitted to your mother all those years, but you did it to protect me. That shows true strength that very few people possess."

I shoved my arms through the stiff brocade sleeve and held it to my chest as Becka cinched it in the back. "What if this whole thing is just false hope?"

Becka stopped what she was doing, grabbed my shoulders, and spun me around to face her. "You stop that crap right this instant. I get that all this is throwing your past in your face, but I need my queen back... thank you very much. You know the one I'm talking about, the one who scolded five clan leaders, left dragon riders to rot in the desert, and faced down ten fucking dragons!" As she spoke, her voice kept getting louder until at the end, she was all but screaming at me. "This palace isn't you. This life was never going to be yours. Accept it and own who you are now because I like the Cassarah I've seen over the last week. That Cassarah would take this situation by the reins and steer it in the direction she needed it to go. Now, I'm gonna need you to buck up, fix your crown, and deal with it!"

I wanted to tell Becka off for yelling at me, but it was only because she was right that I didn't. "Fine, but I won't let you guys screw this up for us. We *need* them to have a chance to survive this war."

"Don't tell me that. I know how to behave. The ones you need to be scolding are listening just outside the door," Becka pointed out.

Bunching up my skirts, I hobbled across the room as quickly as I could, throwing the door open. Sure enough, there were my male guardians gathered around the keyhole. "Did you all get that, or do I need to repeat myself?"

"Ah, no, I think you made your stance clear on the matter," Abbott assured me, trying to smooth matters as the others nodded in agreement.

I found that Zan was the only one still in the sitting room, looking as if he was sleeping, but Ezzu was perched on the top of the chair, looking very alert, watching me. It was odd to know that he could see without his eyes open, but I refused to treat him like he was disabled when he didn't see himself that way.

"Do you need me to fill you in on the conversation, Zan?" I asked, putting my hands on my hips.

He grinned and shook his head. "Nope. I may not have been eavesdropping, but I don't intend to stop you from doing what you need to do. I trust your judgment in doing what is best to keep our people safe. Another reason why I'm over here not listening in when Becka started shouting. Words from a woman's best friend are the best advice you could ever get."

"How enlightened of you, Zan," Becka chirped, giving him an approving nod. "Now, did the queen send up shoes, or are we putting your boots back on?"

"I don't care if she did send shoes, I'm wearing my boots. They support my leg better," I stated, shaking out the skirts absentmindedly.

Zan stood and walked over to me, taking my hand and kissing the back of it. "You look stunning in emerald, Cassarah."

Blushing, I offered him a timid smile as I gave him my best curtsy. "Why thank you, kind sir."

"If I'd known getting her to Royal City would give me a chance to see her in a dress like that, I would have made it happen sooner," Payson whispered loudly to Dayson, who nodded in agreement.

May slapped them both on the back of their heads. "Stop looking at her breasts. Just because the dress puts them on display doesn't mean you should be gawking at them."

Dayson muttered something and turned away, rubbing the back of his neck while Payson scowled at May. "No need to get violent over the matter. It's not a sight we'll get to see very often, if ever again."

Thankfully, a knock sounded at the door, ending this conversation. Izel opened it, stepping aside for a page boy to enter. "Your Highness, I am here to escort you to dinner."

"One moment, please," I addressed the boy, slipping back into the dressing room to get my boots on.

As I did that, Becka slipped on the circlet once more and pulled my dragon necklace out of the bodice. "We can't have them forgetting who you are."

"Was that one last reminder for myself as well?" I quipped.

"I have no idea what you're talking about, Your Majesty. I am but your humble servant." Becka gasped, clutching her chest.

Rolling my eyes, I stood and slowly limped out of the dressing room, where Abbott was waiting for me. He seemed to be able to always tell what I was feeling and knew my leg was not pleased with me walking on it so much. Allowing myself to lean on him, we slowly followed the page boy through the castle's hallways until we reached a small, intimate dining room filled with candlelight and a brightly burning fire. King Edward and Queen Mary were already there, along with Gavin and his younger brother, Prince Phillip.

"Ah, Queen Cassarah, it's lovely to see you again," King Edward greeted as we entered. "I believe you know everyone but my second son, Prince Phillip."

Phillip bowed in greeting, and I smiled, giving a polite head nod. "It is nice to make your acquaintance, Prince Phillip. Prince Gavin has told me much about you."

He looked surprised to hear this and glanced questioningly at Gavin. "Good things, I hope."

"It would seem that we share a love of scholarly things that he finds rather dull," I shared, grinning at him.

Phillip laughed. "That sounds like my brother. He would rather do almost anything than attend his lessons, which then caused him to always beg for my help."

"If the tutors weren't so dull, learning would have been easier. When Queen Cassarah explains things, I understand," Gavin muttered, coming to his defense.

"I'm sure it has nothing to do with the fact you like her," Phillip said, giving his brother a knowing look.

"Boys, that's quite enough," Queen Mary cut in. "Queen Cassarah is an honored guest, and I'll not have you both causing a ruckus. Now take your seats."

The five of us settled at the table while my guardians stood along the wall behind me and near the room's entrance. Servants came from another entry point with large trays of all kinds of steaming meat, vegetables, and bread. Conversation lulled as we filled our plates, and as much as I liked the cooking back home, it was nice to get a change and enjoy some foods I've missed.

"Queen Mary has informed me that your visit isn't a social one," King Edward mentioned when the servants left the room. "It's also very unusual for us to entertain in our personal dining hall, but my queen says I must hear this directly from you, Queen Cassarah."

I glanced at the queen before I set my silverware down to give the king my full attention. I was irritated she was making me break this news to him, but I also understood it in a way. Finding out that your husband fathered a child before your marriage didn't have the best ring to it.

"Prince Gavin and I were kidnapped by the same person... your first-born son, Henry," I confessed, feeling it was best to just put the truth out there. "Currently, he is referring to himself as the Lost King and is on his way to Royal City to take his rightful place on the Norden throne."

The sound of King Edward's knife hitting his plate echoed around the room as we watched him absorb this information.

"I believe it's also fair that I tell you Porvan has shared everything he knows about your son with me. While gathering current information about this matter, I discovered that not only does Henry have power over Utros but Errit as well," I divulged, trying to save him from having to explain everything since we didn't have time to rehash information.

"You're sure it's him?" King Edward whispered.

"Without a doubt, Your Majesty."

King Edward dropped his head into his hands, unable to look at anyone as he spoke. "I should have killed him when he was born. The only reason I didn't was to honor his dying mother's wish to let him live. The gods are punishing me for being selfish and wanting to love someone I couldn't love."

As much as I felt for the king, this didn't help matters now, but I didn't want to appear insensitive toward his suffering. "I'm sorry to come to you with this news, King Edward, but the threat he poses is real, and we need to address it, or all will be lost. There hasn't been a war like this for hundreds of years."

"Do you also know about his Birthright?" he asked, looking up at me.

"I've experienced it myself, but thankfully my dragon was able to break his hold on my mind," I answered truthfully. "That gift makes him even more dangerous than the average power-hungry tyrant. I'm sorry to ask this, but who was his mother?"

"She was a dragon rider in our military. She was stationed as a palace guard, which is how I met her. We fell in love," King Edward answered, his voice void of emotion. "She had a strong Birthright, giving her the ability to soothe those in pain. Why couldn't he have taken after her? Why must I be the one to have given him his Birthright?"

"Knowing what Prince Gavin's is, I can guess at the nature of yours. Personally, I think it's a twisted version of both your Birthrights," I shared. "He warps the mind of whoever he controls and can inflict pain on them when they fight him, making it easier to slip farther into their subconscious."

No one seemed to have anything to say after that tidbit of information, and we awkwardly kept eating in silence.

Once the dishes were cleared away, Queen Mary cleared her throat, drawing our attention. "My King, we only have Queen Cassarah for a short while, and I think it's best if we use that time wisely to start on a plan. She has shared much of the information she's gathered with me, and I believe time is of the essence. I've sent a messenger to my sister asking for help."

"What is there to do but kill the bastard and all his men?" King Edward growled.

"Yet many of the men are enslaved by his mind-control. It's not their choice to be a part of this war," Queen Mary countered.

Gavin reached out and rested his hand on his mother's arm. "No, Mother, once he takes their mind, there is no saving them. His power turns them into mindless puppets who slowly drift into madness until they are killed and left behind. The merciful thing we can do is kill them before it gets to that point."

"So, there is no hope for them?" she pleaded to her son.

"It could be as simple as killing the head of the snake," Phillip interjected. "If Henry is the source behind the control, and you cut off the head, the body dies, but it could also free them from his poison."

"Hmm," I mused, tapping my chin. "It's something to consider. If no one is feeding into their minds, what's to stop them from returning to normal?"

"This is exactly what I was talking about. You two are on another level of smart." Gavin huffed, sitting back in his chair.

Ignoring his comment, I pressed on to other matters. "What we need right now is to find out where his armies are. My people found a second branch coming from Utros' southern border into Norden, hidden in the mountains. If we could send out riders first thing in the morning to locate where the original army is, that would give us a gauge of how much time we have." I turned to Gavin. "When you were there, did you get any sense of why they were waiting in the woods? I know they sent the ransom letter, and he was also trying to draw my people out, but to what purpose?"

Gavin sat up, now fully engaged in the conversation. "I assumed it was to get Mother and Father to send out an army after me, leaving the castle more vulnerable. It would take time for the troops to gather and be sent out since the military base isn't located here in the city. It still wouldn't have given the second wave enough time to hit us, though..."

Then it hit me. "If he had me under his control, he would already have a second wave of people who are far closer. The troop from Utros wasn't planned, but because we got away, he had to change tactics. That still doesn't explain what his plan is for the city." My body twitched with the need to get up and move, giving me space to think about this more on a larger scale.

Unable to keep my frustration in, I shoved my chair back and limped the length of the room, chewing on my bottom lip. I was so close to seeing the last piece, but it kept slipping away from me just as I thought I had it. Then it all clicked into place, and I turned on my heel, meeting the Queen's gaze.

"Lord Everett's been working for the Lost King the whole time."

TWENTY-EIGHT
THE PRINCE IS MINE

"I don't understand. What does that have to do with anything?" King Edward demanded, slamming his fist on the table.

"Oh God, we're done for," Queen Mary gasped.

Gavin lunged to his feet, his face full of terror. "We need to get everyone out of the castle... hell, the whole city, if there is a chance for anyone to survive."

"Your Majesties, if you could indulge us and explain what's going on?" Izel asked as he came to stand beside me, giving me something to lean against.

"Lord Everett has been the captain of the king's personal guard since King Edward took the throne thirty years ago. He has been the one to implement all the changes and matters of castle security, meaning he knows all the tricks. There is nowhere to hide, no passage to use that he doesn't know about. If the Lost King has been planning this for years, then he probably already has people here in the castle to take it whenever he wants," Queen Mary explained.

I visualized the map Gavin made me with all the secret passages and hiding spots in the castle. As the captain of the personal guard then, Lord Everett would have been told about them to make sure the royal family could get away safely. *So what do we do now that we know this?*

"Vasin! I need you and all the dragons in the roost to fly around the city and tell me if any suspicious groups of people are hiding near any of these entrances or exits."

Closing my eyes, I let him reach into my mind and see the map I was talking about.

"WE WILL GO NOW. OUR NIGHT VISION IS FAR SUPERIOR TO ANY OTHER ANIMAL, SO WE WILL BE ABLE TO SEE THINGS CLEARLY."

"I might have just walked right into a trap, Vasin."

"YOU HAVE YOUR GUARDIANS, THE OTHER DRAGON RID-ERS, AND US DRAGONS THAT YOU TRUST. ALL IS NOT YET LOST. LET US FIND OUT WHAT WE CAN BEFORE YOU MAKE ANY MOVES THAT WOULD GIVE ANYTHING AWAY."

"Yes, we have to act normal."

Opening my eyes, I was met with curious looks from the royal family.

"She was talking to Vasin. You'll get used to it," Gavin shared, giving me a weak smile.

"The dragons are going to take a flight around the city and see if there is anything to worry about near the tunnel exits or entrances," I explained. "We need to continue to act like nothing is wrong until we decide on the best course of action. Shall we retire to the sitting room for drinks and entertainment?"

Payson stepped away from the wall, catching my eye. "Your Majesty, might I suggest that one of us remain in your rooms so that an assassin doesn't get in?"

"It's not a bad idea," Izel murmured.

"I leave the task to you. May, you go with him as well," I ordered.

"If I may," Payson interjected. "My Birthright is to give off illu-sions so I can make myself all but invisible to the naked eye, but I can't do that for others. Leave this task to me. You need the protection with you, not in your rooms."

Too preoccupied to argue, I waved him off. "Very well, I will leave the matter to you." With a bob of his head, he left the room.

Our party adjourned to a sitting room, where drinks were poured, and a woman came in to play the piano and sing softly in the corner as we talked about nothing.

"It seems that the rains have been rather scarce this season. I do hope we'll get a decent crop," King Edward mused, tapping a finger against his glass.

"Mother, Father, I want to abdicate the throne to Phillip," Gavin blurted. "You know I'm not the right choice to rule."

King Edward groaned and rubbed his forehead. "Not this again. What would you even do if you didn't rule? Think of how it would look to all the other kingdoms."

"I'm going to be the Norden ambassador to our allies, the mercenaries," Gavin stated, his voice firm in his resolve. "I can be of help to them and support our kingdom at the same time. The mercenaries have such a different lifestyle it could be beneficial to learn from each other. I've been with them and seen firsthand what their lives are like when they're not even in their homes."

"You can't really be serious," Queen Mary pressed, watching her son, and then turned to me. "Are you to blame for this foolish idea? He is the crown prince, and he will be the Norden's next king."

Taking a deep breath, I tried to calm the surge of excitement at hearing Gavin say he wanted to stay. "When we talked about the war and the need to build an alliance, I suggested that if he wanted to be your ambassador, I would gladly allow him to fulfill that role."

"Mother, you know that Cassarah isn't behind this. I've told you for years that Phillip would be a better king," Gavin countered.

Queen Mary's brows shot up. "You use her name so casually... are you sleeping with her? Is that what this is about? You think you're in love with her? There are other ways to deal with this than to give up your throne to a legitimate kingdom. Queen Cassarah, on the other hand, has a group of rebels who were created from a man who was banished from Norden."

"Mother," Gavin snapped.

To hear the queen so casually talk about our history surprised me. This part of our creation wasn't something that was well known, even among the mercenaries. Like Sal said, our texts had been lost in the Great War long ago.

"I'm surprised by your knowledge of these matters, Queen Mary," I commented. "Most assume that the Norden royal family would find it beneath them to learn about our humble culture."

"When a black dragon shows up and bonds with the only member of our court who has any ties back to the mercenaries, you pay attention. I made sure to have my people gather what they could, and it seems to have paid off since you are now trying to steal my son," she all but growled.

"Gavin is a grown man who can choose the life he wants. You have another son who is able to take Gavin's place, and from what I can tell, would be better suited to the job," I shot back. "All you see is your son, and all you care about is how the other kingdoms view you. Well, guess what? They are already trying to kill you all and steal your throne? How much worse could it get?"

The king and queen looked like I slapped them with my declaration, but I wasn't wrong. The only kingdom that wasn't at their throat was Creisal because they were family. Letting Gavin choose the life he wanted, if we survived this, would be the least they could do.

"She has a point, Mother," Phillip spoke up. "You've been wanting to join Norden to Errit with a marriage, but clearly that isn't going to happen. If we do win this war, we'll have leverage to gain a treaty another way or take over their kingdom entirely. I love my brother, but he is not the best person to rule in a world of politics."

"Oh, and living with cutthroats and thieves is better? They will use him against us!" Queen Mary yelled, thrusting a finger in my direction.

Within seconds, I felt two of my guardians come up behind where I was sitting, ready to act if need be.

"If I were going to do that, then why did I let you know we had him and brought him back to you?" I challenged. "I could have used him to get what I wanted more easily and faster than becoming your ally because this is clearly not going to work."

Getting to my feet, I started out of the room, but someone reached out and grabbed my arm.

"Cassarah, wait, please," Gavin begged, pulling me back against him so he could murmur in my ear. "This isn't about you... they're mad at me. Once again, I've disappointed them. Only this time, I did it in front of you instead of keeping it a private matter. Stay with me. I can do this. I can set myself free if you tell me right here and now I can be by your side."

"Is this what *you* really want?" I asked, turning my head to look up at him. "Don't do this for me, Gavin. Make this choice because you and you alone want to do this."

"Yes, this is absolutely what I want."

Letting out a heavy sigh, I took his hand in mine, and we faced his parents. "Gavin is already one of my consorts, and as such, if you do not release him of his duty to Norden as crown prince, that will make me the one who will rule over Norden when the time comes. If Phillip were to take the role of crown prince, then I would have no claim on the throne. We had hoped to do this in a more amicable way, but it's clear to me you won't see me or my people as anything other than pests in your kingdom. I will remain your ally in name only because I won't remain here to be disrespected any longer."

I signaled to my guardians, and we left, not stopping until I reached a dead end on a balcony that overlooked a massive flower garden.

"Um, love, when I asked for your help, that wasn't quite what I had in mind," Gavin said as he leaned against the stone railing, grinning at me. "You never do things halfway, that's for sure."

"Vasin, any word?"

"There are no signs of anyone around the areas you showed me, but that doesn't mean they aren't hiding in the tunnels."

"That's fair, but I'm glad to know they aren't sitting outside the wall, waiting for us to fall asleep tonight."

"We could just go home."

"No, we will remain the night and leave first thing in the morning. I planted the seed of doubt with the servants who were listening in on our conversation. If they believe we are divided, it will be a bigger surprise when we back them up."

"So that was all a ruse?"

"No, not all of it. I stand behind what I said about Gavin. He should make his own life choices."

"Hmm, you play this game far too well for my liking. Make sure to let me know when things you say should be ignored, or else I might eat someone I shouldn't."

"Hello, earth to Cassarah," Gavin called, waving a hand in front of me.

Shaking my head clear, I looked around to see my guardians in a semi-circle, blocking me in. "Sorry, I was checking in with Vasin—"

"What the hell was that back there, little mouse? Gavin is a consort now?" Cole demanded.

"In the eyes of the clan leaders, Gavin has held that position since he came to stay with us. I needed the leverage to free Gavin from the throne and cause a good enough reason for the palace staff to think there is a division between us," I explained, frowning at them. "If we assume that Lord Everett has been working for the Lost King this entire time, it means we don't know who is with or against us. Personally, I would like to believe they are all out to kill us than find out later when we are able to leave this place in one piece."

"Wait, does that mean you didn't really mean what you said back there?" Gavin asked, his face betraying his hurt.

Reaching up, I cupped his cheek with my hand, turning him to meet my gaze. "Nothing I've ever said has been a lie. How others interpret things is on them, but you asked to be by my side and for my help to stay there, and I gave you both. Gavin, I don't want you to leave, but I'm not ready to take any of the feelings I have for any of you further now. There is too much at stake, and I can't risk clouding my judgment, or any of yours, with emotions. I'm not saying no... I'm asking you to give me time." I dropped my hand and looked at the other men standing around me. "Will you all give me time?"

Izel was the first to drop to a knee, and the others, including Gavin, followed suit.

"As My Queen requests, we shall honor," Izel said with his head bowed.

"So shall we all honor," the others echoed, their voices ringing in the night air.

Twenty-Nine

Boys Make Things Complicated

"Do you think it would be better to stay here with you guys for the night since my rooms are in another part of the castle," Gavin asked once he led me back to my rooms.

"Vasin and the other dragons are out scouting the grounds. If they try to attack us, I'll know well before they make it into the castle," I assured him. "There will be servants around if I need to get a message to you, right?"

Gavin stepped inside and grasped a thick golden rope hanging near the door. Moments later, a page boy appeared and bowed. "How may I be of service, Your Highness?"

"Please make sure there is a runner with you all night in case Queen Cassarah needs to get word to me at any point," Gavin instructed.

"It will be done," the boy answered and left to disappear back to wherever he came from.

I peered down the hall, trying to see where the servants' halls might be, but it was deftly hidden away from sight. "Where is the entrance?"

"Behind the tapestry. Each floor has a room where servants wait in case we need them," Gavin informed me, pointing out the large door-sized wall hanging.

Seeing how easy it would be to be attacked made me uneasy, but I had to trust that not every person in the castle was against us. We just needed to survive the night, and I could be off to help the search for the Lost King's army.

"I'll see you in the morning. Don't you dare think of leaving without me," Gavin warned, giving me a stern look before he kissed my cheek and left.

"Did I miss anything exciting while I was here all alone?" Payson asked in greeting.

Sinking into one of the armchairs, I kicked my feet up on the stool. "Nothing worth mentioning."

"Oh, you mean other than the queen thinks you're trying to steal her son, the king is useless, and Prince Phillip is going to be the crown prince?" May scoffed, sitting across from me on the couch.

"May, you skipped the best part," Becka said, leaning over the top of my chair. "She announced that Gavin is her consort and that if they didn't let him off the hook of being king, she would be the one to rule Norden when King Edward died."

"Damn, that's what I get for opening my damn mouth and coming up with the guard-the-rooms idea. Next time, I'm going to take you up on your offer and have another one of them with me. It was way too boring being here alone." Payson sighed dramatically. "Although, I did get to try out all the couches in the room before all of you. I call dibs on the one in Cassarah's bedroom. That bad boy is plush in all the right places."

"Speaking of, I think we need to have one of us awake at all times to keep watch," Izel interjected. "I don't trust anything or anyone in the castle but the people who came here with us."

"I agree. We need to make sure no one can slip in through any secret passages," Jade added. "One person out here in the sitting room and another awake in her bedroom unless we all agree to sleep in one room."

"Cassarah is not sleeping on the floor, and we can't all be in her room," Abbott stated, crossing his arms. "Yes, we are her guardians, and we need to keep her safe, but that doesn't mean we can't give her some privacy. If Becka, May, and Payson are in there, they can rotate who is awake and allow her to get some sleep. Clearly, none of you have noticed her leg has been bothering her all day."

"Because she keeps walking on it and won't let us help her!" Cole snarled from where he was leaning against the wall. "If she weren't so stubborn, then it wouldn't be as big of a problem."

Having reached the maximum amount of drama and arguing I could stand, I stood and headed into the bedroom without giving Cole a response. Becka followed right on my heels as I entered the dressing room and started to help me get undressed.

"You know they mean well," Becka murmured as she freed me from my corset.

"I do, but sometimes it gets overwhelming," I answered. "They all have their own way of looking after me, and I value that, but when it turns into them fighting with each other, it just drains me. All they have as a common goal is me. They don't know each other, making me wonder how being with any of them would work. Obviously, I don't expect them to be best friends, but I want them to be family... to look after each other as well as me."

"So much has happened in the past few days, I think you forget it hasn't even been a week yet," Becka pointed out. "Think about how long it took for you to let Cole and Abbott become part of your family. Just like you asked for time, I would suggest doing the same for them."

"How is it you're always right about this kind of thing?" I huffed as she helped me pull on a simple night shift that had been left in the dressing room.

Becka spun me around and sat me on the stool to take my hair down. She caught my eye in the mirror. "First of all, I have way more experience dealing with you than those idiots. That, and I was raised like a normal human being with childhood friends and the like. It's a skill you have to learn. You're just a little late on mastering that one."

"At least I've mastered it enough to keep you around. I don't know what I'd do without you to explain their crazy behavior." I smiled. "Can you let one of them in? My leg hurts, and it would make them feel better to carry me a few feet to my bed."

"See, you're already learning." Becka winked and opened the door. "Payson, could you help Cassarah to the bed?"

It only took a moment, and he was there, ready with his ever-present smile. "In need of a ride, m'lady?"

Laughing, I nodded, and he scooped me up. "Thank you, kind sir. I would have been lost without you, stranded in the dressing room."

"It's never good to leave a lady all alone, even more so a queen. It's a good thing you have so many guardians to keep an eye on you," Payson teased as he sat me on the bed. "Need anything else because once you lie down, none of us will allow you to get up. You need to rest your leg."

"Maybe some water... that wine is sitting heavy on my tongue," I relented, trying to allow them to feel useful.

Payson wandered off to find me some water while I settled into the large feather-stuffed bed. It was luxurious and far too big. You could fit another two people into the bed without touching one another. Who needed that much room to sleep?

"Becka, why don't you and May share with me? It will be like when we were little, and you snuck in my bed when I was having nightmares," I offered.

"May is going to take the first watch, so we'll switch out if you don't think it will bother you too much. Staying out here together will make it easier if anything happens," Becka reasoned. "If we have to stay here, then the least we can do is be smart about it."

I sighed, staring up at the mural painted on the ceiling. "You know, they make being queen out to be something amazing, and you get all this special treatment. They forget to mention that you think someone is out to kill you most of the time."

Payson reentered the room and handed me a glass of water. "Who would sign up for the job if they knew the risks? Nah, it's better to believe in the illusion than to see the reality of it all. Now try to get some sleep."

Gulping down the cool water, I curled up on my side and watched the flickering flames in the fireplace as I drifted off to sleep.

"You finally decided to come see me again." Miranda smiled as she appeared. "I've been waiting for you. There is so much I want to tell you that has been lost to our people. I see you've learned about Sheca and its people who were left behind."

I glanced around, surprised to find myself again in Vasin's vast memory bank. "How do I keep coming here when I'm asleep?"

"The subconscious mind is a powerful thing. You needed my advice, so you called out for me," she explained.

"Did you know about Sheca?"

Miranda's face fell slightly. "Yes, I knew the Norden royalty was getting too involved in our business and needed to cut ties with them.

I'd learned of our ancestral city and planned to make a trip there to see what was left. The problem was, I didn't want to say anything outside of my men because what if it was all for nothing? Why get my people's hopes up when it might be a dream that never came true? In doing that, Emery didn't know to look there for a safe haven, and we lost many people and valuable information about the clans."

"I feel like I'm back at the same place you were. The king and queen don't see us as a people unto ourselves. They see us as their subjects to be used at their bidding. As you said, there has been so much blood spilled, and I will not *give up what we've fought for, no matter how badly we need their help."*

"Cassarah, you don't need them. Go to Sheca... that is where your path leads you. Don't relive the life I failed," Miranda pressed as she reached out to grasp my shoulders. "Being a part of the dragon consciousness, I know all they know... every secret and detail they hold to keep themselves safe as well as their pair-bonds. You, my dear sweet girl, are meant for such amazing things, and the road will be hard, full of loss, betrayal, and mistakes. These are what shape us into stronger leaders who will do what is needed to save those we care about."

"What if I don't want to go through all that? Why does my life have to be so hard? Why do I have to be the one to give up everything for everyone else?" I demanded as anger bubbled up inside me. "My whole life, I've lived for others, and now you are asking me to do the same when I've just found my freedom!"

Miranda pulled me into a tight hug, almost crushing me in her strong arms. "Those who lead the best are those who understand what it is to be controlled. Your mother was cruel, and no child deserves to be treated that way, but you will never act in violence toward another without good reason because of it. When it's time to dole out punishments, you will do so fairly, not out of a vindictive nature. That will gain you the respect and loyalty of your people more than anything else." She pulled me away from her so she could look into my eyes. "There is also so much love waiting for you, Cassarah. Those men will become your everything if you let them. Trust me, I know how amazing it is to be loved so fully by so many.

"Fate doesn't choose the weak, my dear girl. You just haven't realized that not all strength is loud and flashy. There is an even more formidable power in those who don't feel the need to show what they are capable of just because or to get praise from others, the ones who do it because it's the right thing to do without the accolades or even others knowing. That's far superior in my book. That is the fierceness I see in you and something I failed at. The time of the Dragon Queen has come, as the tales have foretold. The lands will prosper, dragons will roam the skies once again, and all people will flourish like never before. All thanks to the watchful eye of the Dragon Queen and her loyal guardians holding those who rule accountable," Miranda recited before she bent down and kissed my forehead. "I believe in you, little Dragon Queen. Now wake up!"

THIRTY

BETRAYAL

"Wake up, Cassarah! Come on, we need to go. The castle is on fire!" Payson shouted at me, shaking my shoulders.

The groggy, disoriented feeling of being out of my own body seemed worse than usual as I tried to focus on what was happening around me. Finally, I could open my eyes without the world spinning, but everything seemed so hazy, and the air was caustic, making it hard to breathe.

"What's going on?" I croaked before falling into a fit of coughing.

"The castle is on fire. We're under attack, and we need to get out of here now!" Payson explained as he bundled me into his arms. "Come on... the others are already heading for the roost and holding them off so we can get out."

I was still having trouble seeing or controlling my body, almost as if I still wasn't fully back in my own brain. Payson burst through the doors and out into the hallway, and I could hear the sounds of battle all around me. I fought Payson's hold, trying to see what was happening, but he held me tightly to his chest, my face pressed against his shirt.

"Stop fighting me, Cassarah. I need to get us out of the castle. It's full of smoke, and I can't risk you breathing it in," he snapped.

Payson dodged and kicked out at someone, who grunted at the blow, but he kept moving forward. "Dayson, I need a little help over here! They're trying to cut us off from the balcony!"

"I'm on it," Dayson answered, as I heard him rushing past us with a battle cry, followed by the sounds of people dying.

"Cassarah, I need you to hold on to me as tightly as you can. I'm gonna have to jump off the balcony into the pond below. They've cut off all other exits, and the fire is getting worse."

"What about the others?" I cried, twisting my arms and legs around his body.

"They are right behind us, but they won't do anything until you are out of harm's way." His grip on my body was so strong I thought he might break a rib. "Are you ready?"

"Does it matter?"

"Guess not. Here we go and remember to hold your breath," Payson reminded me as I felt him leap off the balcony.

As we fell, I could lift my head to see what was happening around me. The castle was aglow with a haunting orange color from the flames inside, smoke billowing out as if it was a dragon blacking out the moon as it looked down at us from above. I could see my other guardians fighting off a mixture of palace guards and other unknown assailants dressed in all black. Then I was engulfed by cold, dark water. I had to fight the urge to gasp at the shock. Payson kicked out and brought us back to the surface, but he was struggling to swim and hold on to me.

"Let me go, or I'll take us both down!" I yelled to be heard over the fighting.

"You can't swim, though," Payson argued. "Here, get on my back so my arms are free, and I'll get us out of here."

I did as he said, and it allowed me to help keep myself afloat like Abbott had been teaching me, making it easier for Payson to pull me to shore. Once we got out of the water, Payson pulled me up, wrapped an arm around my waist, and dragged me after him.

"No, we need to wait for the others," I demanded, dragging my feet. "They won't know what happened to us if we leave them."

"It's fine. We made a plan to meet at the roost if we got separated. Let us do our job and keep you alive. You can always get new guardians, but we can't get another queen," Payson growled out as he tossed me over his shoulder like a sack of grain.

I knew he was right, but my heart cried out at leaving them behind. What if they got hurt or killed? I never wanted my life to mean more than another's, but they weren't giving me a choice in the matter. Payson ran, bringing us out into the open fields of the stable area where horses calmly grazed, totally ignorant of what was happening back at the castle. We came to a stop, and I was dropped unceremoniously onto the ground as Payson watched the sky for something.

Now that I wasn't touching him, my brain started to clear, and I noticed there was no longer smoke in the sky or the acrid smell of soot burning my nose. Something was wrong...

"Payson, how did you know I couldn't swim?" I asked, brushing my wet hair out of my face.

He glanced down at me with an irritated frown. "You don't think the others would have shared a fact like that? How can we protect you if we don't know your limitations?"

That sounded like it should make sense, but my gut was telling me otherwise. "What are we waiting for? The roost is in the opposite direction from here. I thought that's where we were meeting the others?"

"Took you long enough," Payson said, letting out a cruel laugh. "No one is coming for you, Dragon Queen. They are back in the castle, sound asleep and ripe for the killing."

I scrambled to my feet and lunged at him, but whatever he'd done to me to make me more lethargic still wasn't out of my system.

He backhanded me, sending me sprawling to the ground like I was nothing.

"Vasin! They're going to attack!" I screamed as Payson withdrew his sword. *"I think they might have been drugged or had some sort of spell put on them. They need to wake up!"*

"WHERE ARE YOU? I FEEL YOUR FEAR. I WILL COME GET YOU."

"No, deal with the castle. We can't let everyone die."

"I'M NOT GOING TO LET YOU DIE, EITHER!"

Payson lunged at me, and I rolled out of the way. "That's enough talking with that lizard of yours, the self-entitled bastard. I'm to keep you busy until the rightful king can come and deal with you."

Shock froze my body for a moment too long, and I couldn't dodge the next attack. I gasped at the burning pain as his sword sliced my shoulder. "No! You are my guardian. There is no way that you can be working for the Lost King. My powers would have never chosen you!"

He tossed back his head and laughed. "You stupid woman, for all that you claim to be so smart. I wasn't chosen to be one of your guardians, but you fell for it so easily that I used it all to my advantage." Yanking back his shirt sleeve, he bared his arms to me, which were now clear of any guardian mark. "I'm blessed with the power of illusion. It was child's play to replicate the mark. Then, all I had to do was play the part of doting helper, and you ate it up, allowing me to be a part of all your secret meetings and plans. I was already a spy for my king, but you made it so much easier to get what I needed."

The realization of what that meant sank like a rock in the pit of my stomach. The Lost King knew everything—where we were hiding, what we knew about him, and that we would be making an alliance with the king and queen. "That's why you wanted to guard the rooms... you needed time to tell one of your men in the castle what was going on! I figured it out, and you couldn't wait any longer, which is why you're attacking tonight."

"*Cass, they locked up the roost, and this time they made the doors out of metal instead of wood. I don't have fire, so I can't melt them to let the others free.*"

"*How many of you are free?*"

"*I'm the only one outside. It was my turn to scout. We didn't want them to notice abnormal dragon activity.*"

"By the crestfallen look on your face, I'm guessing your pet just told you we made a few changes to the roost since the last time you visited. It's sad that the king is so easily persuaded when the queen isn't there to make the choices for him, but then again, slaughtering people in the city is a valid distraction." Payson grinned.

Wing beats sounded above, and I spotted a purple dragon circling before it started to land.

"The king has arrived to take his throne. Too bad you won't be able to enjoy the perks of being a part of it. Those who he takes control of rarely remember who they are after a while," Payson sneered as he reached down and grabbed a handful of my hair, yanking me to my feet and lifting his sword to my throat. "Do be a good girl. I'll get into trouble if I end up killing you."

Too bad for him that I would rather be dead than a mindless slave used to further a mad king's plans. Lifting my arm, I slammed my elbow into his gut, then gripped the arm around my throat, leaning forward and tossing him over my shoulder. Payson landed on the ground with a grunt, and I took off back toward the castle, pushing away the pain from my leg, using it as a reminder that I was still alive.

"You bitch!"

I heard his pounding footsteps as he took off after me, and I pushed myself harder to get away from him. My foot caught on a stone hidden in the grass, and I went sprawling to the ground. As fast as I could, I picked myself up and lunged forward, but a body tackled me, sending us both into the grass. Payson no longer held his sword, giving him both hands to grapple me with. This had always been one of my weaker skills, being so much smaller and having less muscle. I tried to remember everything Cole and Abbott taught me as I kicked, bit, and scratched anywhere I could to get him to loosen his hold on me. Nothing I did could free me from his grasp, and he managed to get his legs wrapped around mine. He wrapped his arm around my throat and tightened. The feeling of him crushing my neck sent me into a panic, but he hid his face and didn't budge.

"No matter how hard you fight me, I will always win. How do you know that this is even happening to you right now? What if it's all an illusion?" Payson whispered in my ear. "How do you fight something if you don't know it's real? The Lost King is coming for you, and when he does, the fabled Dragon Queen will be brought to her knees."

He was right. What if none of this is real? What if he allowed me to believe he'd freed me from his illusion but hadn't? I closed my eyes, and in a last-ditch effort, I let myself slip away, reaching out to Vasin, allowing our minds to meld as we harmonized. When I opened them, I found the castle was indeed on fire and swarming with men. The dragon riders were attacking the wave of men pouring out of different tunnels coming from all directions.

"Cass, where are you? Why can't I feel you?"

"Payson is a mole. He isn't one of my guardians, and he's working with the Lost King. I don't know where he has me or what he's really doing to me. I'm trapped in his endless loop of illusions."

"Now that you are with me, I should be able to locate where your body is."

"Are the others all right? What about Gavin and the rest of the royal family?"

"Tahir and Ifra tell me their pair-bonds are fine, but I haven't seen any of your guardians with my eyes. When I checked your rooms, they were on fire but empty—"

"That is something at least."

Vasin flew around the castle, trying to pinpoint where I was and circled out wider when he didn't find a trace inside the castle. As he ventured out farther, still finding nothing, he returned to the battle.

"Something about having you trapped in an illusion is keeping me disconnected from you. There has to be a way to break free from it."

"Can I die in an illusion?"

"If your brain believes that you've died, then yes, it could truly kill you. The power of suggestion is no small trick."

"Then I will do my best not to get killed. I'll have to find another way to shock myself out of his hold."

"Please be careful, my dear Cass. You already know the pain of losing one's pair-bond."

My mind flashed back to my first memory I had of Miranda, the Raven Queen, and experiencing her losing her men and dragon. The pain had been unbearable, ultimately leading to her choice to take as many soldiers down with her before she lost her life.

"I'm not giving up, Vasin. There is too much that I still need to do in this life." With that, I pulled myself back into my body and opened my eyes, renewed with determination.

THIRTY-ONE
TRUTH IN THE ILLUSIONS

When my eyes adjusted, I found myself not in a chokehold out in the fields but tied to a chair in a small stone-walled room with one torch and Payson sitting in front of me. His hands were on either side of my head near my temples. Sweat was pouring off his body, and he tried to force me back into the illusion, but it didn't work for some reason. His eyes snapped open, and he met my gaze with hatred glaring back at me.

"How the hell did you break out of my trap? There should have been an endless loop of changes when you caught onto something not being right," he ranted, dropping his hands. "It couldn't have happened. It shouldn't have been possible!"

A look of fear passed over his face, and he shot up from his seat and looked around the room wildly. "No, no, no, no, no, no. He can't be here. We got rid of him so this wouldn't happen! Where are you hiding, you bastard? I know you're near... there's no other explanation. No dragon can get through my guard. I've trained myself too well for that."

"A dragon didn't get in, I got out," I whispered, my throat sore from the illusion of being choked out. "There are things that happen between a black dragon and their pair-bond that nobody knows. I know what's really going on in the castle, that we are under attack."

Payson whirled back around to me. "You know nothing! There's no way *you* could have bested me!" He slammed his hands on either side of my head once again and dug his fingers into my scalp. "There is no one more powerful than the Lost King. He is the only one who has ever been able to free himself. You, a stupid noble woman, could never match the like of a god-made man."

The roar of a dragon could be heard overhead, and Payson gave me a maniacal grin. "See, he comes for you, little queen. He's been waiting for the day he could crush the one who is fated to kill him. Just wait, you will become his puppet and beg for death, only to be denied time and time again."

A creaking noise came from above as someone pulled open the trap door I hadn't noticed in the gloom. A figure dressed in all black with a wide hood covering his face dropped down, landing in a crouch. With the flick of a wrist, he tossed back the hood, and there stood a man who resembled Payson almost identically. There were subtle differences, like his hair was a slightly darker blond than his brother's as was his skin, but the piercing light-blue eyes gave him away. They matched his father's along with his twin brother.

"How? I killed you! I watched as your body was pulled under the current of the Darsor River. No one could survive the stab wound I gave you to the heart," Payson screeched as he backed himself as far away from him as he could.

This could only be Paxton, Payson's missing twin, or so he and their father would lead you to believe.

"Too bad for you that my heart wasn't in the same place as yours, *brother*, if you even have one," Paxton sneered. "I see that I've stayed away for far too long. Once I heard the Dragon Queen was found, I knew I'd have to come back, seeing as I'm her guardian and all." Yanking back his shirt sleeve, there on his arm was my guardian mark. "Hurt like a bitch and almost cost me my life as I was flying on my dragon at the time."

"Why do you always take everything away from me? What have I ever done to deserve this kind of life? All I wanted was to be valued, but instead, I was never trusted because of my Birthright. The Lost King saw the gift I could give him... only I could do this job," Payson snarled as he shoved off the stone wall, lunging at his twin.

Paxton drew a short, slightly curved sword and met his brother head-on. "I will show you one last moment of mercy and end your miserable life quickly. Something you neglected to do for me. But I'll make sure you don't come back from the dead."

With a swift and practiced movement, Paxton sliced his brother's throat, causing blood to spray all over the room. Payson's hot blood burned on my face where it landed, telling me that what my eyes were seeing was not an illusion. Payson was dead. He'd betrayed me, our people, and tried to hand me over to the Lost King, all for someone to tell him he was valued.

"My Queen, I'm sorry you had to see that," Paxton said as he sat in the chair across from me and used his cloak to wipe my face. "Are you hurt? Do you know what's going on?"

Numbly, I blinked at him. I heard what he said, but I couldn't seem to find the ability to answer.

"We need to get you out of here. The castle has been overrun, and we can't save it," Paxton explained as he cut away the ropes holding me.

I reached out, grasped his left arm, pushed back his sleeve, and ran my fingers over his mark. I could feel the raised skin that was like my own before I met his gaze. "How did you find me? Vasin, my dragon couldn't do that, but you did..."

"My Birthright is to stop others from using theirs. To me, each Birthright *feels* different, and having known Payson all my life, I could tell it was him. He was trying so hard to break into your mind that he became a beacon, so I followed it. I had no idea you were here, but I'm glad I got to you in time. I don't know that anyone else would have found you tucked away in here," Paxton shared, giving me a tentative smile. "I know this is a lot to take in, and I want to give you that time, but we can't wait. You need to get to safety. If we lose you, we lose all hope of beating that crazy bastard who calls himself king."

Gently but firmly, he pulled me up out of the chair. Once I was standing, he tossed me over his shoulder, causing me to let out a squeak of surprise as he started to climb the ladder. Out of what I could only guess was once a cellar, Paxton set me down, giving me a chance to look around and see that I was in the barn. All the horses were gone, but the stalls gave it away.

"Ninnat is waiting right outside. She'll take us to where the others are," Paxton coaxed, wrapping an arm around my shoulders. After a few steps, he noticed my limp and scooped me up in his arms. "We'll have to look at that later, but it doesn't seem to be bleeding so that's a good sign."

"It's nothing to worry about, just an old injury that's not quite healed yet," I murmured as Paxton kicked open the barn door, revealing the chaos of battle.

The glow of the castle was just as real as it had been in the illusion, which made me think that not all of what I'd been seeing was fake. Paxton turned to the left, and I found myself face-to-face with a stunning golden dragon. Her scales glistened in the firelight as if they were gems, making her seem as if she was made of liquid metal. The dragon snuffled me a moment then crooned a sad sound as she shifted so Paxton could hoist me up on her back.

"This is Ninnat, my pair-bond," Paxton explained as he started to strap me in. "Are the clans at the hideout or still in their normal areas?"

"You know about the hideout?" I questioned, looking at him over my shoulder.

"That happens when your father is a clan leader." He smirked. "By your reaction, I'm going to guess that's where they are."

"No! We can't leave without the others," I snapped, the fear of losing them snapping me out of my daze. "If I'm gone, they won't know what happened to me, and they'll get themselves killed looking for me."

"How exactly do you suggest we go about finding them?"

"Give me a moment to reach out to Vasin. He's been keeping an eye out for them," I answered as I closed my eyes.

"Please tell me you found them!"

"Cass, what happened? I can feel you now. Are you safe?"

"Yes, it's a long story that we don't have time for. Have you found them?"

"I've found some. May, Dayson, and Becka got the king and queen out safely, but I haven't been able to find the others."

"Where are the ones who got out?"

"I led them away into the woods surrounding the city, but that won't last long before they are discovered."

"I'm safe and with a golden dragon myself, but I'm trusting you to keep looking for the others while I get people to safety. The king and queen have their own dragons, so I'll work on getting a dragon rider to fly the other two out of the city."

"Is the plan to regroup back at the hideout?"

"Yes, but we will need to evacuate them as well. The Lost King knows everything."

"ONE THING AT A TIME, CASS. WE WILL FIND YOUR MEN AND THEN GET THE HELL OUT OF HERE."

Opening my eyes, I turned slightly to see Paxton's face. "I'm going to show Ninnat where some of my people are hiding and call over one of the dragon riders to help evacuate."

"You can do that?"

Now, I smirked back at him. "Being queen gives you some extra perks."

I settled deeper into my mind and reached out, feeling for one of the dragon riders. Kormark, one of the Bronze Reapers, is who I found first on his dragon, Grim, who kindly opened up to me. Then I took a moment to find the king and queen's dragons, only to discover those two were already guarding the area around where they were hiding. Satisfied with that, I returned my focus on Grim.

"I need you to come with me to this location. We need to get our people back home." Grim sent back his acknowledgment and accepted the images of the location Vasin showed me.

I did the same thing to Ninnat, who was more than eager to help in any way she could. Thankfully, I was strapped in because once she knew where to go, she took off running and leaped into the air. The rush of wind had me opening my eyes, peering over the side, searching everywhere for any sign of my lost guardians.

"Ah, where exactly are we headed?" Paxton asked.

"The king and queen, along with some of my guardians, are hiding out in the woods. They need to leave the city before they get caught or killed," I explained, not taking my eyes off the battle.

"You realize talking to different dragons like that isn't normal, right? Guess if I had any doubt of who you're supposed to be, that would clear things up for me." Paxton laughed.

I elbowed him in the gut before I thought it through, causing him to let out a muffled grunt. "This is no time to be making jokes. People's lives are at stake, and I would appreciate it if you took things more seriously. I will not lose more people than I have to. In my mind, even one is too many."

"My apologies, Your Majesty. I just can't believe this is really happening, but you're right. That's a conversation for another time."

Ninnat nimbly sat down near the edge of the forest, and I was already ripping at the straps and tumbling off her back before she tucked her wings. "Dayson! May! Becka!"

I couldn't see well in the darkness now that the glow of the fire wasn't lighting everything up. Dayson was the first to emerge from the forest, and I ran over to him the best I could and all but tumbled into his arms as he rushed toward me. He swung me up so I could wrap myself around him and bury my face in his neck as he clutched me tightly.

"Thank God you're safe, Cassy-bear," he whispered as he kissed the side of my head.

I leaned back and grasped his face in my hands, searching his expression before I kissed him soundly on the mouth. Seeing we had an audience and were in the middle of a battle, it didn't last long, but I couldn't stop myself. "Are you all right?"

"I should be asking you that. What happened?" he demanded, his brow creased in worry. "Where is Payson? He was in charge of getting you out and to the meetup point. When we arrived outside the roost, there was no sign of either of you."

"It's a long story, and we don't have time to get into it, but Payson is dead, and his twin, Paxton, rescued me," I admitted, turning back to where he was still sitting on Ninnat's back.

Dayson's eyes grew wide as he set me down and looked up at Paxton. "Where the fuck have you been?"

"Nice to see you too, asshole," Paxton called back with a grin. "As much as this reunion is lovely, we need to get the hell out of here."

Gripping Dayson's arm, I drew his attention back to me. "Go with the king and queen back to the hideout. I'm going to look for the others. Kormark will be here shortly to make sure everyone has a ride." Dayson looked like he wanted to argue, but I narrowed my eyes at him. "This is an order from your queen. Get them back to the hideout. Once you're there, collect the clan leaders, tell them what happened, and that we have to get our people ready to move. Day... Porvan is a mole for the Lost King. He will need to be dealt with. Can I trust you to make sure that happens?"

Dayson's face sobered, and his gaze grew hard. "As My Queen commands, it shall be done."

"We will be right behind you once we find them, I promise."

"You better be, Cassy-bear, or I'll hunt you down to the ends of the earth," Dayson promised as he leaned his head against mine, then kissed my forehead. "Go, find the others. I'll deal with everything else."

THIRTY-TWO

TWO BAD CHOICES MAKE A RIGHT... RIGHT?

I stayed long enough to see Kormark land, giving me peace of mind that they could get out of here safely.

"We need to head to the roost. That is where they decided to meet up if they got separated," I stated as we took off into the sky.

"No way... that is crazy. One of the tunnels they are using is in that area... it would be suicide. Once they figured that out, they wouldn't stay there," Paxton argued.

I gritted my teeth, holding back the urge to jab him in the stomach again for arguing with me. "We at least need to fly over the area to check."

"Women! Why are all of you so goddamn stubborn? Fine, we'll fly over it, but that's all I'm agreeing to," Paxton growled out as he relented.

It didn't take us long to reach the roost, and just as Paxton warned, it was swarming with enemy soldiers. Then I noticed that the roost doors were closed like Vasin had warned me about while I was trapped in the illusion.

"Fly closer to the roost, I need to get a look at the doors," I called out to Ninnat.

We banked and circled back, cutting as close to the roost as we could while still being out of reach. At the last moment, Ninnat shifted sideways, so I had an up-close-and-personal viewing of the doors—they were in fact, steel.

"Son of a bitch!" I swore as Ninnat shot up to safety.

I let my senses reach out, searching for Tahir and Ifra, not having seen them with the other dragon riders. When I connected with both of them, I felt fear and pain. Something had happened, and they were trapped.

"Vasin, where are you?" I screamed, fear making my chest tight.

"A WAVE OF ROGUE NORDEN DRAGON RIDERS IS AFTER THE KING AND QUEEN. I'M TRYING TO HOLD THEM OFF LONG ENOUGH FOR THEM TO GET AWAY."

"Do you need us? Tahir and Ifra are trapped in the roost."

"I'M THE BLACK DRAGON, REMEMBER? I'LL MANAGE THIS. YOU SAVE THEM SO WE CAN GET OUT OF HERE."

"Be safe!"

"ONLY IF YOU ARE."

Pulling away from Vasin, I shifted my mind to Ninnat. *"I need you to get as close to the top of the roost as possible."* I could feel her hesitation, but when I showed her what I was going to do, she relented.

"What did you just tell her to do?" Paxton yelled at me as we turned back to the roost.

Not bothering to answer, I glanced down on either side and spied what I was hoping to find. As Ninnat got closer to the roost, I hit Paxton in the gut, snatched his knife out of his boot, and cut myself free of the harness. Before Paxton could figure out what I was doing, I wrapped a part of the harness around my hand and slid off Ninnat's back, dangling until she lowered me enough to land on the roof.

"Are you fucking crazy?" Paxton roared as Ninnat continued ignoring everything that her pair-bond was saying.

Drawing on my Birthright, I pulled back the bow string as far as I could and focused on the massive metal padlock on the top of the roost. It took four hits before it broke open, and I was able to kick it loose. I waved my arms to get Ninnat's attention, and she flew over once again, but this time, she latched onto the metal covering the hole on the top of the roost for dragons to enter and leave by. Being a slightly smaller dragon, it took all her strength thrusting downward with her wings before it started to lift. Finally, she managed to get it high enough for me to slip under it. The part I didn't account for was the fact it was still twenty feet in the air with only sand below to save me. I held onto the lip of the opening and swung myself toward the wall, aiming for the cubby that had been carved out. Slamming against the stone wall, I clawed at whatever I could get ahold of as I slid down toward my death. Then my fingers latched onto a ledge a few feet down from where I aimed and scrambled to safety, panting as I caught my breath.

"When they find out about this, they might kill me themselves." I gasped as the metal covering slammed back down.

If I couldn't get the other dragons freed, then I was trapped here until this battle ended. Since that wasn't my plan, I crawled to the edge and looked down to see if there was a better option to get down to the floor than tossing myself at the wall. Sure enough, hand and foot holds had been cut into the stone for people to reach these cubbies. Gingerly, I lowered myself until my foot caught on the first step and began the slow process of making my way down. I was a few feet away when the step I was looking for wasn't there, and I fell backward, my arms wheeling, trying to will myself back against the wall, but it was no use. The abrupt stop onto the sands of the roost knocked the air out of my lungs, and it took me a solid five minutes to calm down before I could breathe again.

"Cass, why is Ninnat telling me you jumped into the roost from the top?"

"There was no other way to get in. They made the front doors of metal, and I wouldn't be able to do the same trick we did last time. This way, I wasn't in danger of getting stabbed while I tried to break the lock."

"You are trying to test the will of the gods. That is the only reason you would do something so reckless."

"I made it down to the ground with no lasting damage."

"I will not congratulate you for that, Cass. What you did was idiotic. I'm coming to get you with Ninnat's help. We'll be able to get the seal off the top of the roost."

"Thanks. I was a little worried how we were going to get out." Vasin snarled in response to that comment, and I could feel his disapproval clearly through our connection.

Slowly, I sat up, making sure I hadn't hurt myself from the fall, and brushed off the worst of the sand from my nightgown. "Why do these things always happen to me when I'm in my nightclothes?"

Hobbling around slowly, I searched the main caves, but I didn't see any dragons. Then I worked my way to the ones deeper in the back of the roost, where Vasin had been attacked as a baby. That's where I found Ifra bleeding and bound by a spiked metal chain that tore at his scales any time he shifted.

"How can that be? Our metals don't pierce through dragon scales..." I muttered to myself as I shuffled my way to him, using the wall to steady me.

When I reached Ifra, I took Paxton's dagger and tried to pick the lock, but it wasn't slim enough to work. If only I had my weapons and tools, but they were left behind in the rooms when Payson stole me away.

"Are you looking for these?" a familiar taunting voice said from behind me. Spinning on my heel, I found Lord Everett at the entrance to the cave, keys dangling from his outstretched hand. "It seems we meet again, little queen. You really should have killed me when you had the chance."

I'd beaten the bastard before, so what's to stop me from doing it again?

"What have you done with the other dragon, the red one?" I demanded.

He dropped his hand and started to swagger his way toward me. "Oh, you mean the one that belongs to the Grim Reaper, the best-known assassin of the clans? The man who killed his own parents because he was paid to? He seems an odd choice for you to pick as a guardian."

No, that can't be true! Then I remembered everyone's reaction to him when they saw him and how Acton refused to acknowledge him as family, saying he was the clan leader, not Jade's father. *Does it really matter, though? Vasin knows the whole story and isn't worried about me. There must be a valid reason it happened.*

"What queen doesn't need a good assassin? It keeps people like you from doing shit like this," I replied, brushing off what he said, not letting him rattle me.

Lord Everett drew his sword as he got closer. "Yes, Payson did share that the assassin was getting quite attached to you and might cause problems... so I eliminated the threat. Much like I plan to do with this dragon and his blind-as-a-bat pair-bond when I can find the little rat."

"Not if I kill you first," I pointed out, clinging to my bravado. "This time, I don't have any reservations about killing you. Last time, I let you live because I wasn't going to be controlled."

"So young and so much to learn about the world. Everyone is controlled by someone. No one is free from their fate, not even the Dragon Queen."

I noticed the shift in his body language almost too late, but I ducked and rolled in time to miss the lunge. Clearing my mind from everything else, I focused on the fight at hand. Taking the dagger, I made a cut at the hem of my nightgown and ripped it all the way up to my hip, freeing me to move easier. Lord Everett was all power and force. He didn't use his surroundings to his strength like I'd been taught, believing that if he can hit you hard enough, you'll just be dead. Well, that could work if he managed to hit me.

Steeling myself for how bad this was going to hurt, I ran right at him, leading him to believe I was going to do a frontal assault, but I slid to the ground and popped up once I was behind him. Using the wall of the cave as a means to spring off from, I leaped up, kicking off the stone and landed on Lord Everett's back. He gripped my arm, locking me against him as he slammed me into the wall, trying to get me to loosen my hold. Using my other hand, I plunged the dagger into his neck, where there was a gap in the armor, severing his artery. Once again, I was sprayed with blood as the man under me started to die, falling forward onto the ground. I refused to move until I knew he was well and truly dead, this time keeping a finger on his pulse, feeling it slow until it completely stopped.

Shoving him onto his side, I searched for the keys until I found them tucked in his breastplate. Crawling over to Ifra, I tried each of the keys until one of them worked, and the lock popped open. As carefully as I could, I unwound the chains from around him, talking nonsense in an attempt to keep myself calm. When he was free, Ifra slowly started to move out of the cave but paused and looked back at me, letting out a whistle to follow him. I'm sure the sight of us together was frightful, both of us covered in blood and tattered, but we were still alive. Ifra led me to another deep cave, where I found a large cage with Cole, Abbot, and Izel, but no Zan or Jade, knocked unconscious and trapped inside. Tahir was there too, bound just like Ifra was.

"Where is your pair-bond, hmm?" I asked, running a hand over his snout. "Does he at least have Ezzu with him so he can see?" Ifra hummed his answer, making me feel better that Zan wasn't lost and blind out in the battle. "Can you find him and tell him it's time to go?" Ifra butted his head into my chest and let out another hum before he started to shuffle out of the cave.

I decided to start with Tahir first, hoping everything Lord Everett told me was a lie. "Easy, boy, I got you. Don't struggle or you'll make it worse."

Just as I got him free, a horrible screeching sound came from above, followed by an explosion that shook the whole roost. Rock started to break free from where we were in the cave, making me very worried it might collapse on us.

"Tahir, I need to put them on your back. There's no way I can get them out of here without your help," I pleaded with the dragon, knowing he would want to find Jade if he was still alive.

In answer, Tahir laid down next to the cage and gave me a nod. As quickly as I could, I found the key, unlocked the cage, and started to pull them out. I forgot that many of my guardians were large, muscular men, but I managed to drag them far enough that Tahir could help me lift them. With all three of them on his back, it didn't leave any room for me, and the ground started to shake yet again as there was another explosion.

"Move, Tahir, get them out of here. I'm right behind you!" I cried out as it started to get hard to see through all the falling debris.

Just as Tahir cleared the cave, it started to collapse, and I couldn't move fast enough to get out of the way. *"Vasin, I'm sorry."*

"You should be sorry," Vasin snapped. *"Why did you insist on doing this alone? How many times do I have to tell you we are a team, and we do things together?"*

I opened my eyes to find I was shrouded in Vasin's wings, his glowing amber eyes glaring at me with disapproval. I all but fell to the ground sobbing as he nuzzled me gently.

"You reek of blood... are you hurt?"

"It's not mine..."

"All right then, can we go now?"

"What about Zan, Jade, and Gavin?"

"They can take care of themselves, I'll have you know. Ifra is on his way to pick them up."

"Okay, if we have everyone, then let's go home. We have a long journey ahead of us."

Vasin shifted, pulling back his wings, and rubble surrounded us, showing me how close to death I'd really been if Vasin hadn't arrived. I heaved myself onto his back, and we made our way out to the middle of the roost or what was left of it. It seems the explosions had been someone blowing a massive hole into the side of the ancient building.

"What happened?"

"Paxton. That boy is a wild one. He might even have a larger death wish than you do. He piled up explosives and had his dragon set them on fire. Thankfully, I got here in time. That boy is reckless."

"I kind of like him. He's my real guardian, you know."

"THAT'S THE LAST THING WE NEED. SOMEONE TO ENCOUR-AGE YOUR NEWFOUND THRILL OF CHEATING DEATH."

I couldn't help but laugh at that. If you'd told me six months ago I'd be leaping off dragons and fighting off knights, I would have told you, you were crazy. Now, here I was escaping an epic battle that lost us the Norden kingdom. The Lost King might have won this round, but little did he know that I'd kept some things to myself. Payson had no idea where Zan really came from or what was waiting for me when I got there. Looks like it was time to stop putting off the inevitable.

Thirty-Three

Home for Now...

As I arrived back at the hideout with the early morning light peeking over the mountains, I let out a sigh of relief. Vasin refused to let me stop and see everyone before we headed back, saying something about nine lives and having used up three.

I changed my mind. They will be fine without us. The other dragon riders are meeting up with them instead. I can't trust that you won't do something entirely too stupid, and I've had all I can take of that for a lifetime.

The moment we landed, Dayson was there, pulling me off Vasin, fear written all over his face. "Are you hurt? Why are you covered in blood? Where is everyone else? Are you alone?"

"Easy, cousin, let the poor woman speak if you want answers," May suggested as she joined us, wrapping a cloak around my shoulders.

The shadow of another dragon passed overhead, and I looked up to find Paxton and Ninnat coming to land beside Vasin. Paxton hopped off his dragon and stormed over to me, his face turning purple with the anger he was holding back. "You are goddamn crazy, you know that? Why didn't you tell me what the hell you were thinking? I could have helped you, but no, you had to go and leap off a perfectly good dragon and do it all yourself!"

"Look who's talking. You're the one who blew up one of the oldest buildings in our country, not to mention almost killing me as it collapsed!" I yelled back, meeting him toe to toe. "I was handling it just fine, but you had to let your crazy out."

"Oh, ho, ho, is that what you think? Well, *Your Majesty,* the next time you get kidnapped, locked away in a cellar, tied to a chair with a psycho-manipulative fake guardian, I'll be sure to leave you there since you can handle it just fine."

Reaching the end of my limit on things I could handle in one night, I punched him right in the face, catching him so off guard he fell on his ass. "If you wanted me to say thank you, that's all you had to say, no need to be a dick about the whole thing! It's not like I asked you to come save me, goddammit."

Paxton looked up at me, eyes wide with shock as he cupped a hand over his eye. Then in an odd turn of events, he started to laugh. He laughed so hard he fell onto his back, and even his good eye started to well up with tears. "Holy shit. How is there someone as perfect as you in this world? You just decked me in the face and scolded me for being a dick."

"Yes. Yes, I did. Now I'm going to my room to wash off Lord Everett's blood, get some real clothes on, and tell everyone we have to leave this place because it's no longer safe... that okay with you?" I growled.

Paxton stopped laughing, dropped his hand, showing his already swelling eye, and opened his mouth to say something else, but Becka stopped him. "Dayson, would you please take Cassarah up? I'll get some ladies together and bring up the water for a bath."

Bless that woman to know when I've had enough. I was barely holding it together now that the adrenaline was wearing off and the full reality was hitting me. "Thank you, Becka. When the rest of them get back, can you please send Jade to me?"

"Of course," Becka assured me.

Dayson lifted me into his arms, so I snuggled against his chest and closed my eyes, listening to his heartbeat. These men and women were becoming everything to me. They were my family, my best friends, and people I wanted to trust with anything and everything. In a blink of an eye, one of them betrayed me. Granted, he was never truly one of my guardians, but I had started to let him in. Could I trust that the others wouldn't turn on me as well?

"Cassy-bear, it's going to be all right," Dayson murmured as he cuddled me. "We are all okay and made it out of there alive. As long as we are together, we'll be able to make it through this."

"He sold me out, Day. I trusted him to keep me safe, and he was going to deliver me to the enemy. Then his brother, my real guardian, killed him and slit his throat without a second thought. Paxton doesn't even know me, but he killed his flesh and blood to keep me alive. Why would he do that?" I asked, reaching out to clutch Dayson's shirt with my hand.

Dayson took a deep breath and let it out slowly. "Paxton has never shown loyalty to anyone or anything, but now it makes sense as to why. His father and brother were selling out our people for what... power, fortune, approval? He tried to tell the clan leaders, but they wrote him off as a boy who was mad at his father and always caused trouble. What Pax did today was nothing unusual. He's always been known as the act-first-ask-questions-later type. I can't tell you why he did it, but that is the first time he's ever picked a side that wasn't himself."

"Vasin thinks he's a bad influence on me." I chuckled.

Dayson let out his own bark of laughter. "No, what I saw out there was a woman standing up for herself when her guardian was being a dick. I've never seen you get so heated before. It was quite impressive, totally made you even more attractive. I don't know what it is about a woman who can lay out a man, but it just does it for me."

That had me snapping my gaze up to his. "Is that your version of expressing interest in me?"

"We are way past interest, Cassy-bear. I'm halfway in love with you..." He paused when he saw the look on my face. "Now, don't start frowning at me like that. I know you asked for time, and I'm more than willing to give it to you. I'm not pressuring you for anything, but I will damn well make sure you know how I feel about you."

When we entered my room, he set me on my bed, kneeled in front of me, and pulled my injured leg to rest on his. Slowly, he started to undo the filthy-looking bandage to reveal the wound underneath. It was puffy and red. The stitches looked like they tore a little, but it wasn't as bad as I thought it would be.

"Looks like it's going to scar... I'm sorry about that," Dayson said as he pressed around the wound, looking for any infection.

I glanced at the jagged mark and thought of all that had changed because of it. "Scars are moments in our lives that we will never forget. So far, this one has a pretty amazing story to tell."

Dayson looked up at me with pride shining on his face as he smiled. "Paxton had one thing right. How in the world did a perfect woman like you come to be?"

Unsure of how to respond to a question like that, I was thankful when the door opened and four women entered, all carrying buckets of water. Soon, the tub was filled, and I asked to be alone as I cleaned up. I just needed some time to process things. The water turned pink as I washed all the blood from my body, making it so I had to have Becka bring up another bucket of water for me to rinse off with. Finally clean and dressed in the softest leather pants I could find, along with a loose, billowy navy blue shirt, I lay down on the bed.

I didn't fall asleep. Instead, my mind went over the night's events on a loop, looking at every detail, trying to figure out what I could have done differently. There had to have been a way to avoid what happened, but on the other hand, how long could Payson have hidden in plain sight? If I hadn't figured out the plan for the castle, would the attack still have happened? I covered my face with both hands, rubbing my aching eyeballs. When I lowered them, I found Jade's light green eyes staring down at me, his body covered in blood, dirt, and soot. Before my brain could catch up, Jade had me in his arms, kissing wherever his lips could find skin, murmuring endearments and nothingness as he wrapped himself around me on the bed. I decided I didn't care what happened in the past because this was the Jade I knew and was falling for. As we held each other, I cried while he told me everything was going to be all right, we all survived, and made it back home.

At some point, I drifted off to sleep, and when I woke, it wasn't Jade who was sleeping next to me but Cole. I was sleeping on my side while he was flat on his back, arms tucked behind his head, chest rising and falling steadily. His face was relaxed, void of the scowl it's had on it lately—the one I seemed to keep putting there. I reached out and ran the tip of my finger along the bridge of his nose to see if he was really sleeping. His hand shot out and gripped my wrist before one eye slowly cracked open to look at me. "About time you woke up, sleepyhead. It's well into the afternoon."

"Says the man taking a nap beside me." I grinned.

Cole shifted onto his side, so we were all but nose to nose. "Getting drugged and hit over the head will do that to a guy. What's your excuse?"

"Saving the guys who got drugged, hit over the head, and locked in a cage. Oh, and a few dragons too."

"Wow, sounds like that person had some pretty impressive training. I wonder who her instructor was…"

"I think you would like him. He comes off as kind of an asshole, but once you get to know him, he's just a big, overprotective teddy bear," I teased, then reached out and cupped his cheek. "Are you sure you're okay?"

Turning his head, he kissed my palm before he clasped it in his hand. "I feel like a horse kicked me in the skull, but I'll be okay. You going to be all right? Dayson told us about Lord Everett."

"I'm not sure if I'm being honest. He would have killed me without a thought, so he didn't leave me any choice in the matter," I answered. "Is everyone back?"

"Yes, most of them are resting at the moment. We thought it best to let everyone sleep since we didn't get much shut-eye last night. Rumor is that you have a plan."

"Haven't you learned yet that I always have a plan?"

Cole reached out and tapped a finger on my nose. "Not all of them are smart plans, like jumping off a dragon, for instance."

"Saved you guys, didn't I? I'd say it's well worth it," I argued.

"That's where you have things a little backward. The guardians are supposed to do the saving, not the queen."

"Why can't the queen also do the saving from time to time?"

Cole groaned and rolled onto his back again. "I'm not going to win this discussion, am I?"

"Sorry, I don't think so." I slowly sat up, my body screaming at me from all the abuse it'd gone through last night as I swung my feet off the bed.

"Where do you think you're going?" Cole demanded as he got out of bed to head me off.

"We need to call everyone together. It's not safe to stay here for too long. The Lost King might have won Royal City, but we are next on his list," I stated, waving him down to pick me up.

Cole scowled as he lifted me and headed for the door. "Where exactly can we go? This is the safest place we have."

"No, there's another place that not even the Lost King knows where to find. The mercenaries are going back to the motherland. We're going to Sheca, where I'm ready to claim the lost throne of the Dragon Queen."

The End

To be continued in *The Forgotten Throne*

About Author

Elizabeth is originally from Illinois but is now living in sunny Phoenix, Arizona. Though she is newer to publishing, Elizabeth has been writing for nine years. She started in YA Fiction but recently found herself loving the Reverse Harem genre. Like her favorite books, Elizabeth loves to write about strong women of all varieties. Not all strength is flashy or apparent at first glance—some lie just under the surface.

Don't Miss Out!

Be the first to know what is coming next by following Elizabeth's social media! You never know when or what will be coming next!

Website: ElizabethKnightBooks.com

Facebook: Elizabeth Knight's Unicorn Queens

Instagram: elizabethknightauthor

TikTok: elizabethknightauthor

Newsletter: sign up here

Also By

Mercenary Queen – Complete Series
Birthright
Dragon Queen
The Forgotten Throne
The Final Battle

Sunshine & Rainbows Omegaverse
Bailey-Rose Book 1 - Clouds & Daydreams + Petals & Promises

Omega Assassin - Complete series
Book 1 - Dual Nature
Book 2 - Hidden Nature
Book 3 - Perfect Nature

Knot All Omegaverse
Knot All Is Lost: Part 1 & Part 2 (Complete)
Knot All Is Ruined: Part 1 & Part 2 (Complete)

Caprioni Queen – Complete Series
Book 1 – Glitter & Guns
Book 2 – Blood & Heartache
Book 3 – Revenge & Truth

Book 4 – Love & Power

<u>Standalone Books</u>
Nicolette: Ladies of the MC
Lying Lainey: Underground Omega Syndicate

<u>Hidden Empire Series</u> – Complete series
Book 1 - Two Tricks
Book 2 - Three Tricks
Book 3 - Four Tricks
Book 4 - More Tricks
Book 5 - Our Tricks

<u>Hidden Empire Novel</u>
(SUGGESTED TO BE READ AFTER FOUR TRICKS)
Harper's Renegades

www.ingramcontent.com/pod-product-compliance
Lightning Source LLC
Chambersburg PA
CBHW070455300726
48975CB00007B/2186